THE AURA READER

BY

BARRY HOMAN

ISBN-10:0692899278

ISBN-13:978-0692899274

DEDICATION

This book is dedicated
to my father,
John C. Homan, Sr.
who probably never believed
in the metaphysical
while on earth,
yet has visited with me
many times
since his passing.

ALSO BY BARRY HOMAN:

Whispers Through Time:
A Reincarnation Novel

Traces of You

Cover Design by Corey Mastrapasqua

PROLOGUE

The boy was three when he first realized that he was unique.

He saw auras around people; had seen them from the day he was born, or at least as far back as he could remember. The shimmering colors that surrounded every living being, but that most people never see, were as clear to him as his own fingers. Before he spoke his first word, he learned to tell whether his mother was happy, sad, or angry by the colors emanating around her body. He hadn't known the names of the colors back then, but he knew their meanings.

Once he learned his colors and began talking in formative sentences, the question he asked most of his mother or father was not, "Why?" It was, "What color am I?" His parents didn't understand why he kept asking this, and simply replied that he was white, or sometimes pink.

The reason he asked the question was quite simple. While he saw colors vibrating off the bodies of everyone else, he could never see the aura around his own body. This would perplex him for many years, but as he grew older he began to understand that it was probably for his own good.

He was happy on the day it finally dawned on him that not everyone saw colors the way he did; in fact, it appeared that no one did. It made him feel special, and that was a good feeling. However, his parents would always get upset with him every time he brought the subject up.

"Stop doing that," his father would say. "People do not see colors around other people. That's just silly."

His parents were constantly mystified, however, about their child's ability to sense things. He had a penchant for going to his room and closing the door just before a fight broke out between them. When a co-worker of his father's passed away, he climbed into his father's lap and asked, "Why are you sad, daddy?" although he had no idea what had happened. Another time he proclaimed, "Mommy's really happy," even though she hadn't told anyone yet that she was pregnant again.

By the age of five he thought he had all the colors figured out. The way they flowed off people told him who was calm, who was agitated, and who was downright angry. He knew a peaceful red from an angry red; could tell a calm green from an envious green; knew a relaxed brown from a tired brown.

However, one day he learned that a new color could enter a person's aura.

Black.

He quickly learned that black was not good.

It happened during a visit from his grandparents. He had a particular fondness for his grandfather, a gregarious, out-going individual who emanated love and warmth every time the boy saw him. On the evening in question, he heard his grandfather's car pulling into the driveway. He knew from experience the sound of the automobile, even if he couldn't tell you it was a 4-door Chevrolet Fleetline Sportmaster Sedan with built in trunk.

He ran to his upstairs window and watched as his grandparents exited the vehicle and headed for the front door, and then he hurried down the stairs to greet them, holding tight to the railing so he wouldn't fall, as he had a few weeks before.

They had already entered the house and were taking off their coats as the boy raced through the living room. He entered the kitchen and ran right into his grandfather's outstretched arms.

"Grampa!" he shouted, hugging the old man with all the ferocity a five year old could muster.

"Well, well, well; who do we have here?" said the man, a huge grin on his face.

"It's me, grampa," he said.

"So it is," the man replied, and everyone in the room laughed.

As his grandfather put him down, he noticed a sudden frown come over the boy's face. "Is something wrong?" he asked.

"Where's all your bright shiny colors?" the boy said. He had been told many times not to bring the subject up when his grandparents were around, but he couldn't help himself this time.

"What bright shiny colors?" asked the man, who turned to look at his daughter and son-in-law with a questioning gaze.

"Son," said his father, a stern look moving across his face, "we've talked about this before. People don't have colors all around them."

"But I see them!" he insisted.

His father started to speak again, but the old man held up a hand to stop him. "It's okay," he said. "Let's hear what the boy has to say." He turned back to his grandson and said, "Tell me what you see."

"Well," the boy began, "you usually have such nice colors around you. Blues and greens and yellows, and they're always so nice and smooth. But tonight you're grey, and a little black."

"Oh my," said his grandfather, "and what color is your grandmother?"

The boy turned to his grandmother and quickly said, "Orange and yellow, and some red on the side of her face." Before his parents could object, he looked at them and continued on. "Mommy is red and green and purple, and daddy is ...."

He stopped talking again. His father's color was a deep red all around his head and shoulder area, and instead of flowing in a smooth and gentle manner they appeared as spikes jumping every which way. The boy had seen that before and knew what it meant.

"And daddy's mad," he finally said.

"You know," his grandmother said, "I've read somewhere about people who claim to see auras around everyone. It sounds just like what our little angel here is talking about."

"Well," said her son-in-law, "I don't believe in any of that crap, and I'd like it if your grandson would stop talking about such things. Next thing you know he'll be telling us about his invisible friends."

They all moved into the living room a few moments later. The boy sat on the couch between his grandparents while his father sat in his favorite chair. His mom made coffee for everyone, and then she sat on a chair that she brought in from the kitchen.

The boy remained relatively quiet, not wanting to embroil himself in any more trouble. His little sister, who would turn two next month, remained asleep in her bed, much to her grandmother's dismay.

The grown-ups chatted, but the boy spent most of the time watching television, a nine-inch Zenith with a circular screen, aluminum foil permanently attached to the rabbit ears in the back.

The visit lasted just over an hour, and then his grandmother suggested to her husband that it was time to leave. Everyone arose and headed back into the kitchen, but his grandfather motioned to the boy to stay behind.

"I have something for you," he said.

The boy was quiet as he watched his grandfather take something out of his pocket.

"This is my lucky coin," the man said. "It's called a Barber quarter. Look here." His grandfather pointed to the date on the coin. "This coin was minted, that means made, in 1909. That was a long time ago. And this little letter here, the O, means it was made in New Orleans."

The boy had never heard of New Orleans, but nodded as though he understood.

"This coin is worth much more than a quarter now," his grandfather continued, "and I'm going to give it to you. But you must promise me something."

"What?" the boy asked.

"This is not to spend. You keep it, okay? Someday when you're my age it will be worth a lot of money, but only if you keep it in perfect condition. It's best if you put it away in a safe place and never take it out."

"Okay, grampa," he said, although he couldn't imagine ever being his grandfather's age. "I'll put it in my special hiding place."

"You promise not to spend it?"

"I promise," he replied, and his grandfather put the coin in the palm of the boy's hand and closed his tiny fingers over it.

The boy put it in his pocket, and then the two of them headed back to the kitchen to join the others.

He was still wondering why his grandfather's aura—he had made note of what his grandmother had called it—continued to be so dull and lifeless. In fact, as the man put on his coat, it seemed to be turning more black than grey.

He accepted a kiss from his grandmother, turning at the last moment so that it landed on his cheek instead of his lips, and then he hugged his grandfather tight as he whispered in his ear, "I love you, grampa."

He watched with a worried look on his face as the couple made their way back to their car. They both turned around and waved one final time. The aura around his grandfather scared the boy. He didn't know why, but he started to cry.

"What's the matter now?" his father asked.

"Something's wrong with grampa," he said.

"Oh, stop it," his father said. "Your grandfather is as strong as an ox."

The boy was back upstairs ten minutes later. He put on his pajamas, brushed his teeth, put the coin in a small box where he kept his collection of special items, and climbed into bed. His mother entered his bedroom a short time later to tuck him in.

"I don't know what you see around people," she said, "but you need to stop talking about it in front of your father. You know how mad he gets. I don't mind if you talk to me about it when he's not around though. It can be our little secret, alright?"

He nodded his head and said, "Okay, mommy."

She gave him a kiss on the forehead and told him to get some sleep. He tossed and turned for a little while, thoughts of his grandfather running through his head, but eventually he dozed off.

He had only been asleep a short while when the phone rang. He awoke on the second ring and listened intently as his mother answered, but from his room upstairs he could hear very little. Suddenly she screamed, however, and he heard that plain as day. When his mother started crying, he knew something bad had happened.

Grampa, he thought. Then he went back to sleep.

He learned the next morning that his beloved grandfather had died of a massive heart attack just ten minutes after arriving home.

His ability to see auras never wavered over his lifetime, although he would never see his own. He would see the black aura of death countless times; from kids in his school to strangers he passed on the street. Eventually, he came to believe his gift was more of a curse than a blessing.

He prayed countless times for God to remove it, but God never did.

And he and his mother never spoke of it again.

ONE

Simon Taylor awoke from his dream with a start, momentarily wondering where he was. The room was dark; what little light he could see entered through his open bedroom door from the living room.

He rolled onto his side, about to turn on the light, and then thought better of it. The psychologist mumbled "Nora" as the still fresh story of his dream rumbled around in his mind. He tossed the covers down and glanced at his bedside clock. The large, bright digital readout told him it was 4:16.

He felt a warm glow coursing through his body, a feeling unlike anything he had ever felt before upon awakening, and he suddenly realized he was extremely happy. He had been talking to Nora, his late wife. In fact, he had been sitting right next to her, and it was the most awe-inspiring sensation he had felt in years. Perhaps the most wonderful moment of his life, and it had been a dream.

Or was it more than a dream?

He reached under his pillow and found the pen and yellow legal pad he kept there. It had been the idea of Paul Tracy, a friend and fellow psychologist, now retired, who once had an office down the hall from Simon.

"Write your dreams down," Paul had told him. "All of them, no matter how silly or crazy they appear to be. Their meanings may come to you at a later date, or you may see patterns developing that will reveal something to you."

Paul had told him to write down the dream immediately and not to turn on a light, for that might cause the dream to disappear from his memory banks quicker.

"Write in the dark," Paul had admonished, "even if you put one line on top of another. You can make it out in the morning and rewrite it if need be."

The advice made sense to Simon, who knew how fleeting dreams could be. He had rarely remembered his dreams in the morning. They seemed to vanish before his eyes as he tried to recapture them, except for the nightmares. He had been haunted by nightmares ever since Nora had died.

Nora had been an emergency room nurse who loved her job immensely. She and Simon had been married for twelve years, and were making plans for their thirteenth anniversary. She had been getting ready to leave work one night when the police brought in a young man high on drugs. She approached the side of his bed as the police were attempting to handcuff him to the railing. One hand was still free, however, and he used it to grab a billy club from one of the officer's belt. He swung wildly, and fate intervened. The club slammed into Nora's face, pushing her nose back into her head and killing her instantly.

Simon had been devastated. He had always considered Nora his soul mate. He was forty-one years old at the time, and suddenly alone, with a feeling that no one could ever replace his beloved Nora.

He tried to carry on in his hometown of Willis, South Carolina, but as time went by he knew he had to move. Sarasota, Florida was now home for Simon, but the nightmares that had plagued him in Willis had followed him here; lessening as time went on, yet still awful to bear when they appeared.

Besides being a psychologist, Simon also did past-life regression work. It had started innocently enough. He had seen fellow doctors have some success using hypnosis to help their patients quit smoking or lose weight, and he thought it would be a handy tool to have.

One day a young girl troubled by back pain had come into his office. She had been to countless doctors to find the cause and cure for her ailment, but none had been able to help. Most believed it was all in her head. Simon had been her last resort.

During her regression, she claimed to have been hit by a car when she was twenty-six years old. Simon, puzzled when she said this, took a quick glance at the information sheet she had filled out. It stated that she was now twenty-one. After questioning her further, Simon discovered that the year had been 1919, and that she had died from her injuries. Not sure how to react, Simon told her she could leave the pain of that injury in the past, and she would no longer be affected by it in her current lifetime.

He had heard from the girl about a month later. Her symptoms had disappeared.

The experience had opened up a whole new avenue of study for Simon, who had always been open to the idea of reincarnation. He started setting aside Tuesday mornings, and eventually the entire day, for past-life regression work. Eventually he wrote a book on his experiences. *Past Life Memories* had become a best-seller.

After moving to Sarasota, he had continued his regression work. He was currently in the middle of writing a second book, about two clients of his, Hannah and Hollis, who had been married in a previous life and who he had brought together again a few months ago. They had married on New Year's Eve, and two months ago Hannah had called to tell him she was pregnant.

His nightmares had let up lately, although he still woke up in a cold sweat every time he had one. Tonight, however, had been totally different. He noticed he was still smiling and felt incredibly happy, and his body felt light with love and joy coursing through it.

He sat up straight in his bed, crossed his legs yogi style, and put the pad on his lap. He clicked the Papermate pen into position and began to write.

I was walking in a field, heading for water that I heard lapping in the distance. It was probably the bay, or perhaps the Gulf of Mexico. I was alone, enjoying a quiet stroll, when suddenly I heard a voice calling my name. I looked around but saw no one, yet I heard the voice call me a second time, and then a third. I recognized it. It was Nora!

"Where are you," I called, for I still could not see her.

"You must come to me," she said.

"But how?" I replied. I desperately wanted to see her, for she had never come to me in such a way before; only in those horrible nightmares, where her death was repeated over and over to me.

Suddenly the scene changed. I was no longer in the field, but was floating in the air. Higher and higher I went, until her beautiful voice called a final time, saying, "Over here."

I found myself in the highest row of what appeared to be a large auditorium, and as I looked down I saw Nora sitting many rows below me. I instantly began heading her way, and soon I was entering the row where she sat.

She seemed to glow as I sat next to her, her smile as radiant as I had ever seen it, and I thought for a minute it was the Virgin Mary herself that I was next to.

She smiled that smile that always made my heart sing as she said, "Simon, you came."

"I've missed you so much," I said.

"I've been here," she said, "doing what needs to be done."

I took a moment to look all around the auditorium, wondering where we were. There were probably twenty thousand seats, yet we were the only two beings present.

As if reading my thoughts, she said, "It is a meeting room for loved ones who are in need."

"What I need is you," I said. "Come back with me. Please."

"You know I can't," said Nora. "My time on that side is finished for now."

"But why did you leave me so soon? We could have had many more wonderful years together." I sounded whiny at this point and I knew it, but I couldn't help myself.

"I had accomplished what I had set out to do, and had learned what I needed to learn. There was no need for me to stay on that side."

"I need to be with you," I pleaded.

"No, you've moved on, as you should have. Don't look back," she said softly, as she placed a hand on my cheek. She gazed deeply into my eyes, a gaze that I will never forget. "You have many years yet to live and many lessons to learn. They are the reasons you were born. You must fulfill what you went to the earth plane to accomplish."

I was lost for words, and I knew our meeting was almost over. "Stay with me," I pleaded.

"Oh Simon, you have so much more to discover. I will be watching you on your journey, but do not cry for me. My journey there had been completed, but you have much to do. Let me go now, and live your life."

I felt a tug on my back, as if someone or something was pulling me away. I looked behind me for a moment, and when I looked back she was gone. I woke up seconds later.

It was by far the longest dream sequence he had ever written, and as he gently put the legal pad and pen back under his pillow, Simon knew somewhere deep in his being that Nora, or perhaps his guides, had helped him remember it all.

He lay back down and pulled the covers up to his chin. The joy he felt continued unabated. He realized that it had been foolish of him in his dream state to ask his late wife to return with him, and yet there was nothing more in the world that he wanted. He had moved on, yet he still missed her dearly.

He didn't know it at the time, but he would never have another nightmare.

TWO

One week later, Simon woke up and noticed immediately that the warm feeling that had been coursing through his body for the last seven days was gone. The buzz, as he called it, had been strong for the first few days after his dream of meeting Nora, and then it had slowly begun to ebb. Now he was apparently back to normal.

He was disappointed, and felt a sense of loss. The feeling had been hard to describe, yet it had brought about a noticeable change within him. He had been happy and smiling all week, and it seemed as though he were on some kind of wonderful high. How could one dream be so magical?

Had it been a dream? Was it something more?

He had called Paul Tracy to ask about it just yesterday, and Paul seemed to think that perhaps he had astral projected. Paul explained that many people believed that while your body is sleeping your soul, or spirit, can leave the body and travel almost anywhere.

It had reminded Simon of a former client of his named Jill Palmer. She had been the major story in his first book. She had a unique ability to pick up a past life story line from one week to the next, continuing on as though reading from a book. No other client of Simon's had ever done such a thing.

On one occasion, she had just died after a lifetime in England, and was floating above her body, looking down on the scene. Her adoptive father had been in Spain at the time, and when Jill's spirit thought of him, she immediately found herself with him in Spain. Her spirit had traveled hundreds of miles in just a few seconds.

Simon hadn't died in his dream, of course, but he wondered if the theory was pretty much the same. The dream had also reinforced his belief that Nora was his soul mate; someone he had lived many lives with, and would again. He had believed it all during their marriage, particularly once he started doing past-life regressions and heard other people's tales of soul mates reunited.

The only fly in that ointment was Maria Vasquez.

Maria had come to his office twice for regressions. She was one of the most beautiful women he had ever met; tall, with long black hair and the most gorgeous emerald eyes he had ever seen. After her last appointment, she had called him and asked if she could come visit him at his home to talk. Simon had agreed, but was perplexed as to what she might want to talk about.

Maria told him that in both of her regressions, Simon had been *her* soul mate; once as a husband and once as a brother. Her marriage to her abusive husband in her current life had just broken up, and she let Simon know that she was hoping to get together with him again.

Simon hadn't believed a word of it, as Maria had expected. She had finished the visit by saying, "I hope someday you will ask me out, even if you don't believe me."

Simon had agonized over what Maria had told him for weeks. He still wanted to believe that Nora was his one and only. Still, the fact remained that Nora was gone and Maria was here. He had not had a single date since his wife's passing; had not had a desire to do so. Yet he was still just in his mid-forties, perhaps not even half way through his earthly incarnation, and Maria was stunningly attractive. If he was going to start dating again, she was a logical choice.

He waited over three months after her visit to his home before he finally picked up his cell phone and called her. Christmas and New Year's Day had come and gone, but Simon made a belated resolution that the New Year should be about his finally moving forward.

Maria had seemed relieved to finally hear from him, and she agreed to a simple dinner date the following evening at one of Sarasota's finer restaurants. Their reservation was for seven o'clock. They didn't end up leaving the restaurant until nearly ten thirty.

Their conversation was awkward at first, neither one seeming to know what direction to take. Maria mentioned that her divorce from her abusive husband was about to become final, and that her son, Enrique, had just had his fourth birthday. Simon talked about work and mentioned some of the psychic fairs he had been to recently. The conversation slowed even more when their meals arrived.

It wasn't until the plates had been cleared away and the coffee served that Maria finally looked at him and said, "So tell me, where is your head at? What are you thinking?"

"I'm conflicted," he admitted. "I always considered Nora my soul mate. I loved her dearly, and was lost without her. When you came to me and said I was your soul mate, I just couldn't believe it."

"In all of the work that you've done over the years with regressions, didn't the idea of a *soul family* ever come up? Couldn't there be a large group of people who always come back and spend time with each other? Couldn't they all be considered soul mates?"

That had opened the floodgates. They sat there for the next two hours discussing reincarnation, soul mates, and the many people you meet on the street that you seem to have known forever.

The waiter who refilled their coffees and eventually brought them the dessert tray thought they were his strangest customers of the evening.

The relationship moved slowly at first and stayed that way for nearly two months. If Maria was frustrated with him, it never showed. Then one day Simon finally decided it was time to live in the present and look towards the future. They drove to Key West for a three day weekend and finally consummated their relationship.

"You've moved on, as you should have," Nora had said.

He smiled as he realized that Nora was telling him it was okay.

Simon arrived at his office just after eight. It was Wednesday, the day he had set up to do regressions in Sarasota, and he knew he had a full schedule in the morning.

Grace, his matronly secretary, was seated at her desk. "Coffee's all made," she said, "and it looks like it's going to be a busy one." She motioned to the waiting room, where his first client was already marking time.

"Give me five," he said, "and then send her in."

Grace had been a perfect find for a secretary when he had opened his office in Sarasota. Melinda, his office girl in South Carolina, had also been wonderful at her job, but when Nora died she had tried too hard to help Simon out. It wasn't that he didn't appreciate it, but at the time he simply wanted to be left alone.

Grace, older and wiser and with problems of her own, had done just that after he hired her. She hadn't believed in his regression work and thought it was nonsense, in fact, but she needed the job and was good at it. Her views of reincarnation had taken a hit lately, however. She had been in attendance when Simon had reunited the two lovers from past lives who hadn't known each other in this life. Both had come to Simon for regressions, and when he realized their stories matched he found a way to introduce them.

Grace, set in her ways and slow to change, had finally started to come around to the idea that there might be something to this reincarnation stuff.

By lunch time, Simon had seen four clients and was ready for a break. "I'm going out for a bite," he said to Grace.

"No problem," she replied. Grace always stayed in the office at lunch time, even though Simon had told her numerous times she didn't have to. "You have a one o'clock appointment."

"I'll return in time," he said.

"Oh, and I have a message for you." She picked up a sticky note from her desk and read it to him. "Thomas Mann called. He would like you to call him back when you have time."

"About our little vacation together, no doubt," said Simon.

Thomas Mann was a medium who brought forth messages from those who had passed over to their loved ones. He and Simon worked together at Body and Soul Conferences around the country. Usually they would share the stage in the morning session on Friday, conversing with the audience, answering questions and whatnot. Then after lunch, Simon would do regression work with the attendees from 1:00 to 3:00, and then Thomas would bring forth messages from 3:00 to 5:00. Their sessions were always sold out. On Saturday and Sunday they would work individually with much smaller groups, usually about 30-40 people.

They were scheduled to be in Boston next weekend, and then Simon was going to stay at Mann's home in western Massachusetts for a week. Simon hoped nothing had altered Mann's plans.

He walked to a café not far from his office, ordered a Reuben sandwich and an iced tea, and then punched in Mann's number on his cell phone.

"Thomas," he said after Mann answered, "I'm looking forward to seeing you in Boston next week. I hope nothing has changed that."

"Not at all," said Thomas. "I'll be there with bells on, and then I'm hoping you still plan on visiting with me and my wife."

"Absolutely," said Simon.

"Will Maria be coming with you?"

"No, Maria has a new job that she doesn't feel right taking time off from so soon. So what's up? My secretary says you called."

"Well, Simon, it's like this. I've been asked to do some readings in my hometown during our week off. It's something the local Unitarian Church puts on every once in a while. I wondered if you'd like to join me."

"That would be fine," replied Simon, who rarely did anything outside the office besides the major conferences.

"Great," said Thomas. "And there is one other thing."

"What's that?"

"I'd like to have a regression with you, and in return you may have a private session with me."

Simon was quiet for a moment, processing the request. "You want a past-life regression?"

"I do," said Thomas. "And I have messages for you."

"What!" Simon was astounded. *Was Nora talking to Mann?* "You have messages for me?"

"I do," said Thomas again.

"From Nora?"

Thomas knew all about the death of Simon's wife, of course, for they had been working together for a number of years now.

"No, not from Nora, at least not yet. But if you agree to my request she may show up, and I would really like to have that regression. What do you say?"

Simon could not turn down a chance to hear from Nora again. "Let's do it," he said.

"Great!" replied Thomas, obviously pleased. "We'll work out the timing during our vacation. The dates for our readings in my hometown aren't set in stone yet."

"Well, now I'm really looking forward to our vacation," said Simon.

He returned to his office after lunch, and arrived just as Grace was taking a form from an older gentleman. She had seen the change in him over the past week, noticing how excited he seemed every day that he arrived at work. She didn't know what had happened, but whatever it was had obviously been a good thing.

Now he seemed excited all over again. "You look like the cat that ate the canary," she said. "What happened?"

"My vacation just became a whole lot more interesting," said Simon.

"How so?"

"A courtesy exchange of talents," he said, and knowing Thomas Mann had called earlier, Grace figured it out from there.

THREE

The gentleman who entered Simon's office a few minutes later was older than most of the people who came for a regression. He was six foot tall and probably weighed about one-seventy. The full head of hair was almost completely grey, his forehead held deep wrinkles, and he had the look of someone to whom life had not been kind.

Simon glanced at the information sheet that Grace had handed him a moment earlier. "Mister Wilson," he said, "please have a seat."

"Please, call me Billy," said the man.

"Okay Billy, I'm Simon. So tell me, what brings you here?"

Billy gazed at the doctor for a moment as if sizing him up, then said, "I purchased your book one day. I found it quite interesting, and when I noticed you lived in Sarasota, I decided to come see you. So here I am."

"Have you ever had any ideas about what your past lives may have been like?" asked Simon.

"Oh, I've had people tell me things over the years; nothing that I could actually verify."

Simon had the sudden feeling that Billy Wilson was being a bit evasive for some reason. It was not uncommon for his first time clients to act that way, not wanting to give him bits of information he could use to his advantage in a regression. Of course, it didn't work like that, but some people were just overly cautious.

"Are you open to the idea of reincarnation?"

The man again stared at the doctor for a moment before replying, and then a smile suddenly appeared. "To be honest,

I've never thought much about it. I have, however, delved into other areas of what some would call the New Age movement."

"So it's basically curiosity that has brought you here today?"

"I believe so," said Billy.

"Well, why don't we get started and see what shows up?" said Simon. "Please head on over to the couch, remove your shoes, lie down, and get comfortable."

Billy did as instructed, while Simon settled into a nearby chair.

"We'll start by relaxing your body from toes to head. Tighten the muscles in your toes and feet and hold it for a few seconds, then let it go."

It was a process that Simon had always used since he had started doing hypnosis sessions years ago. It had always worked well, helping his clients release all the tension from their bodies, while also beginning to focus their mind.

"Are you relaxed now, Billy?" he asked, when the process was complete.

"Very much so," Billy replied.

"That's good," said Simon. "Now we are going to concentrate on the mind. I'm going to count backwards from ten to one. As I do, I want you to picture yourself descending a spiral staircase. When I reach one, you will be standing at the bottom of the staircase, looking down a hallway towards a door that is closed. Do you understand?"

"Yes," said Billy.

"Okay then, let's begin. Ten; you're at the top of the staircase, looking down, and you begin to descend. Nine … eight. Heading down the stairs, circling around, becoming more relaxed with each step. Seven … six. Farther down you go, nearing the mid-point. Five … four. Descending lower and lower, your mind becoming completely calm and clear. Three … two. Almost at the bottom now, totally relaxed and at peace.

One. Reaching the bottom and standing in the hallway, perfectly relaxed. Are you in the hallway, Billy?"

"Yes."

"Can you see the closed door?"

"I do," said Billy, his voice sounding eerily calm.

"That's fine, Billy. You're doing very well. In a moment you are going to walk to the door and open it. It is a doorway to a past life of yours. When you step through the doorway, the past life will come back to you and information will pour forth. Are you ready?"

"I am ready," said Billy.

"Excellent," said Simon. "Now walk down the hallway, open the door, and step on through."

"Yes," said Billy a moment later, "I have done that."

"Tell me what you see."

Billy Wilson paused for a short while as if gathering information. Simon noticed his head move slightly from one side to the other, as though Billy were checking out the scene in front of him. When he finally spoke, it was with an assurance that Simon rarely heard in people.

"I am a woman in this lifetime, an old woman. It is quite cold out, but I am dressed warmly. I believe I am in Scandinavia somewhere; Finland, perhaps."

"That's excellent, Billy. Can you describe a bit more about yourself; perhaps tell us what you are wearing."

"As I said, old; wrinkled face, worn with age. My hands are small and have many spots on them. My mother calls them liver spots."

"Your mother in that life, Billy?"

"No, my mother now. She has those spots on her hands."

"Tell me about the clothes you have on. What's on your feet?"

"I'm wearing boots with much fur on the outside. There is snow on the ground, but not a lot. It feels like spring is just around the corner. I'm wearing a warm brown coat, leggings of some kind, and a skirt that goes down almost to my ankles."

"Are there other people with you? Perhaps you could find out what your name is."

"Yes, there are more here. I am in a town, not too big, but there seems to be a commotion going on."

"A commotion?"

Billy didn't reply right away, and Simon quietly waited for him to continue.

"My name is Anna, and it's not Finland, but Sweden that I am in. I live in the town of M-O-R-K-A-R-L-B-Y," said Billy, spelling it out.

Simon noticed the look on Billy Wilson's face suddenly turn serious, but before he could say anything Billy continued.

"I remember this place," he said. "The terror is coming back."

"What do you mean by that? What is the terror?"

"The witch hunts," said Billy. "They have passed this way before. Those were horrible times, involving the senseless killing of man, woman and child; the fear of having to turn in your friends and neighbors before they turned you in. Those times are coming back."

Simon knew of the Salem witch hunts in Massachusetts, of course, and was aware that similar occurrences had happened in Europe, although he knew very little about the European calamities. He was afraid that Billy's recall would end before it began, however, and so he decided to move the time frame back.

"It seems you're near the end of that lifetime now, Billy. Let's try to move back, perhaps when you were just a young girl. Tell me what your life was like. Can you do that for me, Billy?"

Billy Wilson replied almost instantly. "I was skinny as a child, even though I had a hearty appetite. My mother said I had a reverse metabolism; the more I ate, the more weight I lost. That changed as I grew older, of course."

"Tell me about your family," said Simon. "Do you have brothers and sisters?"

"I have a younger sister, Helga, and two older brothers named Olle and Sigge. Our father is a trapper, a trader in furs, but he and the boys also spend many hours fishing in the nearby river. Our village is small, in a secluded part of the country, but we get by. The neighbors come to me for advice, trusting what I say."

"Why is that?" asked Simon.

"I have a gift. I see things, what one would call 'future sight'. I see how things will be. I do not publicize it, for even as a young child I know that the terrors have already started in my country. But the locals know of my gift, and come to me when they need advice. Some come when they are pregnant, to discover if it will be a boy or a girl. They call me a sorceress."

"So you've lived with these terrors all your life then?"

"I've known of them, yes, and I've seen some of them in the visions I receive. They are most ungodly sights."

"Tell me, Anna," said Simon, switching to the name of her past life, "do you know what century you are in, perhaps the years that you lived?"

"I was born just before the turn of the century. I will die when the terrors return to my neck of the woods. The year of my passing will be 1669."

"Earlier you called them witch hunts. They were happening even when you were a child?"

"They happened in Sweden for many years. Things would calm down for a little while, and then they would start up again. I was fortunate to live as long as I did."

"What was your life like? Did you marry?"

"It was a wonderful place to live during the quiet times; peaceful, serene. The area was beautiful. The mountains would glisten with snow during the winter. We spent much time down by the river in the summer, fishing and bathing, although the water was always cold. It was refreshing."

"Tell me about your family," said Simon.

"My father was a big burly man, stout of heart, but as kind a man as you could find. My mother died young, God rest her soul. She was not a woman to tangle with; very opinionated. Olle also died young when his boat overturned and he hit his head on a rock, but my other brother Sigge lived to be a ripe old age. He was a trapper after my father and was very good at it. He knew the land like the back of his hand. He was there with me when the terrors came back to our village."

"Did you marry?" asked Simon again.

"No, I never did. Everyone knew of my gift, and I suppose it scared any suitors away. It mattered not to me. My brother inherited the land after our father died. He built a small house for me to live in so I could carry out my work in private."

"You mean your work as a sorceress?"

"Yes."

"Can you tell me what happened when the terrors returned?" asked Simon.

"Fear broke out, as always. Women were arrested who had no abilities whatsoever, yet they were called witches. My village had always protected me, but I was old now, seventy years to be exact, and so my name was added to the list. By now everyone knew me as 'the old sorceress', and I was proud of the title."

"Was it just women who were arrested?" asked Simon.

"Pretty much. There was one man taken in my group, but the rest were all women. Two of them were pregnant at the time, and thus their fate was delayed."

"Can you tell me about your final days, if it doesn't bother you too much?"

"We were taken to Mora, a nearby town, for trial and execution. I was the only one there who had any semblance of what you would now call psychic ability. I may have been the only one ever killed during those ludicrous times who actually had a gift. We were all found guilty, of course. That had been determined as soon as we were arrested. The rest was just for show. We all knew what our fate would be."

Simon, unaware of the culture at the time, assumed they would die by hanging. "I can tell you," he said, "that in doing my regression work, I have found that spirits leave the body moments before the life ends. Therefore, you are generally floating above your body when the time comes, feeling no pain, but simply watching what happens. Can you tell me how your end comes in that lifetime?"

"We come up, one by one, and lay our head on a stump. Our executioner will remove it with the swing of an axe."

Simon winced as he heard this.

Billy continued. "Our corpses are then lifted onto a stake with the corpses of others, and then they are burnt. You are correct in your telling, for I am just floating above the scene, watching it as it happens. My soul, or spirit if you will, left the body as I approached the tree stump."

Simon was stunned for a moment, as he oftentimes was, by the amazing stories many of his clients told.

"I am going to bring you back to the present now, Billy. If your body has unconsciously held on to any painful hurts from that lifetime, you may now release them. There is no need to hold onto them any longer."

"I understand," said Billy, and Simon brought him back.

Billy lay on the couch for a minute, not attempting to sit up. "My head seems to be spinning," he said.

"Take all the time you need," said Simon. "Sit up slowly when you feel ready."

Billy did sit up a moment later. "That was quite the story," he said.

"I am always amazed by the memories that people tell me," said Simon.

"Not a particularly pleasing way to die, although I imagine it is better to die quickly than to suffer for weeks on end," said Billy. "I thank you for helping me to recall this life."

"And how do you feel? Did it seem real to you?"

"Oh, I'm pretty sure that it was a factual remembrance of a prior life. There are things that seemed to come back to me as I went through it, and it explains some things for me today."

"Well then, I'm thankful that you came in," said Simon. "Perhaps I'll see you again."

"Oh, I think once was enough," said Billy. "It was a pleasure meeting you."

They shook hands, and a moment later Billy Wilson left the office.

Neither of them had any idea how soon they would see each other again.

Billy left Simon's office feeling as though another piece of his puzzle had been discovered. He walked to his car in the parking garage across the street, staring at the pavement as he went, his beat-up 2003 PT Cruiser awaiting his return. The car had 186,000 miles on it but still ran like a charm, even though it had been in three fender-benders over the years; or was it four? Billy smiled as he tried to remember. *Damn, I'm getting old,* he thought.

He drove home to the small apartment he rented on the Gulf side of Longboat Key. It was only three rooms, with a bathroom the size of a postage stamp, but it worked for him. He had moved often over the years and didn't need the comforts of a fancy place. As long as he was by the water, he was happy.

He made a cup of coffee in his Keurig, one of the few luxuries that traveled with him from place to place, and took a seat in front of his laptop that rested on the kitchen table. He immediately began a search for Swedish witch trials in the 17th Century. The list was quite extensive, but it didn't take long to find the one he was interested in. He clicked on the line that said, *Mora 1669.* You might think he'd be surprised when among the dead that day he found a woman named Anna, who was known as "the old sorceress", but you'd be wrong. He simply smiled when he saw her listed among those brutally murdered.

Doctor Simon Taylor was the real deal, he thought.

He sipped his still hot coffee as his mind wandered. His life had taken many twists and turns over the years, probably more than most people live through in three lifetimes.

It all started, however, that day in the woods some fifty years ago, and eventually his mind returned there, as it oftentimes did.

By the time his reverie ended an hour later, his coffee was cold.

FOUR

BILLY'S STORY, PART ONE
MAY, 1966

The four boys were playing baseball behind Potter's barn when the first drops of rain began to fall. Within minutes the wind picked up, spinning the weathervane on the barn roof so hard they could hear it, and sending enormous black clouds racing towards them.

"I think it's time to go," called out Walter Logan, affectionately known as Pokey.

The last pitch of the day produced a line drive that danced in the breeze like a Hoyt Wilhelm knuckleball and nearly took Billy Wilson's head off. He stuck his glove out at the last moment, guessing where the ball would go as he ducked the other way, and felt the satisfying thump as it landed in the pocket of his mitt.

"Lucky catch," yelled Hank DiPietro, who had hit the ball solid and thought it would be over Billy's head. "The wind knocked it down or you never would have caught it."

"Had it all the way," Billy replied.

"Hey guys, the storm's about to hit," said Vinnie Maki, who had been doing the pitching. "Let's head for the woods."

"Didn't I just say that?" said Pokey.

"Maybe we should just go home," said Billy. The boy's bikes were all leaning against the side of the barn.

"We'd be drenched by the time we got there," said Hank.

The other boys quickly agreed, and they all began running for cover in the trees beyond left field. The three fastest made it just before the cloudburst opened. Pokey was the last to arrive, and he caught the start of the heavy rain, drawing the usual guffaws from his pals.

"Man, you gotta run faster," said Hank.

"Pokey only has one speed, and that's slowww," said Vinnie, drawing out the last word.

Pokey gave them his usual *aw shucks, got me again* look. Nothing much bothered Pokey, who took everything in stride

The boys, all sixth graders and all eleven years old except for Hank, who had just turned twelve last month, played together almost every day. They spent much of their free time at Potter's farm, playing baseball in the spring and summer and turning to football in the fall. Even in winter, when the snows hit, they could often be found in another part of the Potter's yard, sliding down the hills on their sleds.

The boys genuinely liked each other's company most of the time, and when they fought and stopped speaking to one another, it would usually only last for a day or so before they were back together.

Potter's farm was no longer a working farm. In fact, Mrs. Potter was the only one still living there. Her husband had died three years ago, and their children, whom none of the boys had ever met, lived on the other side of the country. Mister Potter had gone somewhat crazy in his final years, once chasing the boys off his yard with a pitchfork.

The Potter home was at the end of a long dirt driveway more than a quarter mile from the main road. The house was on a small rise at the end of the driveway, with eight steep cement steps leading up to the front porch. A faded red barn, once home to dairy cows and chickens, was off to the left about forty yards from the house. One side of the barn acted as the backstop for the boy's baseball games, saving them the need of a catcher.

The woods beyond left field went all the way back to the main road and stretched for nearly a mile length-wise, making them great for exploring whenever the boys were tired of playing ball. Pine trees dominated, with a good sampling of maple, oak and birch mixed in.

"Let's head for the clearing," said Hank, and the other boys nodded their heads in agreement.

The boys had a favorite spot in the forest about two hundred yards in. It had great tree cover, a long forgotten stone wall, and pine needles covering the ground.

Hank was the leader of their group, although they had never voted on it. Size mattered when you were eleven, and besides being the oldest, Hank was also bigger and stronger than the others. He had long black hair that always looked greasy from an overuse of Brylcreem, as he apparently paid no attention to the TV ad that stated, "a little dab will do ya." He had dark eyes that seemed almost grey, and a small scar on his forehead from a sledding accident when he was two. His father was an iron-worker who wasn't afraid to knock his kids around once in awhile, and Hank had received his fair share of blows to the head. It caused him to have a quick temper, and when Hank became angry, you didn't want to be on the receiving end. He was solidly built, and while the other boys occasionally grew mad at him, none of them had ever started a fist fight with him.

Vinnie Maki was an average size kid with wavy light blond hair and enchanting powder blue eyes. If you could say *he was his own man* about an eleven year old, then you would say it about Vinnie. He did what he wanted, and if people didn't like it, he was okay with that. He was constantly being grounded by his parents, but it never bothered him. He was the risk-taker of the group, and if the boys ever found themselves in trouble, it was usually because of some great idea that Vinnie had come up with. He'd tried cigarettes when he was eight, thinking his mother wouldn't notice as packs disappeared from her carton. Billy had gone down with him on that one. They were caught one day in the tree house that Vinnie's dad had made for him. Billy had taken so much grief from his parents over the incident that he never smoked again, but Vinnie just brushed it off as he did everything else.

"You have to live life to the fullest," Vinnie was fond of saying.

When you saw Walter Logan, you'd wonder how he fit in with the other boys. He was of medium height but chubby, with light brown hair and brown puppy dog eyes. He couldn't run fast, threw a ball just a little bit better than a girl, and lived in the hand-me-down clothes of his two older brothers. He was, however, a good-natured kid. *Happy-go-lucky*, Billy's mother would say, and that was just about right. He was easy to pick on, and they all did at times, but he always took it well. His father had run off shortly after he was born, leaving his mom with three kids to raise on her own. He rarely had money to spend on candy or baseball cards, but he never whined about it much, and you had to respect him for that.

Billy Wilson was the tallest member of the group, but was on the scrawny side. He had brown hair, hazel eyes, and was the only one of them who needed glasses, which he had started wearing last year after his teacher discovered he couldn't read the blackboard. A month after the smoking incident with Vinnie, the two of them had lit a hayfield on fire. It quickly went out of control, and the fire department had to be called. The fire chief sat down with them and threatened reform school if their behavior didn't improve. Vinnie had laughed the threat off as always, but Billy had been scared to death. He became the moral voice of the group, and before much more time had passed the other boys were calling him Preacher.

Billy considered himself the voice of reason to all of Vinnie's crazy ideas. He enjoyed being part of this group, not so much because he liked the other boys but because he loved playing sports. In truth, he was a loner who could happily spend time by himself for hours on end.

The rain was steady as the boys made their way to the clearing. Last year's leaves that had survived the winter snows covered much of the ground. A small stream followed them for the first half of the journey before veering off. The dense tree coverage kept much of the rain from coming through, but the boys were all damp by the time they arrived.

They decided to play cards, and Pokey retrieved the deck they kept hidden in the hollowed out section of a maple tree. They sat by the wall, two on each side, and played rummy.

"Guess the Sox will lose again today," said Vinnie, and the others all nodded their agreement. The Red Sox had not started off the year very well, and the boys had little hope that the season would get any better.

"They only had five hits last night," said Billy, who followed the game closely and always devoured the box scores in the daily paper when he arrived home from school each day.

"What did you expect?" replied Pokey. "Dean Chance was pitching for California."

"I thought we'd do better this year," said Billy. "We have a pretty good lineup, what with Yaz and Tony C, and that new first baseman is really good."

"Yeah," said Vinnie, "but our pitching sucks, except for Radatz."

"Is he the one they call *The Monster?*" asked Hank, who loved to play baseball but really didn't follow it that much.

"That's him," said Billy.

Every year, Billy would try to predict the final standings in both the American and National Leagues. He always picked the Sox to finish first, hoping that some day he could say I-told-you-so to everyone he knew. His father always smiled when Billy showed him his predictions, saying maybe he would be right this year. His father had been born in New York and was actually a Yankee fan, but he never flaunted the fact in front of his son.

The rain finally let up thirty minutes later just as Vinnie won the rummy game, and the boys, all of them now pretty much soaked through, decided to head on home.

Pokey put the cards back in the tree. "Almost time to bring a new deck," he said. "This one's just about had it."

They walked slowly through the woods. Hank picked up a stone and threw it at a squirrel, nearly beaning the unsuspecting animal, and soon the four of them were trying to hit the birds that were sitting in the trees.

They were fifty yards from exiting the woods when Hank suddenly stopped short and said, "What the...?"

Vinnie had been walking right behind Hank and nearly ran into him, stopping just in time. "What's the matter?" he asked.

"Over there, behind those trees," Hank said, his arm pointing off to their left. "Doesn't that look like a hand?"

The boys all turned their heads as one and gazed where Hank was pointing.

"Where?" Pokey and Billy cried in unison.

"Right by that birch tree," said Hank.

Vinnie didn't see anything, but he took off running in the direction Hank had been pointing, and the other boys quickly followed. As he drew closer, Vinnie saw there was more than just a hand sticking out of the muck.

"Holy cow," he cried. "There's a dead guy here."

The boys all gathered around and stood side by side, Pokey arriving last as usual. They stared, mesmerized, at the sight in front of them. Pokey was the only one who had ever seen a dead body before, and that was in the funeral parlor.

The man was laying face down, his head looking left. His right hand, which Hank had seen, was draped over a fallen limb. Whoever had dumped him here had covered him with some dirt, weeds, and leaves, but they did it haphazardly, undoubtedly thinking that the body wouldn't be discovered for a long time, if at all. However, the rain had washed much of the debris away. The deceased was wearing a red and black flannel shirt, blue jeans and Keds sneakers.

"Was he here when we came in?" asked Pokey, his mind picturing a band of killers roaming through the woods.

"Geez, Pokey, look at him," said Hank. "He's obviously been here for a while."

"Then why didn't we see him when we came in?" Pokey replied, a nervous catch to his voice.

"It was raining," said Hank, "and the trees were blocking our view from that direction. Good grief, Pokey, I barely saw him this time." He paused for a moment, and then asked, "Anyone recognize him?"

"Hard to tell with all the muck on him," said Vinnie, but he didn't look familiar to any of them. Vinnie leaned down and plucked two leaves off the man's head.

"Don't touch him," said Billy, as Preacher mode began to kick in, but Vinnie didn't listen. The last leaf was actually stuck to the man's hair with dried blood, the rain notwithstanding. Vinnie moved it to one side, and they all saw the bullet hole in his temple.

"Aw man, that's gross," said Pokey. "Billy's right, you shouldn't be touching him."

"Easy, Pokey," said Vinnie, "it's not like I can hurt the guy. I just want to check him out, that's all."

Without warning, Vinnie rolled the body over as the other boys uttered various cries of disbelief. "I'm just looking to see if he has more injuries," he said. Now the right side of the head was visible, and they all saw the huge exit wound the bullet had made in his skull.

Pokey turned around, took two steps, and started to dry heave.

"What do you think this guy did?" Billy asked.

"I guess he messed with someone he shouldn't have messed with," said Hank, and they all nodded as though he had spoken some amazing truth.

"Probably a mob hit," said Vinnie.

"Mob hit?" said Hank, a look of disbelief on his face. "Vinnie, this is Edgeworth, Massachusetts. The mafia doesn't even know this place exists."

"Well, he pissed somebody off."

Hank watched as Vinnie checked the guy's pockets but came up empty. He couldn't believe Vinnie was touching the body. Hank had no intention of doing any such thing. The sight of the hole in the man's head made him want to vomit too, but he managed to hold it together.

"You shouldn't be touching him," said Billy again. He had moved a few steps back, also having no desire to come any closer to the body. He was already wondering how much trouble they would be in for moving it.

"Oh, bug off, Billy," said Vinnie, annoyed by his friends goody-two-shoes attitude.

Walter, unnerved by Vinnie's actions, suddenly did get sick and threw up just below the body's feet, and then he turned and started walking away.

"We need to call the police," said Billy.

"You're right," said Hank. "We can use old lady Potter's phone. Come on, Vinnie."

Walter, Hank and Billy began walking back to the path. Vinnie watched them walking away, and then turned to take a final look at the body. As he did, he noticed that the man's shirt also had a pocket. Vinnie slipped his hand inside and touched something that felt like paper, only a bit stronger. It slipped out of his grasp at first, his nerves getting the better of him for a moment. After making sure none of the other boys were watching, he reached back into the pocket, grabbed the item, and quickly withdrew it.

Hank turned around at that moment and yelled, "Vinnie, let's go!" and Vinnie jumped to his feet.

He took a quick peek at what he had found before rejoining his friends. *A clue*, he thought. He gazed at it for a moment. The piece was torn, but he could still read the writing on it. He recognized it immediately, because he had seen his father with something just like this on many occasions. He was pretty sure he knew where it had come from, and an idea quickly formed in his mind. He quietly slid the item into his pocket, and then he ran to catch up with his friends.

The rain had nearly stopped as they ran across the field to the Potter house. Pokey soon lagged behind, and when the others reached the barn they stopped and waited for him. When Pokey caught up, he put his hands on his knees and tried to catch his breath.

"You really oughta lose some weight," said Vinnie.

"You really oughta kiss my ass," Pokey replied. Under normal circumstances they would have all laughed at this, but the sight of a dead man in the woods had changed things.

"Come on, guys," said Hank. "Let's get up to the house and make our call. Maybe the old lady will give us some towels to dry off with."

They walked to the house and made their way up the cement stairs to the porch. None of them touched the metal railing on the side of the steps, which was more rusted than not and had peeling paint flakes all over it.

The large farmhouse had eight rooms in all, four upstairs and four down. The boys knew Mrs. Potter didn't use the second floor rooms anymore because it was too difficult for her to climb the stairs. She would occasionally invite them in for cookies and lemonade in the summer, or hot chocolate in the winter when they went sledding, but mostly she let them be.

They opened the screen door that led onto the porch and then gathered around her front door. There were two rocking chairs on the right, both old and in need of a good sprucing up, with cushions that should have been tossed out years ago. On the left were boxes of items no longer used by Mrs. Potter, who probably didn't even remember what they contained.

The doorbell to the old farmhouse hadn't worked in years, so Hank knocked loudly on the heavy wooden door. They waited about ten seconds, didn't hear anything, and then he knocked again.

"Maybe she's taking a nap," said Billy. "Why don't we just go to my house?"

"Try the door," said Vinnie. "Just go in and holler."

"That's breaking and entering," said Billy.

Vinnie gave him a look of disdain. "We have a dead body out there, numb nuts. I think that's a pretty good reason to open the door. The old lady won't mind once we tell her what's in her woods."

Hank agreed. "Okay," he said, and turned the knob before anybody could object. The door was unlocked, as he expected it would be. Few people in the neighborhood ever locked their doors at night, never mind the middle of the day. They all piled into the kitchen and were hit by the musty odor of a home that didn't get much use anymore.

"How come all the shades are drawn?" asked Hank.

"I told you she was sleeping," said Billy, deathly afraid that the police were about to show up and arrest them. "Let's just call the cops from my place."

Hank ignored him, and called out, "Mrs. Potter?" as he walked farther into the kitchen.

Pokey found the light switch and flipped it on. An incandescent light above the kitchen table sizzled into life, its outer glass covering in need of cleaning and dead flies lying inside.

"Mrs. Potter?" called Hank again. "We need to use your phone."

Still no reply.

"Stay here," Hank said. "I'm going to check the other rooms. If we all go in, we'll scare her half to death."

Hank entered the dining room and took a quick glance around, calling out her name as he went. A large table sat in the center of the room with six accompanying chairs. Placemats were set at either end. He wondered why there was such a big table, since he had never known there to be anyone here but the two of them, and now just the widow. Against the wall between two windows was a china cabinet. It was full of dishes that looked like they hadn't been used in decades, and the wood was in desperate need of dusting.

He moved on to the living room and took a quick glance around. "Mrs. Potter," he called again. Still no answer. A taste of fear suddenly bubbled up into Hank's throat. He knew the old lady rarely went out.

He entered a hallway, continuing to call out her name as he went. The bathroom was on his right, and a quick glance showed him it was empty. Mrs. Potter's bedroom was at the end of the hall. The door was closed, and he relaxed a bit, suddenly thinking that Billy had been right; she was just sleeping. He figured they should just use her phone and not bother waking her, but as he drew closer he noticed the door was actually slightly ajar. He gently pushed it in as he softly called "Mrs. Potter" one more time.

The rest of the boys were waiting in the kitchen. Pokey noticed a cookie jar on the counter and lifted the lid. There were chocolate chip cookies inside, which were his favorite. He took one and said, "Anybody else want a cookie?"

They were all hungry, but Billy, now fully in Preacher mode, said, "You shouldn't be taking that without asking, you know."

"It's just a cookie," said Vinnie, as he walked to the counter to take one for himself. "Don't be such a ..."

Vinnie never finished his sentence, for suddenly they all heard Hank yelling "OhmyGod" over and over as if it was one word.

A moment later, Hank ran back into the kitchen screaming, "She's dead, she's dead," and when he reached them he said, "I think she's been shot in the head, too. Just like the other guy."

This would prove to be incorrect, as she had actually been shot in the chest near her heart, but Hank had simply seen the blood soaked sheets and made an assumption.

Billy just stood there with his mouth open, while Pokey dropped his cookie on the floor. Vinnie ran down the hall to have a look for himself, but this time he didn't touch the body. Old people really gave him the creeps. He didn't usually like to be around them, never mind touch them, and that was when they were alive. Mrs. Potter was obviously dead. She was lying on her bed, and the white sheets and pillow case around her head were stained with dried blood.

Vinnie ran back into the kitchen. "She's dead alright," he called out, and the boys made a beeline out the door. They bolted through the porch and down the stairs, running as fast as they could. The rain clouds had moved on, and a ray of sunshine was just beginning to peek out.

They all ran to their bikes and pedaled as fast as they could down the Potter's long drive. No one stopped to wait for Pokey this time. He was barely half-way to the main road when the rest of them were barreling through the Wilson's back door.

Billy's mother was ironing in the kitchen when the boys came in all shouting at once, and she only heard certain words from each one of them; *body, woods, Potter, police*. "Whoa," she said. "One at a time, please. Billy, what is going on?"

"We found a body in the woods," Billy said, not realizing that he was shouting. "He was shot in the head, and when we went to use Mrs. Potter's phone to call the police we found her dead too. We have to call the police."

"What? Billy, if this is some kind of joke..."

"It's not, Mrs. Wilson," said Vinnie. "We really need to call the police."

"Oh my word, you boys are serious." She turned and yelled, "Carl," and a moment later her husband came into the kitchen. The boys quickly repeated their story to him, and then Mister Wilson hurried to the phone.

2

Edgeworth, Massachusetts was a small town on the northern fringe of the state, just a few miles from the Vermont border. The population of 1400 souls would double in the summer, as many of the homes were just summer retreats for the big city folks. The most sought after residences were situated around Brooks Lake, which sat in the northeast portion of the town. Between Edgeworth and the Vermont border sat the town of Dearborn, half the size and population of Edgeworth, and to their west was the town of Philbrook, home to nearly 6000 residents.

Edgeworth Grammar School was located in the downtown area, if you could call a one room Post Office, a combination town hall and library, a convenience store and a gas station downtown. The police station was situated on one end of town and the fire station, consisting of one truck and a car for the chief, was at the other end. The school contained all grades from kindergarten through sixth, and included the children of Dearborn, which had no school of its own.

Once the school children of Edgeworth and Dearborn finished sixth grade, they had to go to Philbrook to finish their education. Packwood Junior High School, named for the only local resident of Philbrook to die in World War One, was just a mile and a half down the road from downtown Edgeworth. When the children entered high school, they had to attend North Bishop Regional High School, also located in Philbrook.

In 1966, the police force of Edgeworth consisted of a chief, a sergeant, and four officers, plus two citizens who were called in to help on occasion if someone in the office was sick.

Daisy Monroe, one of the few female policewomen in the state, was sitting at her desk when the call from Carl Wilson came in. At first she thought it was a joke, as the only known murder in Edgeworth had been in 1928. Once Daisy realized the call was no prank, she notified fellow officer John Paul Stephens, who was currently sitting in his cruiser staring out at the waters of Brooks Lake.

Stephens, 29, had been on the Edgeworth police force for seven years. He was momentarily stunned by the call, but instinct quickly took over. "Call Gilmore and let him know," he said to Daisy, "then call Greenfield and get some detectives out here."

Edgeworth, Dearborn, and Philbrook did not have any detectives on their forces, rarely having need of them. Most of the crime in their small towns involved the occasional assault or domestic dispute, and in the summer a home robbery or two.

Gilmore was Sergeant Dan Gilmore, who was currently in charge of the office. The major police department in the area was in Greenfield, just south of Edgeworth on the other side of Route 2.

Stephens immediately headed to the address Daisy had given him and arrived six minutes after Carl Wilson's phone call. Carl and the boys had just gone back outside and were waiting by the road at the head of Mrs. Potter's driveway.

The Wilson and Maki homes sat next to each other, with the Potter driveway in the middle. Carl had suggested that Vinnie go tell his parents what had happened, but Vinnie stated that neither of them were home at the moment.

Stephens rolled down his window upon arriving, looked at Carl Wilson, and asked, "Are you the one who called?"

"I did," said Billy's dad. "The boys say they found a body in the woods, and when they went to use Mrs. Potter's phone they found her dead too. She lives in the house at the end of the driveway."

"All four of you boys were together when you found the bodies?" Stephen's asked.

"Yes, sir," they all replied.

"I'll take two of you boys with me," said Stephens, "to show me where the bodies are located." He pointed to Hank and Pokey and said, "You two get in the car," and then he looked at Carl Wilson and said, "You wait here with the other boys, if you don't mind. There will be more officers arriving, and some detectives from Greenfield will be coming by at some point. They'll want to talk with the boys."

Stephens knew the detectives would want the boys separated so they could compare stories.

Carl Wilson nodded that he understood as Hank and Pokey slid into the back seat of the police car. Walter barely had time to close the door before Stephens took off down the Potter's driveway. He gunned the car so fast that a cloud of dust quickly arose and stones went flying everywhere.

"Why did they get to go and not me?" cried Vinnie, furious that the cop hadn't chosen him. He wouldn't have minded seeing the body in the woods once more, although he had no desire to see Mrs. Potter again.

Carl Wilson was surprised by Vinnie's outburst. He had spent two years of his life fighting the Germans in World War II and had seen more than his share of dead bodies. He wondered why anyone would want to see such a horrible sight again, particularly a boy as young as Vincent Maki.

Billy was more than happy to stay behind, but the fact that he was apparently going to be interviewed by a detective made his stomach churn.

Hank was excited yet nervous as the cruiser made the short, quick trip to the house, but Pokey looked as though he might throw up again.

"Green to the gills," Hank would later tell the others, and Pokey wouldn't disagree.

Stephens parked in the driveway and told Hank and Walter to get out. "We'll start in the house," said Stephens. "Tell me everything you did."

The three of them climbed the stairs to the porch, and Hank described how he had opened the door after Mrs. Potter didn't answer their call.

"The door was unlocked?" asked Stephens. He wasn't surprised when Hank verified the fact.

They entered the kitchen, and then Hank led the officer through the rooms exactly as he had walked them earlier. Pokey, who had no desire to see the body, stayed in the kitchen.

"She's in there," Hank said, when they reached the bedroom.

"The door was open like this?"

"No," said Hank, "it was open just a crack. I opened it and looked in when she didn't answer."

"Did you enter the room?"

"No sir," said Hank.

"Okay. Go back to the kitchen and try not to touch anything," said Stephens. "I'll be right out."

The cop entered the room and found Mrs. Potter sprawled across the bed. She was laying face down, the top of her head barely touching her pillow, and he knew there was no need to check for a pulse. It was obvious to him that she had been dead for some time. The gunshot wound to her chest appeared to be the only injury. He checked the floor for the bullet or its casing, but found nothing.

He took out his notebook, jotted down a few items, and made a quick, crude but effective drawing of the scene. He was walking back to the kitchen when he heard a siren in the distance telling him that the Sergeant was almost there.

3

Sergeant Dan Gilmore had been flabbergasted when Daisy called him, much as Daisy had been when first receiving Carl Wilson's phone call.

"Murders? In Edgeworth?" he had said. Once assured that Daisy was not joking, Dan said, "I'll swing by the office and pick you up. Call in one of the part-timers to man the phones." Twelve minutes later Dan and Daisy were heading for the crime scene even though their part-time civilian had yet to arrive.

Sergeant Gilmore couldn't believe his luck, although he wasn't sure if it was good or bad. The chief of the Edgeworth police department was Oliver Randall, who had boarded a plane for Jamaica the previous morning, taking his first real vacation in three years. Randall would be chief in Edgeworth for eighteen years, and he would miss the only murders to occur on his watch in the week that he was gone, although he would still play a prominent part in the investigation. Gilmore, who was a sixteen year veteran of the force, was in charge during the chiefs' absence.

Daisy Monroe, the first female officer ever in Edgeworth, had been on the force just fourteen months. The two of them arrived at the scene just seventeen minutes after the phone call. When they reached the head of the driveway, Carl Wilson pointed them towards the Potter house. They didn't bother stopping.

Stephens went out to meet his fellow officers after telling Hank and Pokey to wait on the porch.

Sergeant Gilmore noticed the boys, looked at Stephens, and asked, "Those the kids who found the bodies?"

"Two of four," Stephens told him. "The other boys will be interviewed down at the house."

"Good thinking," said Gilmore.

Hank was nervous with all these cops around him. His father had no love for the police, having had more than a few run-ins with them over the years, and his attitude about them had filtered down to his son.

Pokey still looked as though he might faint at any moment.

The five of them were just about to head back inside the Potter home when they heard yet another car coming down the drive. It was an unmarked sedan.

"Greenfield's here already," said Gilmore.

"That was quick," said Daisy. "They must have been close by when they got the call."

The car pulled up in front of the house, and Detective Thomas Gallo exited the vehicle and joined the group. After a round of introductions, Gallo said, "Let's get started," and they all began ascending the cement steps.

Sgt. Gilmore noted the drapes were all closed. "Were these drapes closed when you came in?" he asked Hank.

"Yes, sir," said Hank.

"Where's the body located?" asked Gallo.

"In the bedroom, down the hall off the living room," said Stephens. "She's been dead a while."

"I want you to walk me through it," said Gallo to Hank. "Show me everything you did."

Gilmore went directly to the bedroom to verify for himself that Mrs. Potter was deceased. Stephens again walked through the house with Hank, this time accompanied by Detective Gallo.

Walter once again remained in the kitchen with Daisy Monroe. He saw the chocolate chip cookie he had dropped just a short while ago lying on the linoleum, but he didn't even look at the cookie jar. It seemed he had lost his appetite.

Hank showed Gallo how he had progressed through the house, as he had done moments earlier with Officer Stephens. He was as excited as he'd ever been in his life, but scared too. He hoped it didn't show. When they reached the bedroom, he showed all three men how the door had been slightly ajar. "I pushed it open like this," he said, demonstrating for them, "and looked in."

"Did you enter the room?" asked Gallo.

"No sir. I think I screamed," he said, embarrassed by the fact. "Then I ran back to the kitchen to tell the others. Vinnie came down to see for himself, and then we all ran."

"Did Vinnie touch the body?" asked Gallo.

"I don't think so, sir, but I didn't ask."

"Did you phone the police from here?" asked Gallo, unaware that Carl Wilson had made the call.

"No, sir," said Hank. "We just ran outside, grabbed our bikes, and headed to Billy's house."

"The father of one of the other boys called it in," said Daisy Monroe, who had wandered down the hall. "I took the call." She looked at the body and asked, "Do you think she was sleeping?"

Her Sergeant gave her a quizzical look. "Not laying like that, no."

"Why come in and kill her if she had been sleeping all along?" Gallo asked Daisy. "She must have seen them drive in. Maybe glanced out her window and one of them noticed. They decide not to take any chances, so they come in here and pop her. She sees them coming, panics, and runs to her bedroom."

They left Monroe with Mrs. Potter while the rest of them headed back outside. Gallo looked at the boys and asked, "Do you remember where the body in the woods is?"

"Sure," said Hank. "It's easy to find. We play in those woods all the time."

They traipsed across the field, the wet ground soaking their shoes and Gallo complaining about the mud on his brand new wingtips.

Walter started shivering because he was still soaked to the bone, but he was last in line and nobody noticed. Hank pointed out where they had entered, and said, "It's not far."

They made their way into the woods, Hank in the lead and Pokey taking up the rear. It was harder to see the body walking in this direction, and Hank kept looking to his right, not wanting to miss it.

"There it is, over there," he said when they reached to spot, and he pointed out the dead man lying in the muck.

Once again Detective Gallo asked Hank to tell him everything they did.

"I spotted the body first, and then we all ran over to it. Vinnie bent down and moved some leaves off the guys head. That's when we saw the bullet hole."

"Vinnie did touch this body?" asked Gallo.

Hank hesitated a moment, but he never considered lying. "Yes, sir," he said. "He was on his stomach, and Vinnie rolled him over to see if any of us recognized him."

He knew right away the cops were not happy, and he unconsciously took a step backward. If his dad had been here, he would have given Hank a hard one across his cheek for doing something stupid, even though he wasn't the one who did it.

The boys stayed back as the cops checked out the scene. It soon became obvious to all three of them that the rain and the tramping of the boys had destroyed whatever evidence they might find.

The sun that had broken through the clouds disappeared again and a slight breeze picked up, causing Pokey to visibly shiver once more. This time the cops all noticed, and after a few more questions they sent the two boys on their way, accompanied by Officer Stephens.

When they arrived back at the Potter residence they noticed that the coroner's wagon had arrived. Daisy Monroe was standing outside the porch, holding the screen door open, as a stretcher was being brought inside.

Stephens said, "Get in the car, boys. I'll take you back to your friend's house."

"Thank you, sir," said Pokey.

Once they were settled in, the officer looked at Hank and said, "That was quite a day you boys had. Were you scared?"

Hank, sitting in the front seat this time, turned to look at Stephens. "Not at first," he said. "When we found the body in the woods, it was almost like an adventure. Something you get to brag about to all the kids at school." He paused for a moment, and Stephens glanced at him. "But when I found Mrs. Potter's body, that scared me, because suddenly I thought maybe the person who did it was still around."

Stephens looked in the rear view mirror at Pokey. "How about you, son? Were you scared?"

"Yes, sir," said Walter. "More scared than I've ever been in my life."

The car pulled up in front of Billy's house and the boys started to get out.

"You did well," Stephens told them.

4

Carl Wilson had been about to send Billy and Vinnie back to the house after waving the second Edgeworth cruiser through when he noticed another car headed their way. The sedan carrying the Greenfield detectives pulled up a moment later, and after verifying that they were at the right spot, one of the men got out and approached the trio.

"I'm Detective William Cranmore," he said, as his partner drove off to the crime scenes. "So you two boys found the bodies?"

"Yes sir," said Vinnie, who had suddenly decided that being interviewed by a real detective might be even better than seeing the bodies again.

On the other hand, Billy looked as though he expected to be arrested for murder at any moment.

"There were four boys in all," said Carl Wilson. "The other two went with one of the police officers to show him where the bodies are located."

Carl Wilson led the detective and the two boys inside his home. Cranmore and the boys took seats around the kitchen table, while Billy's dad stood behind his son. Laurie Wilson offered the detective coffee, which he gratefully accepted.

Cranmore took out his notebook and wrote down the names of all four boys, and then began the questioning by saying, "Okay boys, let's start at the beginning. What were you doing at the Potter residence?"

"Playing ball," said Vinnie. "We play over there all the time. They have a nice big field behind the barn, and we play baseball all summer and football in the fall."

"Where did you find the first body?"

"In the woods," said Vinnie.

"So what were you doing in the woods?" asked Cranmore.

"It started to rain, so we headed to the woods for cover."

"Why not just go in the barn?"

"It's locked," said Vinnie. "One day Mrs. Potter put a lock on it, and we think she lost the key because it's been locked ever since."

Billy was more than happy to let Vinnie do the talking. He spoke only when the detective asked, "Is that how you remember it?" which he did about a dozen times. Billy was so scared he was literally shaking. Even though he had done nothing wrong, he was picturing scenarios in his mind of what reform school would be like.

On the other hand, Vinnie was thoroughly enjoying himself. He was impressed by the detective's thoroughness, but secretly delighted by the fact he had a clue in his pocket that no one knew about. He answered each question honestly, until he was asked if they had moved the bodies at all, and then he hesitated, which immediately gave him away to the detective.

"Which body did you move, son?" asked Cranmore.

"The one in the woods," Vinnie said. "He was lying on his stomach, and I rolled him over. I thought maybe one of us would recognize him."

Laurie Wilson, who was pacing the kitchen floor all during the questioning, couldn't believe what she was hearing. "Oh God, you touched the bodies?"

"I didn't!" Billy quickly yelled. "Just Vinnie." He looked at Vinnie and gave him his best *I told you so* stare, and was shocked when he realized that Vinnie was actually enjoying this.

"You shouldn't have done that," said Cranmore, "but what's done is done." He quizzed them for another ten minutes, and then decided he had all he needed for now.

Vinnie had been debating whether to tell the detective that he had taken something from the scene, but in the end he decided not to. He knew that was a big no-no, and after the slight rebuke about moving the body, he didn't want to get into bigger trouble for taking evidence.

Besides, an idea was percolating in Vinnie's mind.

When Hank and Pokey arrived back at the Wilson's, they went inside and joined the other boys, who were upstairs eating sandwiches that Billy's mother had made. She told them the detectives wanted them to stay just a while longer in case they had any more questions, and then she said, "I called your parents, told them what had happened, and that you would be home shortly. I know you're all wet, so if any of you want to take a shower, you can. There are towels in the closet."

Hank hadn't realized how hungry he was. He quickly devoured two peanut butter sandwiches with marshmallow fluff, and drank a glass of Tang that Mrs. Wilson had made for them.

Pokey, who normally never passed up a meal of any kind, tried to eat but found his stomach still too much on edge. He had never thought the killers might still be in the area until Hank had mentioned it to the cop. The idea had scared him more than the bodies did, even though he knew he was now safe.

"Did you tell them I moved the body?" asked Vinnie, after Laurie Wilson had left.

"Yeah," said Hank. "They didn't seem too happy about that."

"I told the detective too, and he said we shouldn't have touched it," said Vinnie.

"I told you not to touch it," said Billy.

"Yeah, yeah," said Vinnie. He was fingering the paper in his pocket and secretly smiling. *If only the cops knew*, he thought. After a moment he looked at his friends and said, "I think we should investigate this case. We could pretend we were private eyes."

The other boys all looked at him as though he had three heads.

"How would we do that?" asked Billy. "We don't know who the dead guy is, where he's from, nothing? What's to investigate?"

"Yeah," said Hank, "I overheard the cops in the woods saying they wouldn't have much to go on. What could we possibly do?"

"Maybe you're right," said Vinnie, but they all saw that look on his face that they'd seen a hundred times before. He had some crazy idea in his head, and it would almost certainly lead to trouble. "Maybe I'll just look into it on my own."

"Who do you think you are, Perry Mason?" said Billy.

The others all laughed, but Vinnie didn't mind. He knew something they didn't, and when he solved the case and went to the police he would be a hero. They wouldn't be laughing then. He would become the top dog, and Hank would be following his rules. They didn't know how much he wanted that, because he had always hid it well, but Vinnie had always believed that he should be the leader of this group, not Hank. He would show them the truth of that by solving this case on his own.

It was the fantasy of an eleven year old.

FIVE

Richie Membrino knew his time was short. He had cheated death on a number of occasions, but death wasn't about to let him slip away this time.

His hospital room was quiet, save for the beeping of the monitors, and he was so used to them by now that their noise didn't even register. The nurse who gave him his medicine had just left, and he figured it would be an hour before lunch arrived. He wanted to get up, get dressed, and go home, but he knew that wouldn't happen. The next time he left this room would be when they wheeled his dead body down to the morgue.

He had survived three heart attacks, a gunshot in his thigh that just missed rupturing an artery, and four knife wounds from two different attackers. However, the one obstacle he could never overcome was cigarettes.

He had been a two pack per day smoker ever since he could remember, and no matter how often he tried to quit, he never succeeded. By the time he finally went to a doctor for his breathing problems, it was too late. The cancer was so prevalent in his lungs they told him he might not survive surgery, and that became a moot point when pre-surgery tests found a tumor on his heart.

Sometimes you have to know when to fold 'em, as the song says, and Richie Membrino knew when they told him about the tumor that his time had come. He opted out of the surgery and decided to let nature take its course. Life had been good to him, and he didn't want to go out bitching and moaning. Even if he had survived the surgeries he wouldn't have a life worth living, so why bother. He wasn't the type of man who didn't fight back, but eighty-eight years was a good long life, so he figured he didn't have anything to complain about.

Richie had been a tough guy his entire life. He was born in Brooklyn to a dockworker and a stripper. Angelo, his father, was a member of the local mob that controlled shipping in New York harbor; an enforcer, to be exact. He had broken a few legs in his time, and had even cut off some fingers from people who needed a little extra urging to pay their dues.

Richie knew all about this growing up, because his dad also liked to brag. Richie and his brother Mike would sit around the kitchen table and listen for hours on end as their father told them his tales. It seemed only natural when they finished high school that they would follow in their father's footsteps.

Angelo had spent a great deal of his free time as a young man in the red district of New York City. He loved to frequent the strip clubs and gin joints with his pals from the docks. He met Anna Karoli in a dive called The Red Parrot, and it was love at first sight. He'd seen many beautiful women in the strip clubs, but there was something about her eyes that drew him in. He dropped about four grand on her over the course of six months before she finally agreed to go out with him.

Anna also lived in Brooklyn and had a lot in common with Angelo. She had grown up poor, and was forced to drop out of school at fifteen, in order to find work to help out her family. Taller than most girls, and well endowed, she began stripping when she was nineteen, easily convincing the club owner that she was twenty-one. She was stunned at first by the money she made. One night's work would bring in what it would take her three weeks to make in her old job.

She met Angelo just after her twenty-second birthday. By then she had bailed her family out of debt and set them up in a nice apartment in Queens.

Anna didn't stop stripping after she married Angelo. She loved the work and the money, and he loved showing her off to all his friends.

"This is my piece of ass," he would proudly say, as his friends watched with envy while Anna swung naked on the dance pole. Even after Richie and Mike were born, she continued on. At thirty-five, she looked better than most girls fifteen years younger, and she had worked her way up to Kinky Dan's, the classiest club in the city.

By the time he turned thirty, Richie Membrino was the only one in the family still alive. His father and brother were both on the wrong side of a mafia feud, dying in a fusillade of bullets on the same day, albeit in different places. Richie achieved a small measure of revenge three days later, when he captured and executed two members of the rival family. In time, the two families ended the conflict and came to a tenuous but lasting truce.

Anna was distraught by the deaths of her husband and son, yet in no time she had suitors galore. She started dating just weeks after her husband's death, seeing different men from one night to the next. Her attitude turned her remaining son off, and a rift developed between them that would never be healed.

Two years after her husbands' untimely death, Anna also met with a tragic ending. She now worked as a hostess in a low-class strip joint. She was leaving work at 2 a.m. one morning when she was approached by a man who frequented the club often. He had asked her out many times before, but Anna wasn't interested in this man. She had rebuffed his advances every time, and he had reached his wits' end.

"This is your last chance," he said to her. "Let me take you home."

She refused him yet again, and immediately saw anger flare up in his eyes.

"If I can't have you, no one will," he cried, and a moment later he stabbed Anna in the heart.

Richie grieved for the death of his mother even though they hadn't spoken in nearly two years. Now alone in the world, having never been married himself, he decided to leave New York.

He moved east to Massachusetts, where he quickly hooked up with a group of small time hoods in Springfield. As their little fraternity grew they branched out, and in 1961 Richie, now thirty-three, became the muscle for Carlo Bianchi in the Greenfield area. They dealt mostly with loan-sharking, gambling, and prostitution at first, but when the drug culture of the sixties exploded onto the scene, they became one of the major dealers in western Massachusetts.

Richie liked being a thug. It gave him a feeling of invincibility and power over the people he had to deal with. After living in New York City for so long, the quiet, laid-back life in Greenfield took a lot of getting used to. At first it drove him crazy. There was nothing for him to do, and he felt surrounded by farmers and country bumpkins. However, as the years passed, Richie settled in and actually came to enjoy the quiet life.

He married for the first time at forty, and had two daughters in the next three years. He worked hard to keep his family life separate from his work. Unlike his father, he didn't want his little girls to know that he occasionally had to break a few fingers or smash a baseball bat on the knees of some recalcitrant businessman who couldn't pay back his loan.

In 1972, he ran for and was elected to the town council. His mob family was working their way into the construction business, and Richie's election helped ensure that any building contracts went to the right people.

All that seemed far away as he lay in his hospital bed. His wife had died in 1992 from breast cancer, and his two girls were now in their forties and had families of their own, one in California and the other in Texas. He rarely saw them, and it appeared they were too busy to visit him on his death bed. Richie wasn't surprised. He gathered that over the years they had figured out what he did for a living, and they were both appalled. He couldn't really blame them. Had they known everything that he had done in this life, he was sure they would never speak to him again. The thought made him sad.

The volunteer candy striper brought him his lunch at twelve-thirty. Noodle soup, with chicken if you could find it, half a tuna sandwich on white with two pickle slices, a tiny bowl of applesauce, two cookies plus milk and coffee. Richie always thought it amusing that they gave two drinks with every meal, one hot and one cold. Why didn't they just ask him what he wanted?

He was hungry, and although he found the food exceedingly bland, he ate it all. He was amazed how tired eating a meal made him, and how long it took him to eat. He drank the milk with the meal, and then had the cookies with his coffee, dunking them in the cup to soften them up.

Doctor Peter Allen began his afternoon rounds at one-thirty after his patients had all had their lunch. He entered Richie's room just after two and asked, "How are you feeling, Mister Membrino?"

"I'm okay, doc," said Richie. "Let's not be so formal from now on, you and me. I don't have that much time left. Call me Richie."

Doctor Allen didn't like being on a first name basis with any of his patients, but he knew this one didn't have more than a few days to live, so he reluctantly agreed. He asked Richie a few basic questions as he checked his medical chart, realized that his patient's pain was increasing, and decided it was time to give Richie control of the morphine.

"We're getting really close now, aren't we?" asked Richie.

"I'm afraid so," said the doctor, although Richie didn't think the doctor cared at all.

"Hey, don't be afraid for me, doc. It's alright. We all gotta go sometime."

The doctor wished all his patients took dying so well. "If there's anything you need, Richie, you just let me know." He put the chart back on its hook at the end of the bed and was turning to go when Richie spoke.

"Actually, doc, there is one thing you could do for me."

"What's that?"

"I'd like to talk to a priest sometime today. Got some things I need to get off my chest, if you know what I mean."

"You wish to confess?" asked the doctor.

"Yes," said Richie. "It's quite important to me."

Doctor Allen wasn't surprised by the request. Most people wanted to see their priest, pastor or rabbi before they died. A devout atheist, he wasn't sure why, other than the fact that it made them feel better. "I'll have one of the nurses take care of that for you," he said.

"Thanks, doc. I appreciate it."

Doctor Allen found Nurse Doris Keaton coming out of room 313. She was thirty-six and married with two kids, yet the doctor had been trying to bed her for the better part of a year. "Hey, good-looking," he said.

Doris thought the doctor was nothing more than an annoyance, and nothing he said or did was going to change that. "I'm busy," she replied.

"Guy in 317 wants to see a priest; you know who's here?"

Doris stopped and looked at the doctor, thinking for a moment. "I saw Father Thomas a little while ago," she said. "He's probably still here."

"Can you track him down for me?" asked the doctor.

"Sure," she said. "317?"

"Yeah, name's Membrino."

Doris Keaton found the priest at the front desk ten minutes later. It appeared he was about to leave. "Father Thomas, do you have a few minutes?" she asked.

"For you, of course I do," he said. "What do you need?"

Doris gave him the message, and the priest said he'd be glad to help.

Father Carter Thomas was in his mid-sixties. He had a thin, grizzled face, small eyes set close together, and a full head of grey hair. He wore silver glasses and carried an old, well-worn bible in his hands. It was not a regular work day at the hospital for him, but he had come to visit one of his parishioners who had recently had gall bladder surgery.

"Mr. Membrino?" he asked, as he entered room 317.

"That's me," said Richie.

"I am Father Thomas. I understand that you would like me to take your confession."

"Yes, Father."

Richie was happy that it was an older priest on duty and not one who looked like he just came out of the seminary. The young ones always thought they knew it all, much like the young punk kids of this generation. Richie couldn't stand that attitude in someone so young. This priest looked like someone who wouldn't treat him like an idiot.

"What church are you from, Father?"

"Saint Anthony's, in Northfield," the priest replied. "Been there for nearly twenty years now. I put in two shifts a week here at the hospital, although today I was just visiting a friend."

"You like working here?"

"I do. To be honest, I've been thinking about retiring from my post at the church. Don't get me wrong, I love the work, but the weekly grind does take its toll. I think I'd like to be a volunteer here at the hospital, where I could make my own hours. My parishioners could probably use a new, fresh voice coming from the pulpit."

"New isn't always better, Father," said Richie. "Myself, I like a man with experience."

The priest's smile told Richie that he agreed. They talked for a few minutes more, and then Richie began to get tired. "We'd better begin, Father," he finally said. "I don't have the strength I used to."

Father Thomas nodded his understanding, and they gave the customary greetings.

Richie crossed himself and said, "In the name of the Father, and of the Son, and of the Holy Ghost, Amen."

Father Thomas replied. "Have faith in God, my son, for the Lord is in your heart. Confess your sins now with true sorrow." The priest looked at Richie. "Do you have a particular verse you would like me to read?"

Richie Membrino may not have lived a particularly virtuous life, but he knew his bible well. He gazed at Father Thomas, gave him a small smile, and then said, "Blessed be God, even the Father of our Lord Jesus Christ, the Father of mercies, and the God of all comfort."

Father Thomas was impressed, but not particularly surprised. Over the years he had met many people who knew their bible well, including some he never would have suspected had ever opened a bible. He gave Richie a big smile and nodded his head approvingly. "Well said, my son."

Richie did not feel nervous about what he was about to do. He had offered his confession countless times in church. He had always left out one egregious sin, however, and it had always bothered him. Today he would finally remove that weight from his shoulders. He liked this priest that he had just met, but he doubted the man would still be smiling at him a few minutes from now.

"Forgive me Father, for I have sinned. It has been three months since my last confession." Richie started with the small stuff, the usual things a priest would hear about in the confessional. There weren't too many, as Richie had lived a quiet life lately, the illness bringing his everyday life to a virtual halt. He quickly reached his reason for wanting to see the priest now.

"I have a final sin I wish to confess. It should have been done years ago, but I was afraid."

"You have nothing to be afraid of now, my son," Father Thomas said, the remnants of the smile still on his face.

Richie was amused with the way this man, twenty years or more his junior, called him *my son*.

"A long time ago, I killed someone."

The priest closed his eyes, and Richie saw his head drop down.

"It was a boy, just a young boy who had his whole life ahead of him. I was ordered to do it, and I was good at following orders. I have done countless other bad things in my life, but nothing else has ever haunted me like this has.

"I was so ashamed I never confessed it, even though it happened almost fifty years ago. I could not go to my grave with this on my conscience. Forgive me," said Richie, who suddenly found himself crying.

The priest had heard many death bed confessions concerning stealing, cheating spouses and the like, but never one of murder. He was shocked by the admission, but recovered sufficiently to give the absolution. He gave Richie a heavy penance, but one that a man lying in bed with nothing else to do could fulfill.

When they were finished, Richie said, "Thank you, Father Thomas. It was something I needed to do before I crossed over, and I feel better for having done it."

"It must have been a heavy burden all these years."

"It was." Richie was quite tired now, and his breathing was becoming irregular, but he had one more request for the priest. "Would you do me one more favor, Father?"

"Of course," said the priest.

"Would you get in touch with the Edgeworth Police Department and ask Officer Paul Stephens to pay me a visit."

"Will he know your name when I mention it?" asked the priest.

"I don't think so, but you could tell him it involves a case his father once worked on."

"I will go to the station as soon as I leave here and deliver your message."

"Thank you, Father Thomas. I wish I had gone to your church once. I would have liked to hear you speak."

Father Thomas thought it just as well Richie Membrino had never attended his church.

SIX

Paul Stevens was spending his day off doing odds and ends around the house. He was in the middle of washing his car when he heard the kitchen telephone ring. He had soap on the roof, hood and one side of the vehicle when Phyllis, his wife of thirty years, came to the door and called to him.

"Honey, you have a phone call. Susan says it's important."

Susan was the combination secretary, dispatcher, and jack of all trades at the office, and she never called him on his day off unless it was important.

Paul gave a deep sigh as he dropped his sponge into the bucket and headed inside. He wiped his hands on his pants as Phyllis handed him the cordless phone and quietly mouthed the word "Sorry" to him.

He grinned at her as he rolled his eyes upward, as if to ask what could possibly be so important.

"Hello Susan," he said. "You do know it's my day off, right?"

"Of course I do, sweetie," Susan said, "but I have a priest in my office and he wants to talk to you right now. He says it's important, Paul. He won't tell me what it concerns, just insists on talking to you. Roger's right here in the office, but he says the message is for you."

Roger was Roger Moore, the officer currently on duty. "Why can't he tell Roger?" asked Paul, wondering what could be so important to the priest.

"He says you'll understand once he delivers the message. His name is Father Thomas. I'm going to put him on now. Here he is."

She motioned to the priest, who was sitting at a desk on the other side of the room, and switched the call over to him.

"Hello," said Father Thomas. "Is this Officer Stephens?"

"It is," said Paul. "How may I help you?"

"I was working at Greenfield Memorial Hospital today and I took a man's confession. He is quite sick, and I'm guessing he only has a few days left. He confessed something most horrific to me, I must say. Of course, under the rites of confession I cannot tell you what he said, but he has asked to speak to you. I do believe he wishes to clear his conscience of the matter and confess to you also."

"Why me?" asked Paul. "Anyone on duty today could talk to him."

"Apparently it involves a case your father once worked on."

"My father?"

"Yes," said the priest.

"Okay, what's his name?" Paul wrote the name and room number on a scrap of paper he found lying on the coffee table, thanked the priest, and then hung up.

"What was that all about?" asked Phyllis. She was a tall, slightly plump woman, with brown hair just beginning to show the first signs of grey. They had met just after high school at a comedy show in Turners Falls. He had fallen in love quickly back then, and was still in love with her now. It turned out they had the exact same birthday, and both were now fifty-two years old.

"Some death bed confession," said Paul. "The guy wants to talk to me for some reason." He had no idea what it could be about, but the sound of the priest's voice told him it must be important. "I have to go to Greenfield Memorial and talk to the guy."

"Now?" said Phyllis.

"Apparently he only has a couple of days to live, so I guess I'd better go now."

He went back outside and rinsed the soap off his car with the garden hose. He hoped no one would notice that one side was cleaner than the other.

After putting the hose and bucket away in the garage, Paul went inside to change. He put on light brown chinos and a dark brown tee shirt, slipped into a pair of loafers, and grabbed a jacket in case the temperature dropped before he arrived back home.

He picked up what he liked to refer to as his official police notebook from his dresser and transferred the information the priest had given him into it.

"Hopefully this won't take too long," he said to Phyllis. She was making a pot roast in the slow cooker, and he knew it would be ready soon. "I'll try and hurry, but you eat if you're hungry."

"Oh, I will," she said, and they both laughed.

The drive to the hospital in Greenfield took about twenty minutes. He found a parking space near the back of the lot. He usually parked a good distance from the door so he could get some walking in. He knew he didn't exercise as often as he should, and that was his way of making up for it. He entered the lobby, bypassed the reception desk, took the elevator up to the third floor, and followed the signs to room 317.

The door was open and Paul peered in. The man lying in the bed appeared to be at least eighty years old and looked as though he were asleep. He was on oxygen, with a breathing tube in his nose, and he had an IV in his right arm. Paul gently knocked on the door and entered the room.

Richie had been dozing off and on for the last half hour, but the knock registered, and he immediately opened his eyes. He looked at the man who was now walking up to his bed and figured it must be the cop, although he wasn't in uniform. He took Paul Stephens to be about five foot eight, maybe one-ninety. Overweight like most local cops, he thought.

"You Officer Stephens?" he asked.

"I am," said Paul. "I understand you wish to speak with me."

"Priest tell you why?"

"No, he wasn't about to tell me anything concerning your confession. Just said you specifically asked for me. Something about a case my dad worked on?"

"Pull up a chair," said Richie. "This might take a few minutes. Oh, and close the door, would you. I don't want anyone else hearing this." Although it was not a private room, the other bed was currently empty.

Paul went to the door and saw a nurse in the hallway. "Excuse me," he said. "I'm Officer Stephens from Edgeworth. This patient has asked for privacy while I talk to him, so I'm going to be closing the door. Shouldn't take long, but can you see that no one enters for the next few minutes?"

"Do my best," was all she said, and Paul closed the door.

He went back and sat in a lime green vinyl chair that he pulled up from the far wall. He took out his pad, flipped it open to a clean page, and took a pen from his jacket pocket.

"Mind if I ask a couple questions before we begin?"

"Sure. You might pass me a glass of water too. I get tired easy, and the throat gets dry."

Paul got up, poured the water, and set it within easy reach, and then he sat back down. "Your name is Richie Membrino. Is that short for Richard?"

"Yeah," said Richie, as he took a sip of water.

"Are you from around here?"

"Born in New York, but lived here for a long time now." Richie let the cop ask him a few more basic questions, and then suggested they get on with it.

"Fine," said Stephens. "You talk, I'll listen.'

"Is your dad still alive?" asked Richie.

"He is," said Paul. "He's currently in a nursing home, recovering from a fall. Otherwise he lives with me and my wife."

"When you tell him my story, he's going to wish he was here."

"Let's hear it," said Paul.

Richie took a deep breath and began. "There were some murders in Edgeworth a long time ago, back in '66. Bunch of kids found a body in the woods and an old lady shot in her bed."

"I've heard the story," said Paul. "My father was the first officer on the scene."

"They never solved the crimes," said Richie.

"Nothing to go on," said Paul. He had heard his father talk about the case countless times, and once he joined the force Paul had looked into it as well. "Rain washed away any physical evidence from the body in the woods, and the only footprints found in the house belonged to the kids. That was way before DNA testing became routine. You know something about the case?"

"I know a lot about the case, but I ain't telling you. That's not why I asked you here."

Paul was confused. He thought this old man lying in the bed wanted to confess, but now it appeared that wasn't to be. "So what am I doing here?"

"There was a third murder that week," said Richie.

"A third? Not that I know of. My dad never mentioned a third murder."

"Cause he never knew. No one did, till today." Paul started to say something, but Richie cut him off. "Just listen, okay. Let me tell it without interruption." Richie took another sip of water and cleared his throat.

"A couple days after the boys found the bodies, one of them came snooping around where he shouldn't have. He was peeking in windows, pretending to be some kind of detective, I guess. We grabbed him and asked him what he thought he was doing, and the kid says he's investigating the murders. Says he found a clue on one of the bodies, and thinks he knows who did it."

Richie had to pause again to catch his breath. "Trouble is, he was talking to the people who did it. Don't know how the hell he figured it out. He didn't have the clue on him, however, and he wouldn't tell us what it was or where it was. He was one tough little cookie for an eleven year old. Had some balls, you know what I mean. But he knew too much, and kids that age, they like to talk. We couldn't let him go."

Paul suddenly remembered one of the boys who had found the bodies had died later that week, but he couldn't remember the name.

Richie paused yet again and took another sip of water. "They found him the next morning floating in Brooks Lake. Everyone thought it was a simple drowning, though what the hell a kid would be doing in Brooks Lake fully clothed in May I never understood. He did drown, but only because I was holding him under water."

He watched for the cop's reaction, but the guy was a pro, and all he saw was a slight widening of the eyes. "Kid was pretty strong for an eleven year old, but he was no match for me. I just held him under until he gave up the ghost. We weren't but ten feet from shore at the time. Poor kid never had a chance."

"Do you remember his name?" asked Paul.

"Of course I remember his name," said Richie, a sudden harshness to his voice. "I thought of that kid every day of my life. It always haunted me, what I'd done. Kid's name was Vincent Maki; they called him Vinnie."

The name sounded familiar. "Did you kill the other two?" asked Paul.

"I ain't talking about the other two. Maybe I did, maybe I didn't. They were all connected, so you figure it out."

"Who told you to kill the boy?"

"Listen, I didn't call you here to rat out my friends. I'm a loyal guy, always have been."

Richie's breathing was becoming labored and his voice scratchy. "I'm not saying anything about the others. I not telling you who did it or why, and I'm not telling you who made the call to off the boy. All I'm doing is confessing to his murder. I wish to God I hadn't done it. Now that's all I have to say."

"You confessed to the priest about the boy's death; why are you telling me?"

"People need to know," said Richie. "Some of them are still around."

"But it was fifty years ago," said Paul. "What's the point?"

Richie Membrino stared at the officer for a moment. His voice was almost gone, and he took a last sip of water, the cup shaking in his hand. Then he wagged a finger at the cop and said, "Doesn't mean that it's over. Now that's all I have to say." Then Richie lay back and closed his eyes.

Paul Stevens spent five minutes trying to get more information out of Richie, but the guy was true to his word. He never made another sound, just shook his head a few times. Paul finally gave up and moved the chair back to its spot against the wall. As he said goodbye to Richie Membrino, he added, "You're right. My dad's gonna wish he was here."

SEVEN

The population in Edgeworth had nearly doubled over the last fifty years to 2600, but the police force was basically the same size as it had been in 1966, mostly due to severe budget cutbacks in the tough economy. Paul Stephens, Roger Moore and Herman Villanueva were the full time officers under the command of Chief William Randolph Soderheim, whom they called Will. Susan Winston was the do-it-all gal Friday, and the town also had three part-time officers.

There were no longer any schools in Edgeworth, as the Edgeworth Grammar School had been condemned for a variety of reasons; leaking ceilings, rats in the basement, a non-functioning heating system being just a few of them. Fortunately, the town of Philbrook had just finished building a new high school, and the old high school became the grammar school for all the kids in Philbrook, Edgeworth and Dearborn.

Paul Stephens left the hospital after talking to Richie Membrino and headed straight for the police station. He radioed in to Susan as he drove.

"Sue, is Will there?" he asked.

"He's home, I think. Do you want me to call him?"

"Yeah, do that for me, would you? Have him meet me at the station."

"Okay," said Sue.

Paul pulled into the station ten minutes later. He had to wait another ten minutes for the chief to arrive, so he made a fresh pot of coffee, which finished brewing just as Will came in.

"Smells good," said Will. "I'll have a cup."

Paul poured fresh cups for all three of them as he said, "Gather round the table, folks. You're gonna want to hear this one." He brought the cups over to the table, fixed just the way each one liked it, as he had done a hundred times before.

"So what's up?" asked the chief. "Sue told me Father Thomas was in here today and that he had an urgent call for you. He's a good man, Father Thomas. I've been to his church a number of times. So what did he want?"

"He told me there was someone in Greenfield Memorial who wanted to speak to me about a confession. Guy's name is Richie Membrino. He has lung cancer, among other things, and only has a short time left. I went to see him, took down his story, and I must admit he seems sincere. You remember the story about the murders back in '66?"

"Sure," said Will, "most famous unsolved case in Edgeworth. Did he admit to them?"

"Nope. Said he knows who did them, and that it might have been him, but he wasn't going there."

The chief had a perplexed look on his face. "So what did he want then?" he asked.

"If you know the story well, you might remember that one of the four boys who found the bodies drowned later that week in Brooks Lake."

"Sure, the Maki kid," said Will. "I met his dad a few times, and his sister Katie still lives around here."

"Well, Richie Membrino confessed to killing the boy. Says he came snooping around a few days after the murders claiming he knew who did it. According to Richie, the kid was right, so they had to take care of him."

"Holy cow," said Sue, who never uttered a swear word of any kind.

"How could the kid possibly know that?" asked the chief.

Paul took another sip of coffee as he gazed into space. As he had done on the drive to the station, he was trying to recall everything he could about the famous murder case. Finally, he said, "According to Richie Membrino, the kid had some kind of clue that led him right there."

"A clue? I don't remember anything about a clue in that case," said Will. "Do you?"

"No," said Paul, "and I think I would remember. My dad and I used to discuss the case on occasion, and I've even looked into it myself in my spare time. I'm pretty sure there was never a mention about any clue."

"But if it got him killed," said Sue, "he must have known something."

Paul nodded his agreement. "Trouble is, Richie won't tell us anything else. Said he wasn't going to rat anybody out, he simply wanted to confess to killing the boy, because it has bothered him all his life."

"Did he tell you what this clue was?" asked the chief.

"Doesn't know," said Paul. "Said the kid didn't have it on him and wouldn't tell them what or where it was."

"That's it?" asked Will.

"That's it. He told me not to bother to come back, because he wouldn't talk to us again. I don't think he likes the police much."

"Your dad really worked on that case?" asked Sue.

"First responder," said Paul. "The boy's drowning always bothered him, but the Greenfield dicks just called it a coincidence. I guess they had no reason to think otherwise."

"Well," said Will, finishing his coffee with a last long gulp, "I guess we'd better inform those Greenfield dicks about this new development. They have that one gal over there who likes to look into cold cases. Remington; I forget her first name."

"Sylvia," said Sue, "Detective Sylvia Remington."

"That's the one,' said Will. "I guess you'd better get her on the phone, Sue."

"There's one other thing," said Paul.

"What's that?" asked Will.

"The last thing he said to me was, 'Doesn't mean it's over.' I don't know what he meant by that, but it sounded like someone still cares about this case."

The meeting broke up. Sue went to call Greenfield, and Will decided to see what they had in storage on the old case.

Paul wanted to drive down to the nursing home to tell his dad, but decided instead to go home and eat. He had a midnight to noon shift coming up, and figured it would be best to go and see his father after that. The old man would probably want to talk about the case for quite a while, and Paul didn't want to rush him.

He arrived home to the delicious aroma of slow-cooked meat and vegetables. Phyllis was dishing up two plates as he entered the kitchen.

"Heard you coming," she said. "Good timing too, because I'm starving, and I wasn't going to wait much longer."

They sat in the living room and watched television while they ate. "So what was the big mystery?" she asked him.

Paul told her the basics between bites of steaming carrots and potatoes. He often told her about cases he was working on, even things he shouldn't be telling her, because she knew how to keep her mouth shut. Not once in thirty years had she let slip information that she shouldn't have known. Paul trusted his wife completely.

"Oh God," she sighed, when he told her Vincent Maki had been killed. "That poor boy. How could he do that to a child?"

"He may have killed the others also," said Paul, as he stabbed a piece of pot roast. "He wouldn't say one way or the other, which of course makes it seem as though he did. If so, only the killing of the boy bothered him. He said it has haunted him all his life."

"As well it should," Phyllis said. "I hope it haunts him in death too." She had great compassion in many areas of life, but murder wasn't one of them. Phyllis Stephens was a strong advocate of the death penalty.

It was an hour later when Detective Sylvia Remington of the Greenfield Police Department called him. "Officer Stephens?" she asked, as Paul answered the phone.

"Speaking," he said.

The detective introduced herself and said she had just been assigned the Membrino case. "Can you tell me what he said to you, exactly as you recall it?"

Paul went over the interview with her after rounding up his notepad. She interrupted him a couple of times to ask pertinent questions, and it was obvious to Paul that she knew a great deal about the case.

"So did you believe him?" she asked, when he finished.

"I did," said Paul. "He seemed sincere about how much it bothered him, and it was a deathbed confession. I don't see any reason for him to make up a story like that."

"I'm going to want to talk to him," said Remington.

"You can certainly try," said Paul, "but he said he was done talking, to me or anyone else."

It turned out to be a moot point. The tumor on Richie Membrino's heart finished him off before the cancer in his lung could. He died that night as Paul was driving to work.

EIGHT

The Conway Manor Nursing Home was a sprawling one story facility in Deerfield, just south of Greenfield. At first glance, the outside almost looked attractive with its faux brick vinyl siding, but you quickly realized the truth as you drew closer. The windows were shaded by red awnings that went out of style thirty years ago and were severely faded, and they had light brown shutters on either side that needed a paint job and a cleaning.

Once inside, the age of the building was even more apparent. The linoleum floors were well worn, with edges coming up along the baseboards, and no amount of cleaning could make them look anything but old. The furniture was all dated and had been cheap to begin with, and the walls showed cracks in spots and were also in need of a good paint job.

Paul Stephens entered the home just before one o'clock. As rundown as the building looked, he knew that the staff were capable and caring, and that his father would be well taken care of. Paul guessed correctly that his dad would be just finishing lunch in his room when he arrived.

"Hey," his father said upon seeing him, "what brings you here?"

Paul ignored the question for the moment and replied, "How are you doing, dad?"

"Okay. I have a physical therapy session this afternoon. Hopefully it will be my last one, but I pray they don't push me too hard. I'm still pretty sore from the fall."

"You'll do fine," Paul said. "The faster you progress, the quicker you can come home."

The elder Stephens had slipped on a rug at home and landed hard on left shoulder, leaving him with bruised ribs and a strained a/c joint. His head had also whacked the floor pretty hard, and he had spent seven hours in the hospital having tests for a concussion before being transferred here. He didn't see the need, but the doctors wanted to make sure his shoulder received some therapy before he returned home, and Paul had agreed. They told him it would probably be for four to six days. This was day three.

They chatted for a few minutes as the orderly came to collect his lunch tray, and then a nurse stopped in to check his vitals and give him an aspirin. When she finished that task, she said, "Let's get you out of bed."

John Paul Stephens was actually enjoying loafing in bed, something he never did at home, but he quickly agreed to get up. He sat in the chair by the window, and Paul plopped himself down on the side of the bed.

"We tossed out that rug and put in a new one that won't slip," said Paul.

"Thank you. I could go home today, you know, and do my rehab at the house."

Paul knew his dad hated being here. John Paul was in great shape for a man about to turn eighty. He participated in 5K races three or four times a year, and six months ago he had run a half-marathon, winning his age group against three other competitors who were over seventy.

"Let's see how you do today, and then decide," said Paul. "Anyway, this isn't just a regular visit. I'm partially here on business."

"Whatever it is, I didn't do it. I have witnesses," his father said, pointing towards the hallway and laughing. Then, in a more serious tone, he asked, "What sort of business, son?"

"Do you still remember that double murder case you worked on back in the sixties?"

John Paul's head snapped up at the question. "Of course I do, I'm not senile. I'll remember that day as long as I live," he said. "Damned shame we could never solve that case. Why do you ask?"

"You remember the boy who drowned a few days later?"

"Sure, the Maki boy. I never did get to talk to him. He and the Wilson kid stayed behind to be interviewed by one of the detectives. The other two boys accompanied me to the scene. Why?"

"Turns out the boy didn't drown on his own." Paul saw his dad's forehead wrinkle as a questioning look came over the man's face. "He was killed."

"How the hell do you know that?" asked John Paul.

"Death-bed confession," he said, and saw his father's face transform into a look of shock.

"Are you serious? I always thought that boy's death was suspicious."

"I was called by a priest yesterday named Father Thomas."

"Sure, I know him," said John Paul. "Real nice guy."

"He took a man's confession at Greenfield Memorial yesterday. When it was over, the man asked to talk to me. He somehow knew that I was on the force and was your son. I don't know how. His name didn't ring any bells with me."

"What was it?" asked his father.

"Richie Membrino."

"Ah," his dad said, a nod of the head signaling recognition. "I think I remember him. He was a small time hood, muscle mostly for some Greenfield lowlifes. Don't remember their names offhand, but you can probably figure that out with a little investigation. He was in on those murders?"

"He wouldn't talk about the murders. Said he knew who did it and who was behind it, even said it might have been him and might not have, but he refused to say anything about them. He did confess to drowning Vinnie Maki, however. Said he was sorry he did it, and that it's bothered him ever since."

"Dear God," said his father. "We never could figure out why the kid was in the water." He paused for a moment as scenes from fifty years ago played in his head, and then he asked, "Why the hell did he kill the boy?"

"You're not going to believe this," said Paul, "but he claims the boy had a clue about the murders that led him straight to them."

"What?" John Paul looked stunned. "How could he?"

"I don't know."

"What was the clue?"

"Don't know that either. Membrino didn't know, because the kid never told them."

"And they never found out what it was?"

"Apparently not."

John Paul was totally flummoxed. He started to speak three times---"Who...What...How..."---and then gave up. Finally, he was able to sum up what he thought his son was saying to him.

"So Vinnie Maki found a clue, didn't tell the cops, and it led him straight to the killers, which got him killed."

"That sounds about right," said Paul.

"Yet neither the cops nor the killers knew what this clue was?" John Paul watched as his son nodded his agreement. "So if the damn kid had just given us the clue, we could have solved that case in no time."

"Apparently so," said Paul.

"What the hell was he thinking?"

They sat in silence for a minute. Paul watched his dad as the old man stared out the window, and then he updated him on the current goings on.

"Sylvia Remington has been assigned the case in Greenfield. From what I hear, she's studied it off and on, much as I have. As I recall, you didn't have any leads in the case? Did you ever have any suspects?"

Paul watched his father, and knew he was reliving the events of the old murder case in his mind. In his time on the force, Paul had only caught one murder in town, and that one was cut and dried. A family dispute out on Cross Pond Road had ended when the wife, who apparently had been beaten once too often, took a cleaver from the chopping block and deposited it in her husband's back, and then sat down next to him and berated him until he died. When her lawyer showed photos of the abuse that she had taken over the years in court, the jury ruled it self-defense. She went home free as a bird, and still lived in the same house today with husband number two.

"There wasn't much," his father finally said. "No clues on the body in the woods. The blood on his hair and shirt all belonged to him. Nowadays they would probably find fibers or whatnot on the body, but back then, well …." He let the comment drift, and Paul understood they were talking about different times, light years apart when it came to forensics.

"We assumed the old lady they shot, um, what was the name, Parker? No, Potter. Mrs. Potter must have been killed because she had seen them. They either made her get into bed or she was already there, because she obviously hadn't been moved. Don't know which one was killed first, not that it mattered, but we assumed it was her."

John Paul paused for a moment as he recalled the fifty year old murder. He was gazing at the far wall, as if watching a movie screen, and Paul held his questions, not wanting to interrupt John Paul's flow of the story.

"Oh wait, there were the bullets," said John Paul. "I forgot there for a moment, but they found both bullets. Plum luck from the one in the woods. He was alive when they brought him out there, of course, and must have been standing when they shot him, because the bullet was found in a pine tree some thirty yards away about a week later. We weren't even looking for it, but the sun hit it just right that afternoon. We found it when we went to see what it was that was shining so much."

"Who found it?" Paul asked, breaking his silence.

"Oddly enough, it was the Chief. Randall found it his first day back from vacation. I took him out to the scene just to catch him up on everything. We had stopped at the Maki home first, so he could offer his condolences. Poor bastard couldn't believe it all happened while he was on vacation. Never liked the man, to tell you the truth."

"You said they found the second bullet too, from the Potter residence?"

"They did, in the box spring. It went through her chest, through the mattress, hit a spring that changed its course, probably hit more than one, and came to rest against the side of the wood frame. They found that one that day. They knew it had to be in there."

"Any other clues?" asked Paul.

"No. Whatever footprints or tire tracks we might have found had been washed away by the rain. Like I said, it was a different time. Nowadays, you probably would have found a dozen or more clues with all the tricks you have to work with. Back then we didn't have much. If you didn't catch the perp in forty-eight hours, chances were you weren't going to catch him at all."

They heard a rap on the door, and a pretty young girl entered the room.

"Hi, Mister Stephens. I'm Gina, your physical therapist for the day. For the next half hour, you're all mine."

Paul rose from the bed and introduced himself to Gina, then turned to his dad and said, "You behave yourself and do what Gina tells you, okay. I'll be back tomorrow."

"You better plan to get me out of here tomorrow," his dad said. "I want in on this case."

Paul just smiled, knowing his father was about to become the world's biggest pest.

NINE

The sound of Beethoven's Fifth Symphony on his cell phone woke Billy Wilson from a sound sleep. He picked it up off his nightstand and gazed at the time, 4:12 a.m., and noticed that it was his sister calling.

This can't be good, he thought. The symphony continued to play until Billy finally answered.

"Hello," he mumbled, his voice still half asleep.

"Billy?"

A crack in her voice; nervous, he thought, or upset. "Hey, Marylou."

"Billy, I have some bad news."

"Mom?" he asked, already knowing what was coming. Marylou wouldn't have called at this time for just any reason.

"She's gone, Billy. She died …" Her voice cracked again, and he heard a sniffle on the other end of the line. "She passed away this morning about an hour and a half ago. I thought I should call you now rather than waiting."

The news was not unexpected. Their mother was ninety-two and had been in failing health for a few years now.

"She lived a good life," he said. "Try not to be sad. Remember the good times."

"I will, Billy, but it's hard."

"You took good care of her for a long time, sis. You should be proud of that."

"I just wish it hadn't come to a nursing home at the end. She always said she was happy there, but … I think she was just saying that to make me feel better."

"You did all you could." He heard his sister crying, and paused for a few moments before continuing. "Do you have any idea about the arrangements?" he asked.

"She wanted to be buried next to dad, of course. We have to transport the body back home, and the funeral home is setting that up for Sunday, so I'm going to try to get the wake on Tuesday and the funeral the following morning."

"Okay," said Billy. "Keep in touch, and I'll let you know when I'll be getting there."

"I will," said Marylou. "We'll be staying at the Charles Hotel as we usually do."

"I will too," he said. "See you soon."

The call ended, and Billy set the phone back on the nightstand. He hadn't seen his mother in over two years, and their relationship had been a tenuous one for a long time now. He had moved farther and farther away as the years went by. His mother had been in a nursing home in Claremont, South Carolina, where Marylou resided with her husband Mark and their four kids: Jillian, Christopher, Rachel and Joseph.

Carl Wilson, Billy's father, had passed away in 2000 when his car hit a patch of black ice, slid off the road into a tree, and he'd been thrown from the vehicle. His dad had been against a law enforcing the mandatory use of seat belts and refused to wear one in defiance. He was buried in the church graveyard back in Edgeworth, not too far from where Billy and Marylou had grown up.

It was a place home to memories Billy generally tried not to remember.

He thought of getting up and making coffee, but it wasn't even 4:30 yet, so he decided to try and fall back to sleep. He wasn't sure how long it took him, his mind racing with countless random thoughts, but eventually he finally dozed off.

Suddenly the sounds of Beethoven's Fifth started playing once again.

"What the hell?" he uttered, as he grabbed his phone for a second time that morning. This time he noticed it was 6:19 a.m. The call was coming from Massachusetts, but he didn't recognize the number. *Little early to be offering condolences*, he thought.

"Hello," he said, a bit of an edge to his voice to show his displeasure.

"Is this Billy Wilson?"

He didn't recognize the voice, and the female caller didn't seem sure she had the right number.

"Speaking," he said.

"Billy, is it really you?"

"It is, and who might you be?"

"It's Katie. Katie Maki, remember me?"

He hadn't seen Katie in at least fifteen years, and he wondered how she had found his number. "Goodness, Katie, it's been forever. How are you doing?"

"I'm fine," she said. "I was wondering if you had heard the news."

The only news Billy had heard was about his mother, and he didn't know how Katie could have found out so quickly. "You heard about my mom?"

"Your mom? No. Did something happen to your mother, Billy?"

"She passed this morning," he said, now wondering what news she could possibly have.

"Oh, I'm sorry to hear that. Had she been ill?"

"For some time now," he replied. "It's a blessing that she has finally passed over. So what is it you're calling about, Katie?"

"It's about my brother."

Billy took a sudden intake of breath. He hadn't expected that for a reply. "Your brother?"

"Have you heard the news at all?" Katie asked.

"Apparently not."

"Billy, Vinnie was murdered. A man here made a death-bed confession. He drowned Vinnie. It's all over the news."

Fifty years is a long time, and Billy occasionally went long stretches without thinking of Vinnie Maki, but Vinnie was always lurking just under the surface of his memory banks. What they had gone through as kids was still clear as day to him.

"Are you kidding? We always wondered about that."

"The papers say the man, who died the other day, was ordered to kill Vinnie because he came snooping around about those bodies you found. Apparently Vinnie actually knew who did it. The guy was sorry about killing such a young boy and wanted to confess."

"That's unbelievable," said Billy, still too stunned to utter much else.

"The police are re-opening the case. They have one of those cold case detectives working on it, you know, like the show that used to be on TV." Katie paused, then abruptly changed the subject. "Billy, will your mom be buried here?"

"If by here you mean Edgeworth, then yes. Do you still live there?"

"Well, I live in Dearborn now. I have a small place out near the lake."

"Brooks Lake?" asked Billy.

"I know, it sounds weird, living near the lake where my brother drowned ... well, was murdered. But it was so long ago. I divorced Dave back in 2004 and took my maiden name back. I found this place in the woods, and it just seemed perfect for me."

Billy remembered meeting Dave shortly after he and Katie were married. "Sorry to hear about you and Dave."

"Don't be," she said. "Over time he turned into a jerk. I'm better off alone."

He let the comment sit there, thinking that alone only works for so long.

"If you're coming home," she finally continued, "the police will probably want to talk to you."

"About a murder that happened fifty years ago? Not much I'm gonna be able to add now."

"Well, they're going to talk to Walter tomorrow, from what I hear. He lives down in Northampton. I spoke with him yesterday."

"Pokey's still around, huh? Guess I'll have to look him up when I get there. I need to book a flight home. Marylou thinks mom's wake will probably be on Tuesday and the funeral the following day. They have to transport her body from South Carolina."

"Do you need a place to stay?" she asked. "I have plenty of room out here, and it would be great to see you again."

"No, I usually stay at the hotel in Greenfield. That's where Marylou and her family will be."

"Oh Billy, that place is a dump; save your money and come stay with me. It's really peaceful out here. My nearest neighbor is a half-mile away. You'll love it, and I'd love to see you again."

He thought it over for a moment, wondering why someone he hadn't seen in years would make him an offer like this, but what the hell, it would be more fun than a hotel.

"Okay, you win. I'll let you know my arrival plans once I have them."

"Not a problem," said Katie. "Give me your e-mail address and I'll send you a map. It's not the easiest place to find, particularly in the dark."

Billy did as requested, and a minute later the call ended.

He had been Katie's date at her senior prom when he was a junior in college. He had been surprised when she had asked him. Katie was one of the most attractive girls in her school at the time, and Billy figured she must have dozens of boys who would be dying to go out with her. Billy had never dated in high school, and that had barely changed in college. He rarely attended school functions, and generally kept to himself.

The prom date had gone well, as he recalled, and when it ended Katie had given him a hug and a kiss on the cheek. Billy had been a perfect gentleman, and if Katie had wanted more from him that night he never knew it. When it came to dating back then, Billy was still a novice.

Now she was inviting him to her home. He wondered if she was still a knockout.

Going to be an interesting trip, he thought.

There was no sense trying to go back to sleep now, so Billy slid out of bed, put on a pair of shorts, and headed to the kitchen. Coffee was the first order of business, and then he went online, found the Greenfield newspaper, and immediately came upon the story of Richie Membrino.

When he finished reading everything he could, he began to wonder what the hell Vinnie had found.

And the regret he had carried for so many years welled to the surface once again.

TEN

BILLY'S STORY
PART TWO

Word of the boy's discovery spread quickly through the school on Monday morning, and by lunch time all four boys were fielding questions from dozens of kids.

Hank was telling anyone who would listen that it was his *eagle eye* that had spotted the body in the woods.

Vinnie enjoyed seeing the shocked looks on all the kids' faces when he told them he had rolled the body over. By the end of the day, he had added some wonderful theatrics to his performance.

Even Mrs. Landis, the fourth grade teacher, had come up to Billy and Walter as they sat at the lunch table to ask them about it.

Both boys, more subdued than Hank or Vinnie, quickly grew tired of being pestered by everyone. Eventually Walter started telling the kids, "I'm busy, go ask Vinnie." Billy just wished that things would go back to normal.

It was much of the same for Hank at home with his siblings. With three brothers and five sisters, ranging in age from nineteen to four, the questions never stopped coming. As soon as he finished recounting the tale to one sibling, another would drop by to ask him all about it. Only his older brother said nothing, but occasionally gave him an index finger to the mouth, signaling him to shut up.

By the time Monday night rolled around, his father had heard enough. He slammed his fist down on the dinner table and yelled, "That's it! I don't want to hear another word on the subject from any of you," and when Hank's dad blew up like that you knew the subject was closed.

The other boys had it easier at home. Billy's sister, Marylou, had lost all interest in the story by Sunday afternoon. It was the same for Vinnie's sister, Katie, also eight. By the time the family returned home from church services that Sunday morning, she too had moved on.

Walter had two older brothers, Gene and Alfred, who knew him well enough to realize early on that he didn't want to talk about it.

By Tuesday, things began to quiet down a bit at school. Only Vinnie seemed to still want to talk about it, and he did so mostly with kids who had missed school on Monday.

Vinnie seemed pensive on the bus ride home from school that day, and Billy noticed.

"What's up with you?" he asked. "You're never this quiet."

"Just thinking about things," said Vinnie.

In fact, he was thinking about the murders and the clue he had hidden in his room. Second thoughts were beginning to form in his head, and he had the feeling he should just turn the damn thing over to the cops before it went any further.

After arriving home, Vinnie stopped in the kitchen for a slice of cherry pie and ice cream, and then he went up to his room. He waited until Katie went downstairs to watch television, and then he retrieved his clue from its hiding spot. He turned it over and over in his hand as he debated what to do. He knew giving it to the cops at this late date would land him in a world of trouble. Yet what could he really accomplish by keeping it? Did he honestly think he could solve a murder case by himself?

No, you can't, shot through his mind, and he supposed that was true. Yet he had no desire to be grounded for the next month, and no idea about how to give it to the cops without getting into trouble. "Who knows," he finally mumbled to himself, "maybe I can solve this case."

Vinnie Maki decided to keep his mouth shut and begin his investigation after supper that night. He hoped perhaps one of his friends would help him out, but if not, he was prepared to go it alone.

Billy Wilson and his family had just finished clearing the dinner dishes off the table when there was a knock on the door. Billy answered it, and saw Vinnie standing on the front steps, motioning Billy to come outside.

"What's up?" said Billy, after closing the door.

"Do you want to go on an adventure with me?" asked Vinnie.

"What are you talking about?"

"Can you keep a secret?"

The look on his friend's face told Billy that Vinnie was up to no good. It was a look that usually ended up getting both of them in trouble.

"I guess," said Billy. "What is it?"

"You have to swear on your life," said Vinnie.

"What are you up to now?"

"I want you to come with me tonight. I'm going to start my investigation into that guy's murder; Missus Potter's too."

"Who do you think you are, Perry Mason?" asked Billy, exactly as he had done three days earlier.

"Can you keep the secret?"

"Sure, what is it?" asked Billy.

Vinnie smiled wide, and Billy knew trouble was looming. "I have a clue."

"A clue? A clue to what?"

"A clue to the murders," said Vinnie. "If you come with me, I'll tell you all about it."

"You don't have a clue," Billy retorted.

"I do, honest. It's hidden in a secret place, but I'll show it to you if you just come with me tonight."

"Are you sure you're feeling okay?"

"Why wouldn't I be?" asked Vinnie.

"I just thought maybe you were coming down with something," said Billy.

"Is that your way of trying to talk me out of this?" asked Vinnie. "I'm just gonna do a little snooping around is all. There's nothing to worry about. Just come with me."

This time it sounded more like a plea than a request.

Once again Billy said no. He was never allowed to be out very late on a school night, and he wanted to watch television. Combat was coming on at 7:30, and then Red Skelton, one of his favorite shows ever, was on at 8:30. He didn't want to miss either of them.

"You're such a wuss," Vinnie said, and he disgustedly turned and walked away.

"Vinnie, just go home," Billy called out to his friend, but Vinnie just waved a hand at him, never turning around.

Billy didn't believe that his friend had any sort of clue. Vinnie had told them all on more than one occasion that he wanted to be a cop when he grew up, so Billy figured he just wanted to practice.

Vinnie was pissed as he headed down the street towards Pokey's house. He had been confident that he could talk Billy into coming with him. *Maybe if I'd brought the clue with me and shown it to him,* he thought.

He had to walk by his house to get to Pokey's. He could run in and get it, but he quickly decided not to bother. If they weren't going to believe him, so be it. The clue was safely tucked away where no one would find it.

He arrived at Pokey's but had little hope that he could convince his friend to come with him. Pokey's mom was pretty strict, and none of her children got away with much. It was she who answered the door.

"Why hello, Vincent," she said. "What brings you here?"

"I'd like to speak with Walter for a minute if I could." Vinnie knew enough to use Pokey's given name with his mother, who hated his nickname.

She invited him in, but Vinnie asked if Walter could just come outside.

"Okay, I'll send him out," she said, "but don't be long. It's a school night."

Vinnie knew he was doomed right there, and after a quick conversation with Pokey, he was once again on his own. *I'll just solve this case on my own and get all the glory*, he told himself.

He headed off, ready to start his investigation. He walked past his house again, then past the Wilson residence. Maybe he wouldn't solve the crime tonight, but he was confident that he would in the end. The police would call him a hero, the mayor would give him the key to the town, and he, Vincent Maki, would be the new leader of their little group.

The Red Skelton show was nearly over when the phone rang at the Wilson residence. Laurie Wilson answered, and soon after Billy heard her say, "Why no, he isn't." After hanging up, she turned to Billy and said, "Vinnie hasn't come home yet, and his mother is worried. Do you have any idea where he might be?"

"Not a clue," said Billy.

Billy was happy as a lark when he woke up Wednesday morning. There were just five more weeks of school until summer vacation. The winter had been surprisingly mild, and only two snow days had been added to the calendar, a rare event for New England.

As he ate a bowl of Sugar Pops for breakfast, Billy wondered where Vinnie had gone last night. He still doubted that his friend had any sort of clue, but even if he had, what could he have done?

His mom entered the kitchen at that point and interrupted his thoughts. "Are you all ready?" she asked. "Bus will be here in ten minutes."

"I'm ready," he replied.

Laurie Wilson put away the box of cereal that Billy had left on the counter, and then walked to the kitchen sink. There was a small window over the sink that looked out towards the Maki residence. She gazed out the window, and suddenly said, "Oh dear."

"What's the matter?" asked Billy.

"The police are over at the Maki's." A worried look came over her face. "They must have more questions for you boys. Why couldn't they wait until after school?"

Billy went to the window and saw the police car parked in front of Vinnie's house, but he didn't see anything happening outside.

"I want you to go out to the bus stop now," his mother said. "If they want to talk to you, they can do it later. I don't want your father to have to take you to school."

"Okay, mom," Billy said. He hoped he never had to talk to the police again. Even though he hadn't done anything wrong, talking to that detective the other day had scared the crap out of him. He didn't understand how Vinnie could have enjoyed it as much as he did. Now he wondered if Vinnie had decided to share his secret clue with them. Billy suddenly realized that if Vinnie had taken a clue from the body and was just giving it to the police now, he would be in a great deal of trouble.

He grabbed his Bonanza lunch box with the picture of the four stars riding horses on it, checked to make sure his mother had already packed it, and then called to his sister to hurry up.

"We still have time," said Marylou, as she entered the kitchen.

"Mom wants us to go now. The police are next door, and she wants us to leave before they come here."

A minute later, they both gave their mom a kiss and then headed outside. The bus stopped next door at the Miller's house, where it picked them up and dropped them off every day. When the bus arrived, all the neighborhood kids clambered aboard. Vinnie and his sister Katie didn't make it, and Billy wondered how long it would be before they showed up at school. He figured Vinnie would come up with all sorts of excuses to keep himself home as long as possible.

Pokey was already aboard, and said, "Did you see the cops are at Vinnie's house again?"

"We saw," said Billy.

"I hope they don't want to talk to me again," said Pokey, and Billy couldn't agree more.

2

There were twenty-two students in Mrs. Fontaine's sixth grade class, fourteen of them girls. Billy sat in the back row as he had all year. Hank had been on his left when the year started back in September, but within three weeks he had been moved to the front so Mrs. Fontaine could keep an eye on him. Walter's seat was three rows ahead of Billy's on the right. The poor slob was surrounded by girls; the penalty you get when you're the last one in on the first day of school.

Vinnie normally sat on Billy's right, but by ten o'clock he still hadn't arrived. Billy was starting to think the lucky son-of-a-gun had somehow talked his mother into giving him the whole day off.

The girls and boys of Mrs. Fontaine's sixth grade class had just returned from lunch and were taking out their math books when Principal O'Malley knocked on the door and entered the room. He didn't look happy, and everyone in the classroom began wondering who was in trouble this time.

O'Malley was in his sixties and had just a few strands of white hair still left on an otherwise bald head. He was short, wore small wire-rimmed glasses and bow ties, and put the fear of God into every kid in the school. He walked up to Mrs. Fontaine and began whispering very quietly to her. Suddenly she fell back into her chair, put her hand to her mouth, and started crying.

Peggy Clark, who sat in front of Billy, turned to her friend next to her and said, "She must be the one in trouble this time."

The principal turned to face the class. "I want you all to listen very carefully," he said. "I'm afraid I have some very bad news to tell you." The room immediately became so quiet you could hear a pin drop. "One of your classmates," said O'Malley, pausing to clear his throat, "Vincent Maki, has passed away."

The gasp in the room was audible. Billy and Walter stared at each other with frozen looks of disbelief on their faces. Two girls started crying immediately, while the rest of the class went into a state of stunned silence.

"It appears," continued the principal, "that he drowned in Brooks Lake. He was found early this morning. I know what a terrible ordeal this is for all of you. I would ask that you each say a prayer for Vincent and his parents. Let's have a moment of silence right now."

For the next minute, the only sound was the constant sniffling of Mrs. Fontaine and the crying of the two girls.

Billy was shaking; he wanted to pray for Vinnie, but no words would come to him.

Pokey, whose mother had brought all of her boys up with strong religious ties, whispered softly for forgiveness of Vinnie's sins, and prayed that Vinnie would ascend into heaven.

Hank, like Billy, was also speechless. The only words that came to him were *Holy shit*.

Principal O'Malley said, "Thank you", and then left the room a moment later. Mrs. Fontaine was too upset to continue teaching and allowed her students to get up and mingle, as long as they did it quietly. Billy, Hank and Pokey immediately grouped together at the back of the room.

"How could Vinnie drown?" asked Pokey. "He was the best swimmer among us."

"What was he doing at Brooks Lake?" asked Hank. "No one goes swimming in May."

"He said he was starting his murder investigation," said Billy. "He came to my house last night and wanted me to go with him. He said he had a clue."

"He came to my house too," said Pokey. "I don't know why he bothered. He knows I can't go out that late on a school night."

"Did he tell you he had a clue too?" asked Billy.

"Yeah, but I didn't believe him."

"He didn't have any clue," said Hank. "He was full of it. Good thing you didn't go with him."

"What do you mean?" asked Billy. "Maybe if I was with him, I could have pulled him out of the water and saved him."

The thought that Vinnie had died because he hadn't gone with him would haunt Billy Wilson for years to come.

Billy and his sister took the bus home after school. Their mother was in the kitchen making cookies, and Billy immediately asked, "Have you heard about Vinnie?"

"Heard what? The police left right after the bus picked you up, and his parent's left shortly afterwards."

"Vinnie drowned last night in Brooks Lake," said Billy, and he watched as his mother uttered a soft, shaky "oh" and stumbled to a chair at the kitchen table.

"Oh no, that's awful," Laurie Wilson finally managed to say. "I thought the police were just there talking about the murders again. Those poor people!"

Billy sat next to his mother for a while, having no idea what to say, and then realized he was hungry. He poured himself a glass of Tang, grabbed a couple cookies that were cooling on a rack, and headed upstairs to his room.

He tried playing a football game he usually enjoyed, but found he was having a hard time concentrating. The thought that he would never see his friend Vinnie again seemed incomprehensible to him. They had lived next door to each other their entire lives. His sister was best friends with Vinnie's sister Katie.

Vinnie might have been Billy's best friend, although that was hard to say. He liked Pokey too, and there were some seventh graders that he got along with. He liked Hank most of the time, but was afraid of him. In truth, Billy was happiest when he was alone. Making close friends would be a life-long issue for him.

Pokey came over an hour later. "I called Hank," he said, "but his dad put him to work and he can't get free."

Billy put his radio on so they could listen to the ballgame. The Sox were in Baltimore to play the Orioles, and it was a good pitching matchup; Earl Wilson versus Jim Palmer. The boys played some Pick-Up Sticks for awhile to help pass the time, and then they decided to go outside and play catch. They didn't talk too much, both of them feeling subdued, but finally Pokey asked Billy if he was going to the funeral.

"I don't know. I've never been to a funeral before. What do you do?"

"Well, first there will be a wake," said Pokey. "That's where you go and look at the body."

"We have to look at the body?" Billy cringed at the thought.

"If it's an open casket," said Pokey. "I think it will be. You just say a prayer, and then you have to shake hands with his parents and tell them how sorry you are."

"Oh God, do we have to?" asked Billy.

"Yeah. Then the next day will be the funeral. You just have to sit in the church for that, then there will be a short service at the gravesite, and afterwards there will probably be a gathering somewhere. That's where we get to eat."

"You mean like a party?"

"It's a celebration of Vinnie's life, short as it was," said Pokey. "I can't believe he's dead."

"Me either," said Billy.

"I keep expecting him to come running over to join us," said Pokey. "I'm still wondering what the heck he was doing at the lake. It doesn't make any sense."

Billy nodded his agreement. "He kept saying he had this clue and was going to investigate who killed the dead guy, but he never showed me anything."

"Me either," said Pokey. "I wonder if he really had something. What could it have been?"

"No idea," said Billy.

"All I know is that after going to the wake, I don't want to see any more bodies for a long time."

Billy remembered an aunt of Walter's had died just a few months ago. "Amen to that," he said.

They went back into the house just in time to hear Earl Wilson hit a tenth inning home run off of Jim Palmer, and the Sox won the game, 2-1.

3

The Thomas Baylor Funeral Home was located in Philbrook about a half mile from the high school. It was an old building in need of some repair on the outside, but the inside had recently been refurbished and looked surprisingly modern. The hardwood floors that had grown uneven and dull over the years had been refinished to a smooth, glossy shine. New draperies had been hung on the windows, replacing the faded, outdated ones that had been hanging for years. The furniture in the foyer had also been replaced, and the room now had a warm, welcoming feel to it.

The reason for the updated appearance was Clinton Baylor, grandson of the home's namesake and son of Philip Baylor, who had recently retired. Philip, a notorious penny-pincher, had let the home slip in the last few years. Clinton had been embarrassed by his father's cheapskate ways and vowed to make changes when he took over, which he had done last year. Clinton had plans to fix the outside of the home once the good weather moved in, despite his father's constant haranguing that he was wasting good money for no reason.

It was Clinton Baylor who welcomed the people of Edgeworth on Friday night as they came to pay their respects to the family of Vincent Maki. Edgeworth, like many small towns in New England, was a close knit community, and the turnout was extremely large. The wake officially ran from seven until nine, but Clinton opened the viewing room early, with the Maki's permission, because the waiting line was already out the door and around the side of the building.

The Wilson's discovered that line when they arrived just at seven. Billy was wearing the new suit that his father had bought for him last night. The tie felt constricting around his neck, and under normal circumstances he would have complained vigorously about having to wear one. Tonight he had simply uttered one, "Do I have to?" and then acquiesced to his mother's wishes.

He was nervous as he stood in the line, which was moving very slowly as far as he could tell. He was about to view a body in a casket for the first time, and he was not looking forward to it. The fact that it was a close friend of his made it seem all the more surreal.

Marylou understood the importance of what they were there for, but it's hard for an eight year old not to fidget, and she was no exception. She wanted the line to move faster, and kept complaining to her mother. She saw friends of hers in line and was constantly running off. Eventually, Laurie Wilson just let her go, as her husband rolled his eyes skyward.

Billy had never really thought of dying. He was a kid, and kids were supposed to become teenagers, then young adults. They would go to college, marry, and have families. Eventually they would become really old like the Potter's and then die, but to Billy and his friends that seemed like a million years away.

Vinnie's death had brought everything Billy had ever thought about dying crashing down, and suddenly he understood his friend's live-for-today attitude. He had been thinking over the last few days about all the crazy things Vinnie had done, and he wondered if he should start being a little more daring too. Then he would begin to question if it were those crazy ideas that had caused Vinnie's death.

Billy had seen Walter and his family when he first arrived. They were already in line and just entering the funeral home. He figured they must be at the casket by now. The Logan's were churchgoers, and Walter would know what to do. Billy had been afraid to ask his mother about proper wake etiquette, wondering if what Walter had told him was true or not, but now he did.

"Mom, what do we do when we get inside?

Her reply was almost exactly what Walter had told him earlier.

His mother was wearing a long black dress which Billy hadn't seen before, and which he assumed she owned just for these occasions. She looked at him and put a hand on his shoulder, which always annoyed him for some reason.

"Just do what everyone else does," she said. "You kneel down, say a silent prayer for Vinnie, and then get up. After that you will go to his parents and tell them how sorry you are."

The line moved slowly, and it was another five minutes before they reached the front door. Billy had to chase down his sister so they could all enter together.

Clinton Baylor thanked them for coming as they entered the foyer. He shook Billy's hand, and Billy wondered how someone who looked so normal could be an undertaker.

Walter came over a few minutes later. "I've already been through the line," he said.

"I know," said Billy. "You were just going in when we got here. What does he look like?"

"He looks like he's sleeping. Listen, when you get through the line, I'm going to be in that room over there," said Walter, pointing towards a room down the hall.

"Okay," said Billy, and he watched as Pokey ambled away.

The room containing Vinnie's casket was off to the left. As they entered, Billy saw a display that had been set up with pictures of Vinnie, starting with the day he was born and ending with the last picture taken of him. That had been at Katie's birthday party back in January, and Billy suddenly remembered Vinnie's birthday would have been next week.

He didn't want to see Vinnie in a casket, but he felt compelled to look anyway once they were close enough.

It was weird. Pokey had been right; Vinnie looked like he was just taking a nap. He was wearing a suit and tie, his hands were folded across his stomach, and his eyes were closed. There didn't seem to be anything wrong with him, and Billy wondered how he could be dead.

When they arrived at the casket, his father and Marylou knelt down to pray. Once they arose, Billy and his mother took their turn. Billy knelt down, and again he didn't know what to say. *I'll miss you, Vinnie*, was all he could think of, and then he started crying.

His mother put her arm around him and guided him up, and a moment later they were standing in front of Vinnie's parents. Alfred and Irene Maki had already shed a thousand tears, and seeing Billy cry sent a new cascade down both their faces.

"I'm so sorry," said Billy. "I'm gonna miss him so much."

They both hugged him and said, "Thank you", and that was when Billy noticed that Katie and Marylou were crying too.

After finally getting through the line, Billy told his mother he was going to find Walter. She told him to hurry, because they wouldn't be staying very long.

Pokey was where he said he would be, surrounded by some of the other kids from school. Billy saw Peggy Clark, Samantha Cousins, and the Johnson twins, Kim and Mary, who were all in Mrs. Fontaine's class with him. Curtis Armstrong and Emmet Nash, two seventh graders, were also in the group. Hank hadn't been allowed to come. His family apparently had plans for Friday night, and they didn't want to change them just to go to a wake.

Billy joined his friends. "Man, that was hard," he said.

"I feel so bad for Katie," said Mary Johnson. "Now she's an only child."

"What was Vinnie doing out at the lake?" asked Curtis, and the conversation turned into a series of guesses about what he had been up to.

"He said he had some secret clue he found on the body in the woods," said Billy, "but he never said what it was, and I didn't believe him anyway."

"He didn't tell you anything?" asked Curtis.

"Nothing."

Walter was shaking his head. "He kept claiming he was going to solve the mystery of who killed the dead guy, but he never told us anything."

"Hmm," said Curtis, and they were all left to ponder what it could have been.

Eventually the talk switched from Vinnie to school, and Samantha said she was disappointed Hank hadn't come, because she had a crush on him. This surprised all the boys, because quite frankly none of them had started to think of girls as anything but annoying, and the thought that girls were beginning to take notice of them was somewhat alarming.

By the time his mother came to get him, Billy had not thought about Vinnie for ten minutes. It surprised him to think he could forget so soon.

The next morning, Billy was once again in a suit and tie as his family attended Vincent Maki's funeral. The service took place at the First Methodist Church in Edgeworth, which stood alone among the trees in a bucolic setting about three miles from the Maki residence.

Pokey and Billy sat together, their families on either side of them. They paid little attention to the service, instead focusing on the baseball cards they had both brought with them. After some quiet haggling and a few "shushes" from both mothers, Billy traded Roger Maris and Joe Nuxhall cards to Pokey in exchange for Pete Runnels and Tom Brewer. Although Pokey only had about thirty cards in his collection, compared to the four hundred Billy had, he always seemed to get the cards Billy needed. The trading ended when Pokey's mom took his cards away from him and told him to sit still and be quiet.

When the service ended, they all followed the casket out the front door and around the side of the church to the cemetery in the back. The service there was short, as Pokey had said it would be, but the finality of it all hit everyone in attendance.

Irene Maki showed great restraint until the final "Amen", but broke done again as she placed a rose on her son's coffin, which was lying next to a gaping hole in the ground. Alfred Maki comforted her as best he could, but he had a glazed look on his face and appeared to be a thousand miles away.

My friend Vinnie is going to be lying there for the rest of my life, thought Billy. The prospect astounded him, and would for many years to come.

Life returned to normal in the days following the funeral. Billy would occasionally see Irene or Alfred Maki in their yard and would wave to them. Occasionally he would stop and talk, but just for a minute. He had trouble making eye contact, and was never quite sure what to say.

Marylou had no such problem. She spent much of her free time over at the Maki's home. Katie remained her best friend until college sent them their separate ways.

The three boys continued to play together for a few weeks, and then Hank suddenly found a new group of friends. From that point on, he would rarely be seen by either Billy or Walter outside of school. However, Emmet Nash and Curtis Armstrong, who liked to be called Cisco after the Cisco Kid, joined their group, and so they were four again.

Billy and Walter were surprised by this development, since Curtis and Emmet were older than them and a grade ahead, but they seemed to fit in nicely. Curtis was taller than all of them and enjoyed playing basketball, much as his father had done. They eventually ended up spending a lot of time at the Armstrong home, which was located on a cross street just past Hank's house. It had a paved driveway with a basketball hoop set up on one end of it, and for a short time basketball replaced baseball as their afternoon sport.

The new group of four stayed together for a year, and then Curtis went his separate way, much as Hank had done before. Emmet, who had been named after the famous clown Emmet Kelly, remained close to Walter for many years, but he and Billy had problems with each other in high school and parted ways.

Curtis graduated a year before Billy and left for USC. He would play varsity basketball for the Trojans, but mostly sat on the bench. He would eventually earn a law degree, return to Edgeworth, and open up a law practice in Greenfield.

Emmet ended up graduating with Billy and Walter's class. He had been forced to stay back a year due to illness; measles, mumps, and scarlet fever all hitting him within a six-month period. He became an investment broker, bought a mansion in Malibu, and was living the good life. Unfortunately, he perished in 1992 in a hot air balloon accident in Santa Fe, New Mexico.

Billy thought of Vinnie often, mainly because his house was right next door. He tried to change his habit of preaching right from wrong, but found it hard to do. At one point, he decided he may as well become a preacher, and that perhaps his nickname was a sign from God. Those thoughts eventually faded, as did his belief in God for a while. He would finish high school and head to college without a clue about what he wanted to do with his life.

Walter and his two brothers also went to college, a tribute to their mother, who worked two jobs to keep the family afloat. Walter would drop out after his sophomore year, and after drifting for a few years he decided to attend culinary school. Cooking would become his passion. He also returned to the area and eventually became the head chef for the Marriot Hotel in Northampton.

Hank dropped out of high school just before his senior year came to an end, going to work full-time at his father's ironworks business. He developed a drinking problem, and spent numerous nights in the Edgeworth jail for drunkenness and disorderly conduct. The day finally came when his father hit him once too often, and Hank hit back. The blow knocked his old man on his ass and gained Hank some respect in his father's eyes. However, it was the final straw as far as Hank was concerned. He packed his bags that night and moved to places unknown. He was never heard from again.

Billy would visit Vinnie's grave often over the next six years, riding his bike to the cemetery when the weather was nice, and later driving his car once he procured his license. He would sit by the stone that had been placed upon the grave and just talk to Vinnie as though he could hear. He would tell him how the Red Sox were doing, what they were learning in school, and what Katie and Marylou were up to.

In the fall of 1967 he made a special trip to Vinnie's gravesite. It would be to celebrate the fact that Billy's yearly prediction had finally come true. The Red Sox had finished first and won the pennant.

ELEVEN

As Billy Wilson was online looking for flights to Boston, Simon Taylor was boarding a plane at Sarasota Airport. The Thursday morning flight was full, but Simon was comfortably ensconced in his first class seat. He was thumbing through the morning newspaper as the plane took off. By the time the flight attendant brought him his coffee he was on page fourteen, where a news headline attracted his attention.

COLD CASE TEAM INVESTIGATING 50 YEAR OLD MURDER

He read the first two paragraphs and then skimmed the rest of the story. He was about to move on when the name Billy Wilson jumped out at him. He had just had a client by that name last week. *Coincidence*, he thought. It was a pretty common name. There must be thousands of Billy Wilson's in the country.

Simon was looking forward to seeing Thomas Mann that night. They had decided to do their exchange of talents that evening, sort of a warm-up to the Body and Soul Conference that would start the next day. Simon had spent a good deal of time in the last forty-eight hours silently inviting Nora to come through and talk to him again when the time came. It had been a suggestion of Mann's.

"Let the spirit world know what we're going to do," Thomas had said. "Invite those on the other side who you'd like to hear from. They're busy over there doing the things they need to do, but they can take time out to come to our little gathering if they know about it, so let them know."

Simon had a number of family members who had crossed over, but Nora was the only one he cared to hear from.

He had told Maria what they were planning to do and immediately wished he hadn't. Her face remained impassive, neither smiling nor showing displeasure, yet it was obvious to him she was a bit put out.

Finally, she said, "She still has a great hold on you, your Nora."

"I'm sorry," he said. "I don't mean to upset you by talking about her."

"I know," Maria replied, "but I look forward to the day when you leave the past in the past."

As his plane touched down in Boston, Simon's thoughts were still very much in the past.

The pricey Boston hotel where the conference was to be held was historic, and when Simon checked into his room he realized you were paying for the name and not much else. The room was old and tired, with a closet door that stuck, carpeting that was well worn and, as he would find over the next three days, hot water that was hit or miss. If it wasn't for the name over the door, the place would have been torn down years ago, replaced by a shiny new model.

Simon unpacked his things and put them in a dresser that had to be seventy years old. After finishing that task, he sent a message to Thomas Mann letting him know he had arrived.

Welcome, Mann texted back, *I'm in Room 416. Want to perform tonight's festivities in your room or mine?*

Your room, typed Simon. *After dinner, say 8 o'clock.*

Meet you in the dining room at 6, replied Thomas.

Simon answered *Ok* and glanced at his watch. He found his stomach churning with excitement at the thought of hearing from Nora, so he decided to take a walk to settle himself.

Ten minutes later, he was wandering around the grounds of the Boston Common, and the doubt in his mind that he had been keeping in the background suddenly came to the surface.

Maria claimed that in both of her regressions with him, he had been her soul mate. Simon put a great deal of stock in that, for many of his clients had found what they claimed to be their soul mates during their regressions. Jill Palmer had found hers in three different lifetimes, and she had been the focal point of his first book.

Simon had no such experience to fall back on with Nora. He had, strange as it seemed to him now, never had a regression of his own. He had simply believed that Nora was his soul mate while they were married, and he had kept on believing it after her death.

Was she? Had he been fooling himself all these years by thinking that his wife was obviously his soul mate? *We all think our wife is our soul mate*, someone had once told him, *until the divorce*.

During Maria's second regression, she said they were brother and sister, not spouses. If he put stock in everyone else's regressions, why was he so resistant to the information she had given?

He was falling in love with Maria, he knew that much, and while being a father figure to Enrique was challenging for him, and quite frankly made him feel awkward at times, the boy was growing on him.

Yet what about Nora? If he and Maria were soul mates, was Nora just a bridge in his life until he found Maria? Perhaps the soul family Maria talked about was true, and they were all connected. Simon wondered how he could have been doing regressions for so many year, yet not have any answers to these questions.

Perhaps Nora would come through tonight and answer them for him.

"Are you excited?" asked Thomas, as they sat sipping coffee following their dinner.

"I think I'm more confused than anything?"

"Confused? Why?"

"This whole soul mate thing," said Simon. "I wonder if it really matters in the long run. We have to live the life we are in now, so does it really matter if we knew our lovers before in prior lives? Shouldn't we just live for today and not worry about what happened two hundred years ago?"

"Sounds to me like your relationship with Maria is making you question your time with Nora," said Thomas.

Simon gave him a bemused smile as he slowly nodded yes over and over.

"Perhaps you'll get some answers tonight."

"Perhaps," said Simon, but he doubted it could be that easy.

"So who should go first?" asked Thomas.

"I guess we should flip a coin," replied a subdued Simon.

"Better than that, let's ask Siri," said Thomas, and he took out his cell phone. "Heads, I bring messages to you first; tails, you regress me."

Simon nodded his agreement.

"Siri, flip a coin," said Thomas.

"It's tails," the phone replied.

"There you have it," said Thomas. "First I get my regression, and then you get your messages. Are you ready?"

"Ready as I'll ever be," said Simon, but his heart was fluttering at the thought of hearing from Nora once again.

They took the elevator to Mann's room, which turned out to be a carbon copy of Simon's. Mann had already rearranged the room, putting a chair near the couch, as if he had known how the coin toss would turn out.

Simon went over the process with Thomas. He occasionally still used his original method of taking the client back through stages of their current lifetime, back to the womb, and then moving to a past life. His instinct told him he should do that with Thomas, and his friend said he had no problem with that.

Simon lead him through the relaxation techniques and then down the spiral staircase. As Mann reached the final step, Simon said, "The door at the end of the hallway opens to a past life that you will recall. As we near the door, you will go back in time in your current life, and I will ask you to describe events that happened at a particular age. Do you understand?"

"I do," said Thomas, his voice clear and almost powerful, unlike the sleepy voice most people had at that point.

Simon wondered for a moment if Mann was completely under, but he decided to move ahead. As it turned out, there was no problem.

"I want you to start going back in time now; just a few years at first, back to some time in your twenties. Can you find a day that particularly stands out to you?"

"Hmm, there were many at that time. My work was really picking up speed at that point."

"How about an interesting reading that really shocked your client," said Simon.

"Oh yes," said Thomas, "I was in Dayton, Ohio. It was a small gathering in the basement of a church. A deacon of that church was in attendance, and it was obvious he didn't believe that I could actually do what I did.

"Suddenly an aunt of his came through, identified by the blue hair dye she always used. She scolded him for not taking care of his mother, whom he had just put in a nursing home. His father had already passed, and he was the only child. 'Get her out of there,' she said, 'and do your duty as a man.' He was thoroughly embarrassed, of course, and snuck out of the room a moment later."

"How interesting," said Simon. "Now let's go back a bit farther, past your teenage years and back to the age of nine or ten. Tell me a day you remember from that time period."

It took Thomas a minute to reply, and Simon worried for a moment if the connection had been lost. But Thomas finally frowned, then continued.

"My friends don't believe what I can do. They think I'm just making it up. That was a hard time for me."

"Is there a day in particular you remember?"

"I had a friend named Maria who lived next door. One day I heard a voice come through who said I needed to tell Maria something. I told her I had a message from her grandmother, although I forget what the message was. She called me a liar, because all of her grandparents were still alive. I realized later that it was a great grandmother whom Maria had never even met, but from that day on our relationship was damaged, and later, when we were in high school, she told all her friends I was a weirdo."

Simon thought it best to move on at that point. "Now Thomas, I want you to go back to when you were first born. Past the ages of three, two, and one. Back to the time you were in the womb. Can you do that for me, Thomas?"

Simon had found great success over the years with messages from the womb. It was amazing what people could remember, and he had also received messages specific to him from guides, whether his own or a clients, at this point in the regression.

"I'm there, surprising to say," said Thomas.

"What do you remember about that time?"

"I'm excited. I know I'm coming back to the earth plane with a gift that can help many people."

"You know about the abilities you will have after you are born?" asked Simon.

"Yes. It is my main reason for returning. I have chosen parents who will be sympathetic, who will believe in my abilities. That was important, for had I not chosen them, I never would have succeeded."

"Did you choose to have this ability, or were you told you would have it?"

"It was a suggestion to me by my guides, and I agreed to it. It was basically the next step in the process I was going through."

"Thank you, Thomas," said Simon. "Now you are standing in front of the door to a past life. It is time to go through that door. Are you ready?"

"Ready," said Thomas.

"Excellent. The door is now opening. Step on through and tell me what you see."

Thomas Mann was silent for the next ten seconds. Then he suddenly exclaimed, "Oh my!"

"What is it?" asked Simon, not knowing by the exclamation if it was good or bad.

"I am sitting with a great yogi, someone whose statue I have on my bookcase at home," said Thomas.

"Who is it, and why are you sitting with him?"

"He is the great Swami Vivekananda, a great spiritual teacher, well-advanced in the spiritual world. He is sitting crossed-legged in front of me, teaching me and many others about the way of the world. It is truly amazing."

"Are you a yogi also?" asked Simon.

A wide smile came over Mann's face at this. "No, not in the least. I am simply attending to hear the great man speak."

"Let's get some information if we can," said Simon. "What is your name and what country are you in?"

"My name is Gopal. As you must have guessed, the country is India. I am twenty-two years old, and I have come to see and hear the great Swami. He is currently traveling across India, speaking his message of love."

"How many are in attendance at this event?"

"The room is small, but it is packed with people. Vivekananda is very well known. I have somehow procured a seat in the front row. I could reach out and touch him if I wanted."

"What is his message about love? What is he trying to say?"

"He is attempting to inspire the poor people of India, of which there are many millions, to believe in themselves. It is a message he has been teaching for years now, for many of the poor in India have given up hope, and he is trying to change that."

"Let's go back for a moment to your childhood," said Simon. "Try to find a time when you were seven or eight years old. Tell me about it. Are you one of the poor?"

Simon watched as Thomas lay still on the couch, slight turnings of his head the only movements.

"I am six," Thomas finally said, "and no, we are not poor. My father is a well-to-do businessman. He feels sorry for the poor who surround him every day, but considers them more of an annoyance than anything else. Many of them are my friends, however, and as I grow older I understand their plight. By the time I am a teenager, I have great compassion for them and want to help."

"What do you do to help them at that point?" asked Simon.

"Not as much as I would like," said Thomas. "I share some of my allowance with them, buy them some rice or candy, but it is not enough."

"Had you heard of Vivekananda at that point?"

"Oh yes, he was already well known at that time, and was one of my heroes. He came to our small village when I was about nine or ten, and I was mesmerized by him. My father did not see him that day, for he was working in a town far away. I think if he had heard Vivekananda speak that day, it would have opened his heart as it did mine."

"What is your day like? Are you in school?"

"Yes, I am a very good student and actually enjoy my studies. My father wants me to be a doctor, but I am not really interested in that. To be honest, I get weak in the knees whenever I see blood."

"What is it you end up doing?" asked Simon.

"When my schooling ends, I convince my father to take me into his business. I think I did it for the travel, for he has seen a great deal of our country, and I wish to do the same."

"So now you are twenty-two and sitting at the feet of the great Swami. What happens to you after that? How does your life go?"

"Well, I am torn at that point. My father is now hoping I will eventually take over the business from him, but my heart wants me to become a disciple of the great Swami Vivekananda. I wish to follow him everywhere and study under him. My father is not happy about that, and I must admit I become a bit petulant. We have many arguments about it, and I finally move out of his home and go out on my own."

"That must have been very hard on you; what happened?"

"I traveled for weeks to catch up to Vivekananda, but the day after I caught up to him, he left on a trip to the west, traveling to London and then to the United States. I discovered that he would be gone for more than a year. My disappointment was tremendous, almost unbearable to me, and I slowly made my way back home."

"Back to your parents?"

"For a short time, yes, although I finally moved into a place of my own with some friends of mine."

"Did you join Vivekananda when he returned to India?"

"Sadly, no," said Thomas. "I followed his teachings, however, and eventually I realized that if I did take over my father's business I would be paid quite well, and could use my money and influence to help those less fortunate."

"So you went back to work with your father then?" asked Simon.

"I did."

"And did you continue to follow the life of the Swami Vivekananda?"

Thomas paused at this point, and Simon noticed the smile slip away from his countenance. "Sadly, he left his body shortly after I returned to my father's work."

They spoke for another fifteen minutes. Gopal married at twenty-four, had three children in five years, and died at age forty-two when he was struck by a runaway cart.

As the session came to an end, Simon asked, "Do you recognize anyone in your past life who you know now in your current life?"

"I do," said Thomas. "My wife now was my sister back then, and my father is once again my father, although the person he married in this life was an aunt of his back then."

"I'm going to bring you back to the present now," said Simon, and a moment later he did.

"That was fantastic," said Thomas. "I never would have thought that my last life was in India, although I have always had an interest in Hinduism."

"You mentioned you have a statue of Vivekananda in your home; how long have you had it?"

"Oh dear, quite a few years now," said Thomas. "I saw it one day when I was about twenty-five, and I just had to have it. I guess now I know why." He paused a moment, and then looked warmly at his friend. "Thank you, Simon. I only hope I can do for you what you just did for me. It was more than I could have asked for."

Now it was Simon's turn, but first Thomas needed to take a few moments to prepare. He poured a glass of water, drank half of it, and then refilled it. He took the chair that Simon had been sitting in, while Simon sat on the couch.

"Oh my," said Thomas, "you've left a good deal of energy in this chair. I could feel it as I sat down."

Simon was aware of energy shifts, but wanted to hear what his friend had to say about them. "Does that happen often?"

"More often than you'd think, although I doubt most people realize it. For instance, you might go into a restaurant and be seated at a table where an argument had just occurred. Suddenly you become more irritable than you had been a few moments earlier. You don't know why this has happened, but what you've done is felt the energy of the person who just vacated that seat."

"Interesting," said Simon. "So besides your gift of talking to the other side, you also receive energy outputs from those around you."

"Everyone does. I just notice it more." Thomas finished his glass of water and said, "Shall we begin?"

"Ready," said Simon.

"Have you been inviting Nora to the party as I suggested?"

"I've spent a great deal of my quiet time doing just that."

Thomas nodded, then closed his eyes and said a short prayer. He took a deep breath as he finished, opened his eyes, and smiled at his friend.

"Let's begin," he said. "The first person coming through is the one who gave me this idea about an exchange of talents.

He says he is an uncle who lived high up. That's all he ever tells me about his whereabouts. He says that you will know."

"That's funny," said Simon. "That would be Joseph, my uncle who lived just outside of Denver, the Mile High city. He passed a couple of years ago."

"Ah, well that answers that," said Thomas. "He wants you to know that he's been trying to contact you, but you've paid him no heed. It's why he finally came to me, so I could make you aware."

"How has he tried to connect with me?" asked Simon.

"Mostly by burning out light bulbs in your condo."

"I always thought that was Nora," said Simon. "What has he been trying to tell me?"

"He wants you to know that dying is not a bad thing, that life is wonderful on his side, and that we all choose our time to go."

"He was only sixty-two when he passed. Wasn't that early? He had a lot to live for."

"He had accomplished what he came here to do. He says it's important that you understand that."

Simon shifted uncomfortably on the couch. It was the same phrase that Nora had told him in his dream. Why hadn't she wanted to live a long life with him? Why leave the earth plane at such a young age? He was still attempting to process it all.

Thomas could see the troubled look on Simon's face. "Joseph is reiterating the statement, a little more forcefully this time. You MUST understand this concept."

"I understand what he's saying," said Simon. "It's just hard."

"Joseph has left, but a number of people are in line wishing to say hello. The first is an elderly gentleman; I'm guessing grandfather. He's short, stocky, with thinning grey hair but a warm smile."

"Yes, that would be my mother's father. He passed quite some time ago; again, too early."

"No, not too early," he says, "but right on time." Thomas looked at Simon with a sympathetic smile. "That seems to be the theme of this session. He just wanted to say hello and let you know he keeps an eye on what you're doing. He says he likes that lady you are with now."

That finally brought a smile to Simon's face.

"Next up, it seems we have a teenager. He's talking very fast and hopes you will remember him. I'm picturing a needle in his arm, so I'm assuming he died of an overdose."

"Oh God, that must be Kevin. He was a friend of mine when we were kids. I'm surprised he's here; I haven't thought of him in years."

"Did he in fact die from an overdose?"

"Yes," said Simon. "We were friends when we were little, but parted ways in high school. He fell in with the wrong crowd and became an addict; died of a heroin overdose, if I recall correctly."

"He's nodding his agreement," said Thomas. "He's happy that you remember him and that he could visit here today. He says he died as he did as a lesson to others about the evils of drugs, and that nearly all of the children dying today in that manner are doing the same, and will continue to do so until the message finally gets across. That is why they came."

"He knew before he was born that he would die of an overdose?"

"He did," said Thomas.

"So he came to teach a lesson rather than learn a lesson?" asked Simon.

"Kevin says he also learned a few things while he was here, and that a karmic lesson was also involved. He shouts out a big *Bye* to you as he leaves."

The line moved on, deceased family and friends mostly stopping in just to say hello, and Simon suddenly had the notion that Nora was not going to visit him today.

But he was wrong.

"Last person in line," said Thomas, "and I do believe you've been waiting to hear from her."

"It's Nora?" asked Simon, a look of hope consuming his face.

"Nora is here, but I'm afraid she says her message will be short and sweet. She's telling me to listen closely, because she is busy and can only say it once."

Thomas paused as he listened to Nora's words, nodding occasionally as if to acknowledge what she was telling him.

He finally looked at Simon, and his first words nearly destroyed his friend.

"I'm sorry, Simon. She's already left."

"No!" cried Simon. "I want to talk to her."

"She wanted you to know she has heard you praying for her appearance. However, she is deeply involved in a project on the spiritual side and was barely able to break away."

Simon's chin dropped to his chest, and Thomas knew how hurt and disappointed he was. He waited a few moments for Simon to run through his thoughts, and then he said, "Are you ready to hear her message to you."

Simon looked up, sadness dripping from his countenance, and mumbled, "Okay."

"Nora is happy that you have finally moved on and found a beautiful young woman to love. She wants you to stop looking in the past. She mentioned that your spiritual path is about to take a giant leap forward, that you're understanding would grow by leaps and bounds, and that she is so very proud of you.

"However, she also had a caution for you, and I have no idea what she is getting at. A situation is arising that has nothing to do with you but will involve you anyway, and it comes with some danger to those around you. Be careful."

"Was she talking about Maria and Enrique?"

"She did not say. Her final words were that she loves you, checks in on you often, and will be there when your time to cross over finally comes."

Thomas watched once again as his words settled in. "I'm sorry," he said, "that's all there is. The window to the other side is now closed."

TWELVE

Saturday night, as Simon and Thomas were in the middle of their weekend conference, Billy Wilson landed at Bradley Airport aboard Delta Airlines flight 671. He grabbed his bag from the overhead compartment and waited patiently for the line in front of him to move. He was tired, having been up since seven that morning, and he still had another hour's drive to Dearborn.

Once off the plane, he headed straight for the car rental counters, having no other luggage. Billy always traveled light. Fortunately, the counters were slow, and he was able to pick up his 2017 Hyundai Sonata in short order. Bradley was an easy airport to get in and out of, and soon Billy was zooming by Springfield on his way north.

He had heard from Marylou again last night. She and her husband would be arriving Sunday morning on an American Airlines flight from South Carolina. His mother's body would also be on the plane, and would be transported to the Baylor Funeral Home upon arrival. Billy wasn't planning on returning to Sarasota until next Sunday, which would give him plenty of time to check out the old neighborhood and catch up with friends.

The Sonata was equipped with an enhanced GPS System, which led him to Dearborn, but then it seemed confused as he hit the woods. It claimed *You have reached your destination* when he was still obviously a mile or two away. He doubted he would have found Katie's house if it wasn't for her map.

Edgeworth was a small country town, "the sticks" to the big city folks, but it still seemed large in comparison to

Dearborn. The roads, some still not paved, were winding as they made their way through the forest, and spring rains had dotted some of them with shock-pounding potholes.

Billy finally came upon Travesty Lane and wondered what had happened here for a street to deserve such a moniker. He saw a mailbox with the address on it that Katie had given him, and he slowly turned into the driveway. The home was a small saltbox design with white shingles and a green roof.

Katie walked out onto the porch as he was getting out of the car. From his vantage point, Billy wondered if it were actually her. She looked younger than he expected as she stood under the pale porch light.

He grabbed his travel bag from the passenger seat and exited the Hyundai. "Katie?" he said, still unsure it was her.

"Hey there," she replied, "glad you could make it. Any trouble finding the place?"

"One wrong turn down the road, but other than that no trouble, thanks to your map."

"I figured you'd need the map. GPS tends to die before it gets here."

"It did. Thanks for inviting me." She had a glass in her hand, and he asked, "What's that you're drinking?"

"Cabernet," said Katie. "Care to share some with me?"

He made his way up the four stairs to the porch and said, "Sounds good. I could use a drink about now."

They hugged, and then Billy stepped back to look at her. He couldn't believe how lovely she was. If he hadn't known better, he would have guessed her age to be forty-five, not the late fifties he knew her to be.

"Wow," he said, "you look fantastic. How do you do it?"

She just smiled at him and said, "Good living, I guess. You look pretty good yourself." They headed indoors, and Katie said, "I have beer if you'd rather."

"No, wine's fine."

They entered her home and she gave him a quick tour. The rooms were small but cozy. The porch led into the living room, where she had a rather large collection of Tom Clark gnomes. The furniture was old but appeared comfortable, and the television was a simple 27" inch set. "I really don't watch much television," she said.

The kitchen was compact but easy to move around in. There was no table, and she told him she usually sat in the living room and listened to music while she ate. The downstairs also contained a pantry and a bathroom.

They went upstairs, where there were three more rooms. Her bedroom was in the front of the house and had a woman's touch to it; lots of fluffy pillows, candles on her dresser, family pictures on the wall.

A small second bedroom in the back of the house had one wall lined with boxes. "This is usually my storage room," she explained. "I had to move some stuff out to make room for you."

"You didn't have to do that," he said.

"Happy to do it," she said. "I'm glad to have the company."

The other room upstairs had been turned into a photo studio. It was cluttered with lamps, backdrops, and half a dozen cameras lying scattered about.

"I gather you like to take pictures," he said.

"Billy, I'm a photographer," exclaimed Katie. "You didn't know?"

"No," he said. When he'd last seen Katie, she had been working at a day care center. "When did that happen?"

"I went to school back in 2005 for it and slowly worked it into my routine. Turns out I'm the only photographer in Dearborn, and there are only a couple others in Edgeworth and Philbrook, so it works out pretty well. Come stand over here."

She positioned him in front of a light blue backdrop, and then picked up one of the camera's that was sitting on top of a desk. "Relax and smile," she said.

She started taking pictures one after another. After what seemed like twenty shots, she changed the backdrop and took ten more.

"Enough," he finally said. "Didn't you offer me some wine a while ago?"

"Oh my goodness," she said. She had set her glass down in the kitchen and forgotten about it. "Sorry about that."

They headed back downstairs, and after Katie poured his wine, they settled onto the couch in the living room.

"You like it out here in the woods?" he asked. "Isn't it lonely?"

"I love it out here," she replied, as she gazed into his eyes. "It's always peaceful. I love nature and animals. They're my favorite things to photograph. I have six feeders on my porch that attract all varieties of birds. Of course, they occasionally attract the deer and bears too."

"Bears? You have bears in your backyard?"

"Of course, silly," she said. "You're pretty deep into the woods out here, in case you hadn't noticed."

As they talked, Billy couldn't get over how great Katie looked. She had short black hair which showed no signs of grey, mystical bluish-green eyes, and a small mouth tinged with the lightest touch of lipstick. He guessed her height to be around 5'4", and her small but perky breasts and flat stomach told him she must work out on a regular basis.

The talk quickly turned to Vinnie. "It must be weird for you, after all these years thinking that he had drowned, to suddenly find out your brother was murdered. How are you dealing with it?"

"It is strange to have something that happened so long ago suddenly all over the papers," she said. "I mean, I was eight at the time. I hate to say this, but I don't remember a great deal about my brother. But to think that he was murdered ...." She let the thought drift as she stared off into space.

They talked about old times through another round of wine until Billy couldn't keep his eyes open any longer.

"I'd better put you to bed," Katie finally said as the clock neared midnight, and minutes later Billy was fast asleep in the guestroom.

Billy slept soundly, a rare occurrence for him. The next morning, he headed downstairs to find Katie scrambling eggs, and there was a batch of home fries with peppers and onions cooking on the stove.

"Hope you're hungry," she said. "There's coffee on the counter."

"Smells great," said Billy. He found the cups and took the largest one he could find, filling it to the brim. Then he noticed Katie's cup was almost empty and filled that one too.

"Thanks," she said. "Do me a favor and put some bread in the toaster."

Five minutes later, they sat in the living room and enjoyed the feast.

"What are you doing today?" she asked.

"I thought I'd go check out the old neighborhood, and then I'm going to take a ride to Northampton to see Walter. He called me the other night about Vinnie. I haven't seen him since dad's funeral."

"That's good. I wouldn't want you to be bored out here all day," she said. "I have a job over in Shelburne Falls and probably won't be home till 5 or so. If you get back before me, there's a key on the porch under the bag of bird seed."

Katie left as soon as breakfast was finished. Billy did the dishes, then showered and dressed. There was a small dresser in his room, so he unpacked his travel bag, which he had been too tired to do last night. He was just about to leave when Marylou called.

"Hi Billy, it's your sister," she said.

"Hey sis, what's up? When did you get in?"

"Our flight landed around nine," she said. "We transported mom's body straight to the funeral home. We're actually still here. I have the final details for you."

"Okay," said Billy

"The wake is going to be from 7 to 9 Tuesday night. I didn't see the need for an afternoon shift. Funeral is Wednesday morning at 10."

"How are you holding up?" he asked.

"I'm alright," she said, but her voice gave away how she really felt. "Are you at Katie's?"

"Yup. Arrived last night around ten."

"I still can't believe the news about Vinnie," she said. Katie had called her last week after talking with Billy. "Can you believe he was murdered?"

"Well, we always wondered. To have it come out after all this time is a bit surreal."

"She said the cops would want to talk with you."

Billy's stomach did a quick flip. Even after all these years, seeing anyone in a police uniform made him nervous. "I guess so, but I don't know what good it will do." Billy wondered if they knew he was in town, and then remembered that Marylou had put the obituary in the local paper.

They chatted for a few minutes more. Billy was surprised to hear that none of Marylou's four children had made the trip, but he didn't ask why. Mark's parents were flying in later that afternoon and would be staying with them at the hotel.

The ride to his old neighborhood took fifteen minutes. He knew times had changed as soon as he turned onto Town Line Road. There were twice as many homes as there had been when he was a kid, and a new condo complex had been built across the street from Walter's old house. His parent's home had seen so many changes he almost drove by it before he realized it was his. He drove down to the DiPietro house and turned around. That was the only name he recognized on the mailboxes, and he assumed one of Hank's siblings owned it now.

Billy drove back in front of his boyhood home and parked the car across the street. He gazed down the long driveway between his old house and the former Maki home. He remembered standing there with his father waiting for the police to arrive, and recalled how happy he had been that the cop hadn't chosen him to go back to the scene of the murders. Even now the memory of the body in the woods still turned his stomach. He sat there lost in his thoughts for another few minutes, and then noticed a man exit his old home and head for his car.

"You need help?" the man asked.

Billy lowered his window and said, "Hi there. I was just daydreaming. I used to live here."

"In his house?" the man said, pointing behind him.

"Yes."

"Well I'll be." The man's face broke into a big smile. "My name's Ted Dalton. I've lived here for nearly twelve years now."

"You must have bought the place from my mom," said Billy.

"Oh," Ted Dalton said, and Billy saw his face drop. "I read about her passing in the paper. Sorry for your loss."

"Thank you," he said.

They chatted for a few minutes more, and then Ted said, "Would you like to come in and see the place? We've made quite a few changes."

Billy accepted the offer, and the two men headed inside. Ted introduced him to his wife Sally and their two boys, Jason and Philip, and then Ted led him on a tour.

Billy couldn't believe how the house had changed since he was last here. A bedroom and a porch had been added to the back of the house, and a wall upstairs had been taken down, turning two small bedrooms into a master bedroom. The two men returned to the kitchen, and after some small talk, Sally said, "Did you hear about the big news this past week? There were three murders here about fifty years ago, and a man confessed to killing a boy after all this time."

Billy gave them a knowing smile. "If I could have a cup of that coffee," he said, pointing to the pot on the counter, "I'll tell you all about them."

"Oh my goodness, you lived here then!" she exclaimed.

"I was one of the boys who found the bodies," he said, and he saw their eyes light up. Sally handed him a cup of coffee, and for the next twenty minutes Billy told them his tale. The story enthralled them. They had known nothing of any murders until the papers had reported the confession of Richie Membrino.

He visited with the Dalton's for nearly an hour before taking his leave. Billy was about to get back in his car when he noticed a slip of paper under the windshield wiper. He opened it up as he sat behind the wheel. What it said shocked him.

Don't talk to the cops. If you do, don't tell them anything. We'll know if you do.

"What the hell," he mumbled. Billy sat staring at the paper for a minute. Who knew he was in town? More importantly, who knew he was here? Was he being followed? Why? "It's been fifty years," he muttered, wondering who would care after all this time.

He started the car and headed out. A visit with Walter was next on his list, and suddenly Billy thought it was the most important thing he had to do.

THIRTEEN

Billy's mind was in a daze as he headed for Northampton. He was mystified why anyone would still care about some small town murders fifty years later. He assumed all the main characters in that play must be dead by now; Richie Membrino probably being the last one.

Walter had asked him to drop by around one, since he had to be at work for four. Billy wondered if Walter had received any messages on his windshield.

Walter was sitting in a rocking chair on his porch when Billy pulled in. He held up a margarita and called out, "Shall I pour another one?" The scene reminded Billy of his arrival at Katie's the night before.

"Absolutely," replied Billy, as he stepped up on the porch and shook hands with his old friend. "I could use one of those right about now."

Walter had a pitcher on a table next to his rocker and filled another glass. As he handed it to Billy, he said, "I was sorry to hear about your mother. She was a fine lady. How are you doing?"

Billy accepted the glass and took two good swallows. "I'm fine," he said. "Mom and I weren't that close in the last few years. It's Marylou who's taking it hard."

"Well, I can understand that," said Walter. "My brother Gene and his wife have been taking care of my mom for the last couple of years. It's not an easy job. I hear you're staying with Katie."

"News travels fast. How'd you hear that?"

"Oh, she and I keep in touch pretty regularly. She comes down to the hotel once or twice a month to have dinner. She told me you were coming."

Walter Logan was a large man, well over three hundred pounds. His face was puffy, his cheeks a permanent red, and what little hair he had left on his head was a dazzling white. His mother had taught all her boys to be careful with their money, and Billy would have been shocked to know how much Walter had in the bank. The house he lived in was nice but small, the car in the driveway was ten years old, and nothing that Billy saw spoke of opulence.

"So you're still at the Marriott," said Billy.

"Sure am. Been over twenty-five years now," said Walter. "Hard to believe."

"Looks like you enjoy your cooking," said Billy, as he patted his buddy's stomach.

Walter just smiled. "I used to try to lose weight, but then I just gave up. I'd rather eat, and yes, I do love my cooking. Got some sandwiches all made in the house if you're interested."

Billy suddenly realized he was hungry again. "That would be great," he said, and they made their way inside.

They passed through the living room, and Billy saw old furniture and a small television. It seemed Walter was barely making ends meet until you entered the kitchen, which was totally different. Billy thought the room could have been featured in one of those fancy magazines. The appliances were top of the line. Pots and pans hung from the center aisle, and everything sparkled and shined.

"Holy cow," was all he managed to say.

Walter smiled. "Can you tell I'm a cook?" he said. He had made ham and turkey clubs with bacon. He removed the wrap covering them and brought them to the dining room table, and then they both dived in.

"This is great," said Billy.

"It's my own secret dressing that makes the difference," replied Walter, "and no, you can't have the recipe."

Billy just smiled and continued to eat.

"That was something about Vinnie, huh?" said Walter.

"Unbelievable," said Billy. "Have the police talked with you about it?"

"They came by last Thursday. They wanted to know if I knew anything about this mysterious clue that Vinnie supposedly had." Walter took another bite of his sandwich and then continued. "Can you believe Vinnie really knew something about the murders? I never believed him, not for a second."

"Me either. Tell me something, Pokey ..."

"Pokey? Wow, I haven't heard that in ages," said Walter. "Anyone still call you Preacher?"

"No, not really," said Billy. He stared at his old friend for a moment, and then said, "Have you received any messages from anyone about all this?"

Walter's head jerked up. He returned Billy's stare, and Billy knew he had struck a nerve. "Why do you ask?" Walter finally said.

"I went to visit the old neighborhood today. Even had a tour of my old house from the fellow who lives there now. When I returned to my car, there was a note on the windshield."

"What did it say?" asked Walter

Billy had a feeling his old friend already knew. "Told me not to talk to the cops, and if I did not to tell them anything."

"Jesus, Mary, and Joseph," said Walter. He arose from the table and went into his bedroom. A minute later, he came back out and handed Billy a piece of paper. "Did it look like this?"

Billy took his note out of his back pocket, opened it up, and compared the two. They were exact matches, and Billy realized they were photocopies of an original. He set them on the table so Walter could see. "When did you get yours?" he asked.

"Wednesday, the day the story broke. I worked a double at the hotel. Got off just after nine. When I went out to my car, I found this."

"You show this to the detective?"

"The detective who came to see me is a woman, one of those cold case investigators; kind of hot looking, too. And no, I didn't mention it." He paused for a while as he sat back down. "What am I gonna tell the cops fifty years later? Who the hell would be worried about this now?"

"No idea. But somebody sure is, and I think we'd better be careful. You said you're working at four today?"

"Yeah, four to nine. I'm always off by nine; it's just room service after that. Why?"

"No reason. Just be on your guard for anything unusual. Something about this whole thing with Vinnie just doesn't seem right to me."

"Well," said Walter, "the way I see it is like this. According to the paper, this Membrino character would have been about thirty-five when he killed Vinnie, so his bosses who ordered it must have been older. Therefore I figure they're all dead by now, and whoever is leaving us these notes must be a son or grandson of the originals."

Billy nodded his agreement. "That makes sense."

"Membrino was apparently a mafia hood, but they're pretty small time out here, and I can't imagine who his boss might have been. I haven't seen anything in the papers about it either. If the lady cop knows anything, she wasn't letting on," said Walter. "And another thing; if they killed Vinnie, why didn't they come after the rest of us?"

"They must have interrogated him before drowning him," said Billy. "I guess he didn't talk. They must have assumed, correctly I might add, that the rest of us didn't know anything."

"I guess."

They finished eating. Walter picked up the dirty plates and put them in the sink, then refilled their glasses with the last of the margarita mix.

They spent the next hour catching up on the last twenty years. It was just after three when Walter said he had to get ready for work, and Billy headed back out to the car.

"Be good," he called out, as he turned to give his buddy a final wave. "Be careful too."

He arrived back at Katie's just before four and was surprised to see her SUV in the driveway. She was refilling her bird feeders, and she turned and gave him a big smile.

"Hey there," he said, "you came home early."

"It was one of those rare days when the photo shoot went smoothly," she said. "Doesn't happen very often. There's fresh coffee inside if you want some."

Billy looked at her a moment longer and felt a tingle go through his body. She really was an attractive woman, and it had been a while since he had been with anyone. He thought of her living alone out here in the woods, and wondered how long it had been for her.

She saw the look on his face and said, "What?"

"Just thinking," he mumbled, but the slight smile that curled the sides of her mouth made him think she knew what was running through his mind. He went indoors, poured himself a cup of coffee, and then noticed a box of apple turnovers sitting on the table and grabbed one of those too.

Katie came in a minute later. "Hey, don't spoil your appetite," she said. "I'm making spaghetti and meatballs with garlic bread for supper."

"Sounds great," he said, avoiding her eyes.

"I need to take a shower and do some paperwork. What say we eat about seven?"

"That'll be fine," said Billy. "I'll think I'll take a little nap."

He awoke later to the aroma of spaghetti sauce and garlic. He immediately slid off his bed and headed downstairs.

"Here's the sleepyhead," said Katie, who was removing the garlic bread from the oven, "I was just about to come looking for you."

She was wearing a beat-up Red Sox jersey with *EVANS* on the back and a pair of blue shorts. She pointed to the counter and said, "Would you open that bottle of wine for me, please."

Billy did as asked, and then filled the two glasses that were sitting nearby.

Katie took the bowl of pasta and plate of garlic bread into the living room and set them on the coffee table. Billy followed her with the glasses of wine, plus a couple of plates and silverware. They sat on the couch, and she said, "Help yourself."

Billy dug in. The meal was delicious, and a second helping was inevitable. He tried to turn down a second glass of wine, telling her about the margarita's he had already imbued at Walter's, but she would hear none of it.

"So tell me about your day," she said. "How is my good friend Walter?"

Billy leaned back on the couch as he turned to look at her. She was gorgeous, even in a rundown baseball jersey, and her long shapely legs were a ten in his book. He wondered how such a woman could possibly be single. Suddenly he saw a smile break out on her face.

"Earth to Billy," she said.

"Sorry," he replied. He told her about his visit to the old neighborhood and the tour he had received from Ted Dalton. He debated telling her about the note on the windshield, but decided to hold back on that for the time being. Then he talked about his visit to Northampton.

"Walter is a very large man," he said.

"Yes," said Katie. "I've been trying to get him to lose weight, but I think he's given up."

"He said he likes his cooking too much."

"He is a great chef. I go to the hotel to eat once in a while."

They chatted for another minute, and Billy thought he was through with his tale. However, Katie suddenly asked, "So are you going to tell me about the note?"

"How do you …?"

"Walter called me as soon as you left. He said your note was exactly like his."

"Ah, you knew about his, huh?" said Billy. "They were photocopies of the original. I don't know why anybody would care about all this now, so many years later. Doesn't make sense to me."

"Well, I know that note scared Walter. He told me he didn't tell the police anything about it."

"That's just the point," Billy said. "How could anyone think we know anything now when we didn't know anything then? It's crazy."

"It may be, but you'd better be careful just the same. Somebody obviously thinks otherwise. Do you think you were followed to Walter's house?"

"I checked my mirror a few times. Didn't notice anyone following, but …." He let the topic slide, and changed the subject. "So how long have you had that shirt? Dewey Evans hasn't played for the Sox in years."

"I know," said Katie, "but it's so comfortable I just can't part with it. I wear it around the house all the time."

Billy started thinking about what she would look like without the shirt on. Unfortunately, his cell rang at just that moment. He checked the caller i.d., then looked at Katie and said, "Sorry, it's my sister."

"Billy," said Marylou after he answered, "we're going to have dinner at the Greenfield Café before the wake on Tuesday. I was hoping you would join us; Katie too, of course."

"Sure," said Billy, "that would be fine." They spoke for another five minutes, and Billy was happy to hear that his sister sounded better.

By the time the call ended, Katie was in the kitchen doing the dishes. Billy turned on the television and found the Sox game, although his mind continued to wander back to his fine looking host.

Unfortunately, when she was through in the kitchen, Katie announced that she had some Photoshop work to do on her computer, and Billy should just make himself at home. She was still working when he went to bed three hours later.

FOURTEEN

Simon Taylor and Thomas Mann stayed at the hotel in Boston Sunday night after the conference ended. The weekend had been a major success. Friday's show where they performed together in the morning had been a complete sellout, and the crowd seemed genuinely disappointed when it was time to break for lunch.

Afterwards, Thomas had taken the stage from one to three, and then Simon took over from three to five. It was a change from the order they normally did things, but not a problem.

Thomas had the most interesting moment of the afternoon sessions. He was bringing forth messages from the other side when a lady named Lily came through.

"Who has someone named Lily on the other side?" he asked the crowd.

Half a dozen hands shot up.

"Okay, let's see if we can narrow it down. I need more information, Lily; something specific."

He stared at the ceiling as he retrieved the message. The six members of the audience were all desperately hoping the message was for them.

"Ah," he finally said, "it seems that Lily used to live in South Africa."

Six hands went down in unison. None of them knew a Lily from South Africa.

Everyone seemed puzzled for a moment, including Thomas. "No one?" he asked.

Finally, a voice arose from the far side of the auditorium. "She's mine," an elderly gentleman called out, "not that I want to hear from her."

It was a response rarely heard at a conference such as this.

"Well," said Thomas, "she apparently wants to speak to you."

The man did not wait to hear what the message was. Instead, he called out, "She was a horrible person and a worse wife. I wish I'd never known her. Tell her to keep her message."

"I'm afraid that's not how it works, sir," said Thomas.

The man stood up and started to walk down the aisle towards an exit.

"Please stay," said Thomas. "She's sorry, so very sorry."

The man stopped, turned, and called out, "She should be."

"What is your name, sir?"

"My name is Arnold."

"Arnold, nice to meet you. Please listen to what your former wife has to say. I think it will be important for both of you."

Arnold returned to his seat but remained standing. "Go ahead," he said.

"Lily knows she was not a good person," said Thomas. "She says she made your life a living hell, but her father had been a tyrant and that was all she knew. She loved you very much, but she didn't know how to show it."

The stern countenance on Arnold's face suddenly changed, replaced by a look of abject sadness. He started to say something, but the words caught in his throat.

Thomas continued with the message. "When Lily arrived on the spiritual plane and saw how she had lived her life, she was devastated. It took her a long time to recover. Just now, after all these years, has she felt strong enough to come through to you with this message."

"I did love her," said Arnold, "but she made it so damn hard."

A look of sympathy came over Thomas's face. "She's so very sorry, Arnold. She wants to ask for your forgiveness, but she's afraid you will withhold it."

Arnold stared at the bald head of the man sitting in front of him, and then he gave a sigh so deep everyone in attendance must have heard it.

"I've learned a great deal over the years coming to these conferences," he finally said. "The pain that Lily caused me was great, but I know holding on to it is not doing me any good." He turned to look directly at Thomas. "Tell Lily I forgive her."

The crowd in the auditorium burst into thunderous applause, and it was a full minute before Thomas could finally speak again.

"Lily is crying tears of joy at your magnanimity. She will remain on the other side until you cross over, and will greet you when you arrive. She says all things will be revealed then."

Simon had enjoyed a long lunch and did not return to the auditorium until just before it was his turn to take the stage. He had missed the exchange between Thomas and Arnold, but Thomas filled him in later that evening.

Simon's regression session with the audience had no such excitement. It went well, as it always did, and afterwards individual members in attendance shared what they had experienced. The most interesting, in Simon's mind, came from a gentleman who claimed that in a prior life he had been a female film star in silent movies.

On Saturday and Sunday Simon had four sold out groups, each limited to fifty people; one in the morning, another in the afternoon. Simon considered each group a success and heard more interesting past-life tales. However, it was during the final group on Sunday when something happened that gave the psychologist goose bumps.

The attendees all wore name tags, yet Simon could only read those sitting closest to him. He performed the past-life session in his usual manner. When it was over, and Simon had brought them back to the present, everyone heard a man in the back sobbing. It was the first time such a thing had happened to Simon in all his years of doing regressions, and he immediately arose and went to the gentleman. "Are you alright, sir?" he asked. It was then that Simon noticed his nametag.

It was Arnold, the man from Thomas's group on Friday.

Arnold had taken a handkerchief from his pocket and was wiping his eyes. "I'm not sure," he said. "This had been an extraordinary weekend for me, and now this."

"Would you like to share with the group what you discovered during your regression?"

Arnold recounted what had happened on Friday, although nearly everyone in attendance had been in that session.

"I forgave her," he said, as he finished retelling the tale, "and she was happy, but now I know why she treated me as she did. It was a karmic payback."

"Do you mind telling us about the regression you just had?" asked Simon. "What did you learn?"

"In our previous life we lived in South America. I think it was Chile, but I'm not sure of that. We were also husband and wife in that life. It was a hard existence. We lived in a hilly area and grew our own food. Most times we barely had enough to eat. I was the abusive one in that life, constantly hitting her to keep her in line."

The room was deathly quiet as Arnold spoke.

"Oh my God," he suddenly cried, "I was an awful person."

Simon knelt in front of Arnold and took his hands. "It's okay," he said. "You need to remember to leave the past in the past. Let it go now."

Arnold sniffled as he looked at Simon.

"You have information now which probably explains a great deal to you," Simon continued. "It's information that you can grow from, and which helps you understand what's happened in your current life. You are right, this life with your wife was probably a karmic payback, and if you both learn from it, than it need never happen again. Release your shame, thank your wife for the lesson, and move on."

Later that night, as Thomas and Simon were leaving the hotel's dining room, they ran into Arnold in the lobby.

"I just want to thank you both," he said. "I'm leaving here tonight a completely different person than I was when I arrived three days ago. A tremendous weight has been lifted from my shoulders."

The two men later agreed that it was the most special moment either had ever been a part of during all the conferences they had done.

On Monday morning, the two men headed to Thomas's home in Northampton. They were both looking forward to a relaxing week off, although Thomas had scheduled the event at the Universal Unitarian Church in the city for Thursday night.

"I know the pastor at the church," said Thomas. "Her name is Martha Gallagher, and she will get the word out. It won't just be church members who show up. We'll probably have twenty or so people attend the session. It should be fun."

The Mann's house in Northampton was just outside the downtown area. The home was over one-hundred years old, yet it had been remodeled numerous times over the years. Simon was impressed by some of the work Thomas had done and told him so.

"If I didn't know better, I'd think you were a carpenter," said Simon.

"I actually learned a great deal from my dad. He worked construction off and on, along with a myriad of other jobs. I guess you would have called him a jack of all trades."

Elizabeth, Thomas's wife, arrived at the house just ten minutes after the men pulled in. She had been grocery shopping for the week ahead. Simon had met her before, as she occasionally attended some of the weekend conferences. She was a tall, thin woman with long brown hair. Simon always thought she needed to eat more.

"Nice to see you again," he said, as he gave her a hug.

"I'm glad you're staying with us," said Elizabeth. "It's too bad your lady friend couldn't make it." The Mann's had yet to meet Maria.

"It would have been nice if she could have come, but she had to work," said Simon.

Later that night, Simon settled into the guest bedroom on the second floor. He was looking forward to a nice peaceful week away from work.

FIFTEEN

As Simon and Thomas were getting ready to leave Boston that Monday morning, Billy was waking up to the sound of Katie puttering around in the kitchen. He tossed on a pair of jeans and a tee shirt and then headed downstairs, where he found her putting what looked like a trail mix concoction into a couple of baggies.

"Hey," she said when she saw him, "are those the best hiking shoes that you have?"

"Hiking? You mean ..."

"I thought we would go for a walk in the woods. I want to show you around." She saw a look of stunned disbelief come over his face and said, "What, you don't like playing in the woods anymore?"

"Well ...," he mumbled.

"Don't worry, it'll be fun."

"Don't you have any work today?"

"Nope, I have the whole day free. But I am sorry; tomorrow I have a major job that can't be changed. I may not make it to your mom's wake, and will certainly miss the dinner beforehand."

"Oh, well that's alright, I guess," he said, but he was clearly disappointed. The more he was around Katie, the more he wanted to be around her. He was beginning to feel things that he hadn't felt for a long time, and he thought there was a good chance the feeling was mutual.

He had put his loafers on, so he went back upstairs, switched to his sneakers, and then headed back to the kitchen.

"Will this be okay?" he asked.

"It'll do," she said. Katie was wearing jeans too, since the morning temps were hovering in the mid-fifties. She was also wearing a black tee shirt, with a checkered flannel shirt unbuttoned over it, and a pair of hiking boots.

Billy had a quick cup of coffee and some toast, and then Katie handed him a small backpack.

"Let's go," she said.

There was an obvious trail leading from her back porch into the woods. The walking was easy at first, although Katie pointed out some areas where she had cut back the overgrowth.

"The last owner obviously didn't roam out here very often," she said.

After a short walk, the path forked. They turned left, which headed farther into the forest. A gentle twenty minute walk from there brought them to a lovely clearing overlooking the valley below. A bench, obviously fairly new, awaited them.

"This is just about my favorite spot," she said, "so I decided to build a place to sit."

"You lugged this all the way out here?" he asked.

"Actually, it took a few trips to carry the wood out here, and then one day I brought my tools and put it all together."

"Wow," said Billy, "you are a woman of many talents."

Katie gave him a most delicious look as she accepted the compliment. "I love to sit out here and just be one with nature," she finally replied.

"It's beautiful," he said, "just like you."

He was afraid that he had gone too far as soon as the words were out of his mouth.

Katie looked surprised at first, but a smile quickly spread over her. "That's kind of you," she said.

They lingered there for another twenty minutes as they shared a bottle of water and some of the trail mix.

Finally, Katie said, "Okay, let's go. I want to show you where the other trail leads to."

As they walked, she pointed out the different types of trees and plants that they passed. She was appalled by his lack of knowledge of the various flowers they came across, and she laughed at his occasional nervousness that a bear might come along.

"You've been away from here far too long," said Katie. "You need to get back to your roots."

Billy looked at the beautiful woman standing next to him and began to think she was right.

They reached the fork once again, and this time they took the path that went right, heading towards the lake. Katie chatted non-stop as they walked, suddenly catching him up on everything that had happened in her life. She talked about her previous jobs, her photography work, and her marriage and subsequent divorce from Dave.

Billy listened intently, wanting to know everything he could about her.

They stopped again ten minutes later when they could go no farther. In front of them was a drop of about forty feet. Below lay huge rocks, with the edge of the lake some thirty feet out.

"The water is usually closer," Katie said, "but we had a quiet winter and not much rain lately." She opened the backpack and took out the energy bars and another bottle of water. "Let's sit and enjoy the view for a while."

This time there was only grass to sit on. "What, no bench?" said Billy.

She knew he was just joking, but shook her head anyway and mumbled, "City folk."

Billy ate slowly as he gazed at the scenery. Their walk reminded him of his days traipsing through the woods as a kid. He turned to look at Katie and found her looking back.

"I can't believe you're the annoying little kid who used to hang around with my sister," he said.

She was quiet for a moment, but he saw a small smile crease her lips. Then she said, "I had a crush on you as a kid, you know."

"You did not," said Billy, stunned by the admission.

"I did. You were cute."

"My sister would have told me."

"As much as Marylou and I hung around, I don't think I ever mentioned that to her. She would have called me crazy. She always referred to you as 'my stupid brother,' after all."

"You never said anything to me about it," said Billy.

"Well, you seemed so much older then," explained Katie. "I mean, when you were a senior I was just a freshman. Three years may not mean anything now, but back then it was a huge gap."

Billy didn't know what to say. He had never imagined that Katie had ever thought about him back then.

They were silent for a long time as they gazed at the scenery, each lost in their own thoughts, each wondering what the other was thinking.

Dark clouds began to appear on the horizon and the wind was picking up.

"We'd better go," said Katie. "It looks like a storm is moving in."

They returned the empty water bottle to the backpack and headed back to the house.

This time it was a quiet trip.

Billy showered upon their return, since he hadn't had time to do so earlier. He thought of Katie the entire time and wished that she were in the shower with him. It had been a long time since he had allowed himself to be close to anyone. He had enjoyed many one-night stands over the years, but they rarely went beyond that. Usually the feeling was mutual, although he knew he had pissed off a number of women who had wanted more.

He did not want a one-night stand with Katie. There was something about her, something special, which made him feel alive. It was a feeling he hadn't enjoyed in a long time. The best part was, he knew Katie was feeling it too. She couldn't hide it from him, even though at times he guessed she wanted to. She had been divorced for quite a while now, and maybe she just wanted some companionship, but he was pretty sure she wanted more than that.

Billy did too.

"Why don't we let Walter cook for us tonight?" said Katie, when Billy came back downstairs. She saw the quizzical look on his face and smiled. "We can spend the day in Northampton walking around the town. They have tons of cute little shops and lots to see, and then we can have dinner at the hotel. I know he's working tonight, and Monday's are usually pretty slow there, so he will probably be able to come out and see us. You can tell him what a good cook he is."

Billy didn't have to think very long before replying. A whole day spent with Katie was suddenly his idea of perfection. "Sounds great," he said.

As Billy drove through Greenfield and headed south to Northampton, he couldn't believe how little seemed to have changed over the last fifty years. There were more houses and different stores, of course, but the countryside still looked shockingly similar to the way it had when he was a boy. He mentioned it to Katie.

"Some people like the simple ways of life," she said, "and don't wish to change."

"Is that why you came back?"

She thought for a long time before answering. "My divorce from Dave, while not unexpected at that point, shook me a great deal. I spent months debating what I wanted to do with the rest of my life. In time, I decided the big cities were not for me. I had an overwhelming desire to return home, to get back to the simple life, as it were. Finally, one morning I woke up, packed my bags, got in my car and drove."

"Was it difficult at first, coming back here?"

"I was pinching pennies for a good long while. You wouldn't believe the little two room apartment I was living in."

"Oh," interrupted Billy, "that I would believe. I've lived in a lot of them over the years."

"Really?"

"Really," he said. "I'm living in one now. So what happened?"

"My aunt died. She had never married, and it turned out she was one of those rich old spinsters you hear about. She left part of her estate to me, not a lot, but enough to get me started in photography school. It turns out I'm pretty good at that, and over time I was able to buy my house in the woods."

They arrived in Northampton just after noon. It was a quirky little place in Billy's mind, lots of little shops selling all sorts of strange merchandise, with street musicians playing on every other corner.

Katie took him into a place called *Willow's Metaphysical Shoppe*. The store specialized in all things New Age, from crystals, books, and tarot cards to a large display of Wiccan items.

Billy was a bit surprised, since he had not seen anything in her home to make him think she was into the metaphysical realm. Of course, he hadn't been in her bedroom yet. A huge grin suddenly overtook him, and he was glad Katie wasn't watching him at that moment, for how would he explain where his mind had suddenly taken him.

Katie was busy slowly making her way through the store. Billy sidled up to her and said, "See anything you like?"

"There's plenty I like, but I'm pretty picky about what I end up buying."

By the time they reached the checkout line twenty minutes later, her purchase consisted of a pack of ten incense sticks.

As they headed for the door, Katie said, "I just want to check out the board before we go."

The board that she referred to was a cork board on which were posted flyers announcing coming attractions, from psychic fairs to local tarot card readers, energy healers and weekly book clubs. A clerk was just adding a new announcement when they arrived, and Katie noticed.

"Oh my goodness, look at this," she suddenly said.

Billy hadn't been paying much attention, but turned to see what she was pointing at. The advertisement caused him to take a sudden intake of breath.

"Have you ever heard of Simon Taylor?" she asked.

Billy gave her a bemused look. "You're not going to believe this," he said, "but I just had a regression from him a few weeks ago."

"What!" cried Katie, loud enough for those standing nearby to turn and look at her. "You must tell me all about it. I'm a big fan of his." She looked at the poster again and noted the date. "He's going to be here at the Unitarian Church on Thursday night. Billy, we have to go!"

"Who's this other guy?" asked Billy, pointing at the poster.

"Thomas Mann; you've never heard of him? He actually lives around here, but he's also very famous. He's one of those people who bring forth messages from loved ones on the other side."

"Have you ever been to see him?"

"No," said Katie, "but I'd like to. Will you come with me?"

"Of course," said Billy.

"There's a deli around the corner. Let's grab a light lunch and you can tell me all about your regression."

They split a corned beef sandwich on rye while Billy told her about his visit with Simon. She was appalled by his brutal murder at the end of the story and pushed the last bite of her sandwich away.

"How did you manage to relay that without jumping off the couch?" she asked.

"It seems the spirit leaves the body before death occurs," he said. "Makes sense, I guess. Anyway, I was just floating over the scene, watching as it happened. As I think of it now, I was feeling quite calm, actually."

Katie gave a look of dreadful unease.

"I think a quick death is much better than a long, drawn out on," he said. "Don't you?"

"I suppose," she replied, "but if that's what my regression would be like, I'm not sure I want it."

"This Mann fellow, do you know much about him?"

Katie thought for a moment. "I saw him once when I was down here shopping. He was talking to a lady in the store, and I sort of eavesdropped once I realized who it was. I know he has five or six books out. He does these local readings once in a while, but I think this is the first time that Dr. Taylor has been here with him."

"Should be fun," said Billy.

They still had hours to kill before going to the Marriott for dinner. They decided to go to a movie and chose a Tina Fey comedy. It was funny in a whacky sort of way, and half way through the show Katie slipped her hand into his and held it for the rest of the movie.

Billy was pretty sure she was feeling the same way towards him that he was feeling for her. His mind went into overdrive about where this was all headed, and when the movie ended, he realized he had spaced out much of the second half of it.

They arrived at the Marriott just after six, and as Katie had expected, the dining room was fairly empty. The hostess, a young girl with a silver hoop pierced in her nose and two more in each eyebrow, brought them to a table with a lovely view of the parking lot.

The waitress, a short, plump lady more their age, came over immediately. They ordered a bottle of chardonnay, and then glanced at the menu.

Most hotels that Billy had stayed at had fairly simple menus, twelve or fifteen selections at the most. This Marriott had three pages worth, and Billy correctly assumed that Walter had a great deal to do with that. "What do you usually order here?" he asked Katie.

"The steaks are always good," she said, "and I love the Chicken Marsala. I tried the duck once, only to find that I wasn't that fond of duck."

"Steaks, huh? A girl after my own heart."

"You mean that wasn't obvious already?" she said.

A tingle went through him, much as it had at the movies.

The waitress returned with their wine, opened the bottle, and poured out two glasses after Billy gave his approval. She came back a minute later with a basket of warm rolls and asked if they were ready to order.

Katie wanted to try something different and chose one of the evening's specials, lobster ravioli in a creamy Newburgh sauce.

Billy stuck with the steak, medium rare with a garlic butter glaze. When they finished ordering, Katie asked if Walter was in the kitchen tonight.

The waitress rolled her eyes to the ceiling and said, "He's here. He's always here."

"Would you please tell him Billy and Katie are here."

They made small talk, and were surprised when their orders arrived so quickly. The steak practically melted in Billy's mouth, and he quickly proclaimed it one of the finest steaks he had ever eaten.

Katie's bowl was filled with ravioli's, and she suspected that Walter had given her a double portion. They were both stuffed by the time they finished eating.

Walter made his way to their table shortly after, stopping to chat with a few other guests along the way. He grabbed a chair from a nearby table so he could sit with them. "Looks like you enjoyed it," he said.

"It was fabulous," said Billy, as he patted his stomach.

"You gave me too much," chimed in Katie.

"Slow night for a Monday, as usual," said Walter. "I didn't want them to go to waste."

He turned to look at Billy and said, "I did manage to rearrange my schedule for the next two days, so I will be at your mom's wake and funeral."

"You better tell the waitress," said Katie. "Apparently she thinks you're always here."

"Monica?" he replied, shaking his head and giving a half-smile. "We're always butting heads, but she's a damn good waitress, so I can't let her go. She's probably upset because it's slow and she's not making many tips."

"We'll be good to her," said Billy.

"Ah, as if I care," said Walter. "Hey, have the cops talked to you yet?"

"Not yet," said Billy. "Not much I can tell them after all this time."

"Keep quiet about the notes on the windshield, okay?"

"I will," said Billy. "I'm not sure talking about them would help."

In truth, he had spent some time thinking about just that. Perhaps letting the police know that someone was still very interested in this fifty year old murder case would help them out. Yet he was also afraid that it might cause trouble, not only for him and Walter, but also for Katie. And that was the last thing Billy wanted at the moment.

They chatted for just a few minutes, and then Walter said, "Well, thanks for coming in, you two. I better get back to work. I guess we'll see each other tomorrow."

Ten minutes later Billy paid the bill, and then he and Katie headed for the door.

When they arrived back home, Katie asked if he wanted to share another bottle of wine.

"I'm still stuffed," he said, "but I don't think one more glass would hurt."

"I have another bottle of chardonnay in the cabinet by the refrigerator. Why don't you pour two glasses? I'm going upstairs to change. I'll be right back down."

"Sounds good," he said, and headed into the kitchen. He found the bottle on a shelf below the breakfast cereal. It was a simple twist cap, as more and more wine bottles seemed to be these days. He grabbed two glasses from the cabinet, moved into the living room, and sat on the couch.

He was staring at an old magazine when he heard her coming back.

She stopped halfway down the stairs and said, "Billy?"

He looked up at her and his mouth dropped open. She was wearing a black lace teddy, easily seen-through, black panties, and thigh hi nylons.

"I'm going to bed," she said. "Why don't you bring that wine and join me?"

Billy continued staring at her before finally managing to utter a "Wow," and then he did as asked.

Her bedroom was dark, save for a candle burning in one corner. She had already pulled the comforter down and was doing the same to the sheet when he arrived. He put the wine on the nightstand, turned her around to face him, and kissed her, softly at first, and then long and passionately.

She unbuttoned his shirt and removed it, then did the same to his jeans.

"Are you surprised?" she asked.

"Happy," he said. "I was hoping things were leading to this."

"I got tired of waiting for you to make the first move," said Katie. "This is something I've wanted for a long time now."

They lay on the bed, gently holding and kissing each other. He removed her teddy and cupped her breasts. Her nipples were already hard, and grew even more so as he gently sucked on them.

They took their time, taking turns pleasuring each other in a way Billy hadn't experienced in a long time. Katie kept bringing him to the brink and then letting up, making him last as long as he possibly could, and driving him crazy. When he finally let loose inside of her she screamed with joy, and Billy thought he was in heaven.

"God," he said, as they lay next to each other, "that was fantastic."

She smiled at him as she played with his chest hair. "It's been a long time for me. You've just made me realize how much I've missed it."

"You're so beautiful," he said. "How could you possibly not have guys falling all over you?"

"I guess I'm too particular. Most guys don't interest me much, but when I saw you get out of the car the other night, I knew right away I wanted you. All those childhood fantasies came rushing back. And I've seen the way you've been looking at me, too," she said. "I knew it was mutual."

They cuddled together as they drank their wine. Billy slowly began moving the tips of his fingers over her body as they talked, and occasionally noticed the goose bumps it caused, and the sudden smile of ecstasy on her face.

"You like that, huh?"

"Oh God, Billy," was all she said.

In time Katie started doing the same to him, but it turned out he was the ticklish sort, and it didn't have quite the same effect.

It did, however, arouse him once more, and Katie noticed.

"I think someone's ready to play again," she said.

And so they did.

SIXTEEN

Tuesday morning broke sunny, not a cloud in the sky, and Billy thought that was wrong. It was the day of his mother's wake, and it should be raining. He awoke in Katie's bed alone. She had a long day ahead of her and had already left.

"I'm really going to try to make it to the wake," she had said, "but I have an awfully long shoot and I'm just not sure."

He had been disappointed, but understood. She had a job to do, after all, and this sounded like an appointment that was going to pay extremely well. As he was about to get up, he found a note on the nightstand.

Billy. Last night was a memory I'll treasure forever. I hope they'll be more.

He smiled. Last night had sparked something in him also, and he definitely wanted more.

He spent the day alone, not having any desire to see his fellow human beings. After lunch, he decided to do a meditation ceremony for his mother. It was a tradition of his to do this when a family member passed over. He found a meditation CD in Katie's collection of music and put that on, and then he lit one of the incense sticks she had purchased yesterday. He sat yogi style on the floor, calmed his mind, and wished his mother a safe journey to the other side. In the end, he apologized for not being as good a son as he could have been. He shed a few unexpected tears along the way.

Billy enjoyed meditating. He had been doing it for a few years now, though it was not a daily ritual. He tried to do it once or twice a week, mostly to center himself after a hectic day. He didn't see guides or angels, as some people claimed they did, but he did occasionally come up with good ideas or receive answers to questions that had been bothering him. Whether it was a message from the beyond, or simply because he had calmed his mind, he didn't know and didn't particularly care.

He spent the afternoon with his thoughts shuffling between his deceased mother and Katie. Occasionally a giant grin would overtake him as he thought about their lovemaking last night, and then he would scold himself for thinking about sex on such a solemn day.

He headed out just before five to meet Marylou, Mark, and Mark's parents at the Greenfield Cafe. He was the first to arrive, so he grabbed a table and ordered a beer.

Marylou and the others came in a few minutes later, and Billy could tell at once how difficult their moms passing had been on her. She looked haggard and strung out. He stood up and gave her a big hug. "Hey sis," he said.

"Billy, it's so good to see you," she replied. "It's been too long."

As they separated, he asked, "You doing okay?"

The sadness in her eyes was palpable. "I'll survive," she said, as they all took their seats at the table. "I thought I was ready for it. I know she's in a better place, but it's been hard. We grew really close while she was living with us."

They spent the next hour reminiscing while sharing appetizers and drinks; no one, it seemed, cared to order a full meal. Billy discovered that his mother had spoken about him quite often while living with his sister.

"She really loved you, Billy," said Marylou. "She just never understood why you always seemed to push everybody away."

"She knew why," he said, and left it at that.

His sister glanced at the others around the table and said nothing.

"Mostly I like to be alone," he finally stated. "Don't you know introverts are in nowadays." Billy knew she would never fully understand. His sister was one of the most outgoing people he had ever met.

"Well, you should have spent more time with mom, particularly after dad died."

He knew this subject had driven a wedge between them over the years, and for that he was sorry. "I know, sis, but there's not much I can do about it now."

At six-thirty they headed over to the Baylor Funeral Home, the name Thomas having long since been dropped, and were greeted by the current owner. Billy was surprised to discover it was a woman.

Amanda Baylor had inherited the place from her father when neither of her brothers had shown the slightest interest in the business. She was a tall woman, nearly six foot, slim and attractive, with shimmering black hair and dark blue eyes.

"My condolences to you," she said as they entered, and then she led them into the viewing room.

Their mother was laid out in a lovely blue dress that she had set aside years ago to be buried in. She looked older than her years, the illness having taken a toll on her. Amanda Baylor held back as Billy and Marylou approached the coffin and knelt down. They each prayed silently for a moment, and when they finished, Amanda showed them where they should stand to greet the mourners.

The night passed slowly as those paying their respects came in. The crowd was sparse, as Laurie Wilson had left the area years ago and many of her friends had passed before her. Most that did come were former neighbors or church-goers that still lived in the area.

Walter came in around seven thirty. After stopping at the casket and offering up his prayers, he shook Billy's hand and then stopped to talk with Marylou, whom he hadn't seen since her move to South Carolina.

The mourners had trickled to a slow crawl as eight o'clock came around, and Marylou was wondering if they needed to stay open until nine

That was when Katie walked through the doorway. She was wearing a knee-length black dress with black nylons, and Billy thought she looked stunning. Black nylons had always turned him on, and even though he knew this was not the place for such thoughts, he couldn't help himself. He gazed at Katie as she moved closer, before receiving a soft elbow in his side.

"It's not polite to stare," said Marylou.

He turned to his sister with a sheepish grin on his face. "It's hard not to," he said. "She's so damn beautiful."

"Oh my," whispered Marylou, "you've got a thing for her, haven't you?"

Billy raised his eyes to the ceiling and said nothing, but he had an idea the cat was out of the bag.

"Well," said Marylou, "she's certainly available. Good luck."

Katie knelt at the casket for a moment, and then came over to them. "I'm glad I made it," she said. "I was afraid for awhile that I wouldn't get here." She hugged each of them in turn, and said to Marylou, "Your mother was a lovely person."

Katie and Marylou stood and chatted with each other for a few more moments before Marylou finally said, "Can we sit down? I'm getting tired."

The two women moved to a row of softly padded chairs and continued their conversation.

It seemed to Billy that Katie was purposely ignoring him, and he thought that was probably for the best. He spent the time making small talk with Walter.

As the wake neared its end, Walter said his goodbyes and left, as did the other hangers on. The five members of the family, plus Katie, were getting ready to leave when another woman entered the room. This one was about 5'8, a bit stocky and wearing a business suit. She viewed Billy's mother for just a moment, not kneeling, and then came over to Marylou and said, "Sorry for your loss."

"Thank you," said Marylou. "I don't believe we've met before."

"I'm Detective Sylvia Remington." She turned to Billy, and as she shook his hand she said, "I'd like to speak with you, if I could."

"You want to speak with me here?" asked Billy.

"Good a place as any, if you don't mind," said Sylvia. "Save me a trip to wherever you're staying."

Amanda Baylor came over at that moment to announce she'd be closing the doors in fifteen minutes. Billy asked Amanda if there was another room they could use after introducing her to the detective, and Amanda escorted them to one off the foyer.

"I heard you'd probably want to speak with me," he said, after Amanda left.

"Oh, from whom?"

"Walter Logan," he said, not wanting to involve Katie if he didn't have to.

"Ah yes, Walter. Interesting man. Loves his cooking a bit too much, I'm afraid."

Billy ignored the comment as he stared at the woman. She had sharp eyes, which almost looked magenta to Billy, and a well-endowed bosom that he hadn't noticed upon first seeing her. "You honestly think I can tell you something new about the murders after fifty years?" he finally said.

"I hope so," she replied. "You've heard about the death-bed confession, I take it."

"Sure. Some thug named Membrino says he drowned Vinnie."

The detective stared into Billy's eyes. "He claimed Vinnie had a clue about the murders. If he did, it was one he never showed the police, and it hasn't turned up since. So I'm wondering if he ever showed it to you."

"Sorry," Billy said. "He told me he had a clue, but he never said what it was. Hell, I didn't believe him anyway."

"You still remember that day?" she asked.

"Like it was yesterday," he replied.

"Take me through it, if you don't mind."

The door opened, and Marylou let him know the rest of them were leaving. *Even Katie?* he thought, but then realized they had come in separate cars and there was no need for her to stay.

He turned back to face Sylvia Remington and once again replayed the story. He could feel the ball he had caught as it hit his glove; remembered the rain pelting his face as they ran towards the woods; saw the body under the leaves and muck. He took her through the whole tale, ending with sandwiches and Tang in his upstairs bedroom.

Sylvia Remington listened to his story, rarely interrupting, but occasionally jotted down a note in her pad. When he finished, she asked, "So to the best of your knowledge, Vinnie never touched the body of Mrs. Potter?"

"No," he said. "I don't think he ever entered her bedroom."

"So whatever clue he found must have come from the body in the woods, unless he found something on the floor or porch of the Potter home?"

171

"I would say so," said Billy. "I know he touched the body in the woods, because he rolled it over. And ..." he paused, thinking for a minute.

"What is it?" asked Sylvia.

"I know he was the last one to leave the body. Now that I think about it, it seems we all had turned away while Vinnie was still kneeling down. We were about to head to Mrs. Potter's house to call the police, and I looked back as we reached the path in the woods and was surprised that Vinnie was just getting up."

"So if he took something off the body, that was probably when he did it?"

"I'd say so," said Billy. "Not that that's going to help you much."

"You never know," she said. "So, is there anything else you can think of?"

Billy thought about the note on his windshield and wondered if he should tell her about it. Walter hadn't, and in the end that was what decided it for him. It didn't occur to him that now they were the ones withholding evidence from the police. "No," he said, "I think that's it."

Sylvia Remington handed him her card. "Call me if you think of anything else. Will you be in town long?"

"I have a flight back to Sarasota on Sunday."

"How about giving me your number in case anything comes up?" she said, and Billy gave her his cell phone number.

"You have much luck in cold cases?" he asked, as she turned to go.

"You'd be surprised. If we have DNA evidence still available, the odds are better than you might think." A minute later she was gone.

Amanda Baylor was waiting to lock up as Billy came into the foyer.

"Thank you for everything," he said, and received a comforting smile in return.

As he walked to his car, something he had just said kept playing in his mind.

Katie was waiting for him on the porch as he drove in, much as she had been the night he arrived. This time she had a beer waiting for him.

"I thought you might need this more than wine tonight," she said, and she handed him a bottle of Guinness.

"Sounds about right," said Billy. He took the bottle from her, and then he gave her a kiss on the cheek.

"Let's sit on the porch," she said. "It's a nice night out."

In fact, Billy thought it was a bit on the cool side, his body used to the warm Sarasota nights, and yet the coolness felt good to him.

"Will tomorrow be hard on you?" she asked him, after they were settled into the rocking chairs.

"Oh, I don't know; I suppose so."

"Marylou says you and your mom weren't close these last years."

"No," said Billy, "we had our differences. Most of it was probably my fault. I put a lot of miles between us, and then used that as an excuse not to visit." He took a good long swallow of beer, and the silence between them suddenly lingered.

Katie finally looked at him and said, "This is probably not the best time to be asking such a question, but …." She paused, not sure if she should continue.

"About last night," he asked.

"Yeah … that."

"I've been thinking about that a great deal today," said Billy.

"You fulfilled a dream of mine," she said, "only forty years later than I'd hoped.

He turned to face her, a quizzical look on his face. "What are you talking about?"

"I told you, I had a crush on you back when we were kids. Why do you think I asked you to take me to the prom my senior year? Did you think I couldn't get a date?"

Katie laughed, seeing the expression on his face. "Geez, Billy, I must have turned down a dozen kids who asked me."

He listened to her, dumbfounded. "I didn't know," he finally mumbled.

"I wanted you to be my first lover. I was sure by then that you must be a horny college guy. Instead, you turned out to be the perfect gentleman."

"I was just trying to behave," said Billy.

"And I wanted you to misbehave." Katie took a sip of beer, and then said, "Hell, if I hadn't pulled you towards me and kissed you before you knew what was happening, I probably would have received a hand shake at the end of the evening."

Suddenly Billy laughed. "I was a dork back then, wasn't I?"

Katie nodded her agreement.

"I hope last night made up for it in some way."

"Last night was terrific. But what was it, a one night fling, or the start of something?"

She watched as Billy turned away from her and ran a hand through his hair. He sighed deeply, and suddenly seemed interested in the variety of trees in front of him.

"It's okay if it's one and done, Billy. I get it. I won't be happy about it, because I've wanted you ever since we were kids, and I still want you now. More than you could possibly know. And I've seen the way you look at me, the way you gaze just above my head."

He finally turned to look at her, a sudden look of terror overcoming him.

"You still see them, don't you?" she asked. "You still see auras?"

"How …?" The words wouldn't come out, as his mouth turned instantly dry.

"You think I didn't know?"

"No one was supposed to know," said Billy. "No one has even talked about it in my family since my grandpa died."

"That can't be quite true," replied Katie, "because at some point you told your sister, and then she told me."

He had forgotten, and he wondered how that was possible. Yet Katie was right. He must have been eight, or thereabouts, and Marylou would have been five. She was in her room playing, and as Billy passed he heard her talking to someone. He went in to investigate, and she told him she was speaking to her invisible friend, a little girl named Penny. She told him what Penny was wearing, and that she once lived nearby but was now an angel.

"Well, I don't see Penny," he had said, "but I can see by your colors that you are telling me the truth, so I believe you."

And when she asked what he meant, he had told her.

He looked down at his feet as he asked, "How did you ever remember that?"

"I've watched you ever since you first arrived. You usually look at the ground as you walk, as if you don't want to look at people. Most people, if they don't want to look you in the eye, will look down at a person's mouth, but you don't. You look up at the top of their heads. You read people when you have to; otherwise you try not to look."

It was true. He'd been that way for more years than he could count.

"The night of the prom, you must have known I wanted you."

"I was going through a bad period then," said Billy. "I hated my ability at that point. I was trying to ignore it, hoping it would go away." He gave her a bemused smile. "I honestly don't remember what I saw around you that night. And I really was still clueless about sex at that point."

They sat in silence once again. Billy lifted his bottle and found it was empty.

Katie noticed and went in the house to get two more.

Billy managed a quiet "thanks" as she handed it to him.

"You must have known I wanted you once you arrived," she finally said.

He gazed into her eyes this time and finally cracked a smile. "Your love meter was running pretty high, and you should know I wanted you too."

"But," she said.

"But it's hard for me to get close to anyone."

"Because of Jenny?"

Billy nodded yes, but both of them understood in that instant that he was not ready to go there. Not with Katie, maybe not with himself.

Katie thought she saw his lip quiver, and knew enough to let it go.

They went inside, turned on the television to get the sports report, discovered that the Sox had lost to Texas 8 to 2, and then called it a night.

Upstairs, they both knew there would be no passion that evening. Billy went to the guest bedroom while Katie was brushing her teeth. He had just slipped under the covers when she popped into his room.

"Billy, there's one thing I have to ask you; please forgive me."

He looked at her and knew from her aura that she was troubled. "Go ahead," he said, and in the instant she asked him the question he knew what it would be.

"Did you know Vinnie was going to die that night?"

He stared at her for just a moment before his eyes turned towards the bedspread. "No," he said, "I didn't know Vinnie was going to die. I just thought he was coming down with something. I told him to just go home."

"Thank you," said Katie, and she looked relieved. "You have another hard day tomorrow. You'd better get some sleep."

Billy did not sleep, not until the clock neared three a.m., because his mind wouldn't stay away from that place where he didn't want it to go.

Jenny.

SEVENTEEN

BILLY'S STORY
PART THREE

Billy graduated from high school in June of 1972, not knowing much of anything except that he didn't want to go to Vietnam. He was still a big sports fan, but he also took an interest in the nightly news, and the images he saw of the war that was some 8,000 miles from home convinced him that he would never survive if he was sent there.

The image of seeing a person he passed on the street with the aura of death around him was bad enough; to see it on dozens of soldiers surrounding him every day in a war would drive him to madness.

He kept his ability hidden from everyone. In fact, he refused to recognize it, and did his utmost to pretend he didn't see the various colors flowing and glowing around everyone he met. He desperately wanted this curse to go away.

About three-quarters of the 97 kids who graduated from Philbrook High School that year attended college. Peggy Clark, who was the valedictorian, received a full scholarship to Brown University, an Ivy League School. Samantha Cousins, however, was on the other end of the spectrum. She had become pregnant back in January and was never to be seen again. Her father, a strict Catholic, sent her to a boarding school for pregnant girls in Virginia. Billy had become friends with Sam in high school and missed her when she was gone.

He applied to three different colleges his senior year, and in the end he decided to attend Penn State to study accounting. The Pennsylvania school was far enough away from family where he couldn't be watched over by them, yet it was close enough to home if he ever felt the need to be there. His parents helped him move into his dorm that first day, and when it was time for them to head back home his dad shook his hand, his mom gave him a good long hug, and Marylou cried.

"It'll be lonely without you," she said, and he knew she meant it. They were close, Marylou and Billy, although little did they know that this day would be the beginning of their slipping apart.

He muddled through that first year of college, his grades nothing to write home about. He was basically holding a C+ average even though his accounting grades were in the B+ range. He made friends with his three dorm roommates and a couple kids who lived down the hall, but that was about it. Two of the fraternities on campus tried to recruit him when pledge time opened, but Billy wasn't interested.

As his sophomore year rolled around, you could have said he was just going through the motions, and you wouldn't have been far from the truth. It appeared from all indications that he wasn't the ambitious type. In fact, Billy thought long and hard about dropping out of school, but that would have made him eligible for the draft and a trip to Vietnam, so he decided to stick it out.

There were females aplenty on the Penn State campus, but Billy was still shy at that point, and always became nervous when he tried to talk to them. For the most part, he left them alone.

His junior year was much the same, although the one roommate he had that year, a member of the Beta Tau Alpha fraternity, did manage to coax him to a couple of the dances the frat put on, and he was even dragged along to a Sorority party that the BTA's were invited too.

179

At the end of his junior year, he returned home and went to Katie's senior prom as her date. He had been surprised to be asked. She had grown more beautiful than he last remembered, and he wondered why no one in her class had asked her. He thought he behaved like a perfect gentleman, and he brought her home on time.

He had no idea she had wanted to lose her virginity that night. She had no idea that would have meant he would have lost his too.

Everything changed his senior year. He went home for the Christmas holidays that year, as always, but returned to Penn State ten days earlier than normal because he just couldn't stand being around the house. He simply told his folks he had to work on his senior thesis and needed to use the Penn State library, none of which was true.

There were few kids on campus at the time, which was fine for the introvert in him. It meant meeting people you probably never would have run into otherwise, however, and one of the people he met was Catherine O'Leary.

Cath, as she liked to be called, was a short blond girl with a bright smile and a quick wit. She spied Billy as he headed to the student cafeteria one night and started walking beside him.

"Hi there," she said, her smile a ray of sunshine on a dreary evening.

"Hi," he managed to mutter, surprised by the sudden advance of this stranger.

"I've seen you before," she said. "You're kinda cute."

No one, except perhaps his mother, had ever said anything like that to him before. He just looked at her, too stunned for words.

"Wanna hang out with me?" she asked.

And before he knew what he was doing, his mouth said, "Sure."

Catherine O'Leary was a wild child. It turned out she had an apartment off campus, a right that senior's had but that Billy had declined, and she took him there that night. There were about eight other kids in attendance, and they all shared some Boone's farm wine and passed around a joint. It was the first and last time Billy would ever have marijuana, and by midnight he was at peace with the world.

As the crowd started going their separate ways, Cath said, "Come with me."

She took his hand to help him up, and then led him down the hall to her room. It was there, in the early hours of the morning, that Billy Wilson had sex for the first time.

He had no clue what he was doing, but Cath was obviously not a first-timer. Over the course of the next three days she taught him what to do, and what not to do, when making love to a woman. She brought him up to speed with what everyone else had been doing all along.

His three day affair with Cath ended as soon as it began. It turned out her boyfriend came back to school on day four. Billy didn't mind. He'd had sex, and suddenly felt a bit more like a grownup than he had before.

Two months later his life changed completely. There was a party on the weekend at one of the sororities on campus, and Billy and his roommates decided to attend. Two things ended up happening that night, neither of which he expected.

The introvert in him had a good time for once, and he fell in love.

Her name was Jenny Kinsman. She had graduated from Penn State a few years earlier, but she often came to the sorority parties as an alumni member. She spied Billy in the crowd that night and started heading his way. When he saw her for the first time, her aura exploded in his mind, and he couldn't help but notice. He knew something special was about to happen.

"Well, here's a face I haven't seen before," she said, when she finally arrived at his side. "What's your name?"

"Billy," he said. "Billy Wilson."

Jenny Kinsman was hot. She stood five-foot nine, and in the heels she was wearing that night she was almost as tall as he was. Her hour-glass figure was enhanced by a low-cut, form fitting dress of blue that matched her eyes and nearly forced him to look at her well endowed breasts, which he did.

Jenny noticed, as women always do.

She took his arm and led him to a corner of the room that was less sparsely populated. At her request, he poured a couple of beers from the keg in the corner, and then joined her on the couch.

"So why have I never met you before?" she asked.

"I'm not much of a partygoer," he replied.

"Tell me all about yourself."

And so he told her the Billy Wilson story, which was about as boring as a story could be; except for the dead bodies in the woods, of course. That part enthralled her. Then it was her turn.

Jenny was twenty-five, four years older than him at the time, and had graduated three years earlier. She had majored in economics, but had turned to real estate upon graduating, working at a company in downtown Pittsburgh and living on the east side in an area called Squirrel Hill. She'd basically gone from one college campus to another, as Squirrel Hill was populated with students from the University of Pittsburgh, which was close by.

Two hours and a couple of beers later, she kissed him for the first time. He had a feeling he was in over his head, but he wasn't about to stop, her aura telling him exactly what she had in mind.

"Let's get out of here and take a walk," she whispered in his ear.

He was more than happy to follow her lead. The cool evening air was sharp and crisp as it hit them. They strolled hand in hand as they walked. He wasn't paying much attention to where they were going until he noticed the parking lot ahead.

"My car's over here," said Jenny.

He thought perhaps she planned on taking him somewhere, and you could say she was, although the car would never move.

Much to his surprise, she unlocked the back door and said, "Slid in," and then she slipped in beside him. They made out for awhile, slowly getting undressed as they did. Billy still had a preacher mode mentality, and the thought that they were about to be arrested for moral indecency kept running through his mind, but a part of him kept saying it would be worth it. He couldn't believe he was fondling and sucking on a pair of breasts so large, and then, well …. He was glad Catherine O'Leary had taught him a few things, because they came in handy that night.

Billy and Jenny were a couple from that moment on. His parents met her at graduation and thought she was wonderful. His dad took him aside at one point and asked, "How did you ever find her?" Billy thought what he was really asking was, *What is she doing with you?*

"We met at a party," he said, "and just hit it off." It may have been the only time he thought his dad was truly impressed with him. Carl Wilson was a strict man, never laughing much or seeming to enjoy life, but he worked his ass off to get Billy through college.

His affair with Jenny Kinsman took everyone by surprise. His roommate, who'd had sex with half a dozen girls but never had a real relationship, was stunned that such a beautiful lady had chosen Billy. Billy himself kept waiting for the break up speech, but it never came. For whatever reason, Jenny thought he was *the one,* and nothing ever changed that.

They were two months into the relationship when his graduation rolled around. The day was sunny and bright, and the ceremony seemed to take forever, but Billy had his Accounting Degree. His parents were as proud as he'd ever seen them, and Jenny was by his side.

Marylou was not at his graduation. She had found love in high school with a boy named Mark McGrath. They had married a year ago, a month after their graduation, and now she was about two weeks shy of having their first child, a girl whom they would name Jillian.

Billy moved in with Jenny after graduation, much to the dismay of both his parents, whose religious beliefs frowned on such things. The free love movement of the sixties had carried over into the seventies, however, and Billy and Jenny were hardly alone.

Jenny was making decent money at her job at the time, and she had a few connections at a local bank. With her help, Billy managed to snag an interview, and then a job, as a loan officer trainee at the First Union Bank and Trust. As soon as Billy saw the aura around the lady who interviewed him, he figured he was in. He also knew that if he ever wanted to have an affair, she'd be a willing partner.

Billy and Jenny finally tied the knot for good on May 19th, 1979. It was a warm Saturday for May, the temps hovering near 85, and since they had decided to have the wedding in the backyard of Jenny's parent's home in Troy, New York, they all felt the heat.

The parents all seemed to get along well. Billy loved Jenny's mom, a vivacious lady who could cook up the most delectable foods. Her father never treated Billy poorly, but Billy had the idea that Thomas Kinsman also wondered what his daughter saw in him.

They stayed in the Pittsburgh area, eventually moving away from the college crowd and buying a home in the northern suburbs. Billy was moving up the ranks at the bank at a fairly rapid clip, which was good, because the economy was in the midst of a downturn, and Jenny's pay went down with it as housing prices tumbled.

Once in their own home, they decided to start a family. Despite how hard she worked, Jenny had a sex drive that never seemed to quit, and Billy was more than happy to oblige. Thomas Michael Wilson was born on October 17th, 1981. Billy had just turned twenty-seven; Jenny would soon be thirty-one. They named him after her grandfather. Two years later, almost to the day, Ruth Anne was born. They thought two kids were enough and didn't plan on having any more.

Marriage to Jenny was everything he could have asked for and more. Billy loved her dearly and she loved him back, and it turned out he was a pretty damned good father too. He taught Tommy everything he could about sports. Billy was a Boston fan for life, but Tommy liked the local teams, the Pirates and Steelers, and Billy supported him much as his Yankee-loving dad had supported Billy's love of the Red Sox.

Then there was Ruth, their little princess. Who knew a little girl could touch the heart of someone so much? Billy adored her, and truth be told she was his favorite child, although he would never admit it. She had curly blond hair and a cherubic round face that made him think of Shirley Temple. They'd watch cartoons together every Saturday morning, and Billy would read to her almost every night.

They barely survived the economic downturn. Jenny had thought of switching jobs numerous times over the course of the decline, but in the end so many other realtors had left that she stuck it out. Things were finally beginning to shift, and as 1987 began the market was starting to pick up again.

Life was good.

And then it all went to shit.

2

There are days in life that you always remember, like where you were when JFK was shot, or the Challenger explosion, or 9-11.

February 10th, 1987, would be that day for Billy Wilson.

It had been a restless night; he couldn't seem to stay asleep for more than an hour at a time. At 5 a.m. he finally arose for good and went downstairs to make coffee. He retrieved the paper from the driveway while the coffee brewed. He had reached the sports section when Jenny entered the kitchen at 6:15 to begin her day.

"What are you doing up so early?" she asked.

"Couldn't sleep," he said.

She poured herself a coffee, gave him a kiss, and tousled his hair. "Gonna make for a long day."

"Tell me about it." He stared at her for a long moment, and then asked, "You feel okay?"

She looked at him with that friendly smirk on her face that he loved so much and said, "What, is my aura telling you I have some deadly disease?"

He had told Jenny about his ability just before they married. Much as Katie would years later, Jenny had noticed the way he walked with his head down nearly all the time. Finally, she had brought it up to him, and Billy, not wanting to keep any secrets from the woman he loved, had spilled the beans. Over the years she had come to count on it, particularly when the kids were coming down with something. Once in a while, she'd see him staring at the children funny and ask him what was wrong. She had become very adept at reading him, almost as if she could see the auras herself. Billy had tried more than once to teach her, but she had never succeeded.

"You look a little pale today, and there's lots of grey around you. I don't like what I'm seeing."

"I'm fine," she said. "Probably just need this coffee."

He watched her closely as she moved about, and after ten minutes or so she said, "You're getting on my nerves. How about you go get the kids up?"

He did as asked, heading upstairs where all the bedrooms were. He entered Tommy's room first and shook his shoulder. "Time to get up," he said, and the boy moaned as he usually did when he had to get out of bed. Then he went and did the same with Ruth. His little angel opened her eyes, looked at him, and said, "Hello, Daddy." Then she sat up and gave him a great big Ruthie hug, as she called it.

It was a Tuesday morning, four days before Valentine's Day, and as he headed back down the stairs, Billy wondered what else he could get Jenny for that special day. She wasn't a flower and chocolates person. He had already made reservations at Niko's, a fancy little downtown restaurant in the heart of Pittsburgh, and had set up the babysitter for the evening. He also had purchased some fancy lingerie from Fredericks, which had become a staple Valentine's gift between them. He was still looking for something special, however, and so far had come up short. He had bought her jewelry last year and wanted something different this time around.

It took the kids a while to brush their teeth and get dressed. Ruth was the first one to make it downstairs, and when she entered the kitchen he was immediately alarmed. Her aura was a ragged mix of browns and grays.

"Are you feeling alright?" he asked, much as he had done with her mother earlier.

"I feel great, daddy," she said, and she sat at the table, where a bowl of Fruity Pebbles was awaiting her.

Jenny gave him a questioning stare? The look he gave her back must have hinted that something was up, but he didn't have time to answer before Tommy came sauntering into the room.

His aura looked much like Ruth's did, and as Billy turned back to Jenny he suddenly noticed her aura was even worse than it had been when he first saw her.

"You two sit at the table and eat," he said. "Mommy and I need to go into the living room for a moment."

"What is going on?" Jenny asked, as they headed out of the kitchen.

"All of your auras are bad," he told her. "None of you feel ill, so whatever is going on is because of your plans for the day."

"Same as every day," said Jenny. "I drop the kids off at Kindergarten and day care, and then I go to work."

"I need you all to stay home today."

"Oh come on," she said. "I have a big meeting with a major potential client this morning. I can't cancel it."

"You have to," he said. "This is serious. All your auras are dark."

She gave him that little sound she made whenever she was miffed at him. "Let's go back to the kitchen and see if it's changed any."

Tommy and Ruth were just finishing their cereal. Their auras hadn't become much worse, but they sure weren't any better.

"You need to stay home," said Billy again. "Just call work and school and tell them everyone has a 24-hour bug."

"Are you sure?" Jenny replied. "This is a very big client I have today. It will be major income for us if I can sell him on the property he's looking at. Major income."

"Whatever it is, it's not worth the risk," he told her. They circled around the issue for a few minutes more before she finally agreed to take the day off and keep the kids home.

Fate can be a fickle thing. On most days, Billy would be the last one to leave the house. The bank didn't open until nine, and he rarely had to be there before 8:30. He had a meeting that morning, however. It was something the bank did about once a month, and this Tuesday was the day. Otherwise he would have been home and made sure that Jenny kept her word. Instead, at 7:30, he headed off to work.

He would never know why Jenny did not heed his warning that morning. Perhaps she thought her client was too important to cancel; perhaps she thought the kids shouldn't miss school; maybe she just decided to be more careful and alert as she drove in order to avoid any problems. He would later determine that Jenny left the house about ten minutes after he did.

Maybe she just didn't believe in his ability as much as he thought she did.

Fate can also be a fierce mistress. Not one to be toyed with, by any means. Fate had a plan that day, and his attempts to overcome it would prove fruitless.

Jenny packed the kids in the car and headed to the school.

They didn't even make it a mile.

The dump truck had a full load and was cruising about ten miles over the speed limit when the light turned yellow. He never would have stopped in time, and so he gave it a little more gas. It was a quick light, unfortunately, and Jenny started forward when her light turned green.

The truck broadsided them and drove them nearly thirty yards before Jenny's Chevy Monte Carlo disengaged as it hit the curb. The Monte Carlo flipped onto its side and took out the better part of a glass covered bus stand, and then flipped one more time before slamming upside down against the side of a flower shop.

Jenny and Tommy, who was sitting in the seat behind his mother, were killed instantly. Ruth, who was sitting in her car

189

seat on the opposite side, somehow survived the initial impact but suffered major damage as the car rolled. She would exit this world in the ambulance on the way to the hospital. In truth she had no chance, the internal injuries being much too severe.

Billy received the news at work when he was visited by a two-man team from the Pittsburgh police force. He knew when he saw them walk into the room that they were there for him and the news would be bad. They were matter-of-fact in the telling of the situation, as policemen often are, though he did see a note of compassion on the younger one's face as he left. Rodriguez, his name was, and Billy would always remember it.

After the cops left, Billy sat in the nearest chair, stunned. His life as he knew it was shattered. He broke down as his fellow workers entered, heard what had happened, and tried to console him.

The higher ups at the bank were tremendously supportive. After the funerals, they gave him plenty of time off, and leeway when he did return. However, his work was not up to par, not even close, and by the end of July he gave them his notice to save them the embarrassment of having to fire him.

And then he drifted.

EIGHTEEN

"Billy, are you up? You need to get ready."

Billy fumbled with the sheets for a moment, cobwebs in his mind, and wondered for a second where he was.

"Billy?" Katie called again.

He suddenly remembered; Katie's home, mom's funeral is today. "I'm up," he called out.

"Okay," she replied, "I'll be downstairs. Would you like some breakfast?"

"Just coffee," he said, and then, "maybe a bagel."

He managed to drag himself out of bed and towards the bathroom. He felt more tired than he had when he went to bed, and realized he had only slept about four hours. Thoughts of his late wife were still rumbling through his brain, but today was about another funeral, and he needed to focus on that.

He showered quickly, and then put on the suit he had worn last night, the only suit he owned; black, of course, for weddings and funerals. That was all he ever wore it for. *I am my mother's son,* he thought.

He headed downstairs, entered the kitchen, and stopped dead in his tracks. Katie was also in black, though this dress was different from last nights. Billy thought she was stunning. He stared at her for a moment, and then he said, "You are a beautiful woman, Katie Maki."

"They'll be time for that later," she replied, a huge grin overcoming her face.

"I'm just saying..."

"You're very sweet, Billy Wilson," she said, as she handed him a cup of coffee. "There's a Danish by the toaster; sorry, no bagels."

They ate in relative silence. Billy's thoughts finally switched from Jenny over to his mother. Their relationship had been strained for a long time, but Billy tried to remember the good times.

Katie eventually interrupted his reverie. "We'd better go," she said.

The funeral for Laurie Wilson was held at the First Methodist Church. Once again the sun shone brightly, and this time Billy was grateful. The attendance was sparse, barely thirty people in all, and the service was short. When it ended, the pallbearers carried the coffin outside as Billy and Marylou watched. It was placed in the hearse, driven about 150 yards to a spot in the cemetery behind the church, and removed.

The mourners made their way to the gravesite on foot. The whole scene inevitably reminded Billy of Vinnie's funeral so many years ago, and he imagined Katie was thinking the same thing.

Laurie Wilson would lie next to the grave of her husband. The final service lasted just under ten minutes. At its end, Billy and his sister each gently laid a bouquet of daisies, their mother's favorite flower, on top of the coffin, and said their final goodbyes.

As the other mourners departed, Billy and his sister spent a few minutes at their father's grave.

"They're finally reunited," said Marylou.

"Oh, I imagine dad's been watching over mom for some time now."

"When you die, you're dead, Billy," she said. "I don't believe in that New Age stuff that's so popular these days and that I know you believe in. I trust in my Bible."

He did not wish to argue with his sister, who he knew was still a devoted churchgoer.

"I know you don't," he said, and the subject was dropped.

There was a small gathering in the church basement after the service; nothing fancy, just some finger sandwiches which Walter had insisted on making, plus coffee and soda. A few people had left after the church service, but about twenty remained. No one from the police department showed up, for which Billy was grateful. Curtis Armstrong had come with his wife to offer his condolences, and Kim Johnson, one of the twins from Billy's sixth grade class, was also there.

Billy sat at a table with Marylou and Mark, Mark's parents, and Walter and Katie.

"Well, Billy, I guess you're the head of the family now," said Marylou, as they quietly nibbled on tuna salad sandwiches.

He could tell by her puffy eyes that she was still having a hard time dealing with the loss of her mother. "I think you're better equipped to take that mantle," he said.

"Well ...," she started to reply, but apparently had no words to offer.

He turned to Katie, who was sitting on his left. "In all this time we've been together, I still haven't asked about your folks yet. How are they doing?"

Billy knew Alfred and Irene Maki had divorced as soon as Katie had gone off to college. Losing a child did that to people.

"Dad's in a retirement home in Oklahoma, of all places," said Katie. "He moved out there to be with his brother, who passed away about three years ago. Mom's doing okay. She remarried about the time I was getting divorced. They live in Connecticut now. She wanted me to tell you she was sorry she couldn't be here, but she doesn't get around too well anymore. She always liked your mom."

She turned towards Billy and her leg brushed against his. As it did, a smile came over her face, and she stared straight into his eyes.

He didn't need to read her aura to know what she had in mind, but Curtis came over just then. He looked at Katie and said, "That was something about Vinnie."

Katie just gave him a small nod of her head, but Billy said, "Took me by surprise, although I guess we were always suspicious back then about what had really happened to him."

"Have the cops talked to you yet?" asked Curtis.

"Yeah. Some lady detective from Greenfield cornered me at the end of the wake last night. Say, you're a lawyer; you think they have any chance of ever finding out what really happened out there?"

"Not unless you or Walter tell them something they don't already know," said Curtis, "and I'm guessing that's not likely."

"No, probably not." Billy shook hands with Curtis and said, "Thanks for coming."

"Here's my card," said Curtis. "If you feel you need a lawyer while you're home, just call."

Marylou arose to say goodbye to the final guests, and Katie joined her.

As they walked away, Walter asked Billy, "What's going on with you and Katie?"

"What do you mean?"

"Come on. I saw the way you two were looking at each other."

Billy paused for a moment, and then said, "Who knew Vinnie's little sister would grow up to be so attractive?"

"What are you gonna do?"

Billy laughed, seeing a stream of envy shoot up in Walter's aura, and looked at him as if he had two heads. "We're letting nature take its course."

"Well, I guess it's about time. Hope you know how lucky you are."

Katie came back around and asked if he was ready to leave.

"Pretty soon," said Billy. "I'm just going to help Marylou clean up."

"Okay," she said. "I'm going to wait outside. Want to join me, Walter?"

Billy watched her walk away, and then he felt a playful punch on his arm from Walter.

"I love you like a brother," said Walter, "but don't you hurt that girl, or I'll be pissed."

"I won't," said Billy, and Walter headed out to join Katie.

Billy and Marylou finished clearing the tables and washed them down, restacked the folding metal chairs, and washed and dried the few dishes that they had used. It was a few minutes before noon when they finished.

"Done," said Billy, and suddenly it hit him that his mother was in the ground and he would never see her again. He looked at his sister and said, "I can't believe she's gone?"

He thought his sister might start crying again, but she held it in. "You should have visited more often, Billy."

He could hear the resentment in her voice and knew he couldn't blame her. "I know," he said. "I'm sorry. I'd think about it, but just kept putting it off. I guess I never thought I'd run out of time."

"Well," she said, "you still have a sister. Come and see me sometime, okay? Or at least call."

He said he'd do his best, and then they shut off the lights and headed outside.

Walter and Katie were standing at the bottom of the stairs, and Billy saw Katie nod her head towards his car. There was an Edgeworth patrol car parked nearby.

I guess I'm going to see a cop today after all, he thought.

The cop got out of his car and walked towards him. "Hi there," he said. "You're Billy Wilson, aren't you?"

"I am. What can I do for you?"

"My name is Paul Stephens. I'm on the force here."

The name didn't ring a bell at first, and Billy just stared at the officer. Then he remembered the newspaper articles he had read online and asked, "Are you the one that guy confessed to last week?"

Paul Stephens nodded.

"I read all about it," said Billy.

"And did my last name ring a bell?" asked Paul.

Billy looked at him a moment, then mumbled, "Stephens? You mean from '66?"

"That was my dad. He was the first officer on the scene."

"Oh. I never really talked to him," said Billy.

"Are you sure?" asked Paul.

"Yes. He took Hank and Walter back to the crime scene with him, and left me and Vinnie to talk to the detective who came to the house."

"Didn't my father come and talk with you after they found Vinnie?" asked Paul.

Billy thought for a moment, and then said, "No. Actually, no one ever came and talked to me after Vinnie died. I remember my mom being all worried about it, but nobody ever showed up. So what can I do for you today, officer?"

"I was wondering if anyone had talked to you since you've been home."

"You mean the police?" asked Billy, and Paul Stephens nodded again. "Sure, a detective showed up at the wake last night."

"Detective Remington?" asked Paul.

"That's the one. Not much new I could tell her after fifty years. Did she send you?"

"No," he said, and Billy noticed a perturbed look on his face. "She took over the case the day after Membrino confessed, and we local guys have been pretty much shut out ever since. You didn't tell her anything she didn't already know?"

"Not really. I told her if Vinnie really did have a clue than he must have taken it off the body in the woods, because I don't think he ever touched Mrs. Potter. That seemed to interest her a bit, although I don't know why."

Paul Stephens chatted with Billy for a few minutes more and then left, leaving Billy to wonder what that was all about.

As he headed back towards Katie, Billy saw Curtis walking his way.

"I saw the cop waiting for you," said the lawyer, "and thought I'd stick around in case you needed me."

"Thanks," said Billy, "but as I've said a dozen times by now, what can I tell them after fifty years? I guess they're just doing their jobs."

Curtis nodded, and then headed back to his car.

NINETEEN

Billy and Katie headed back home after Curtis left. "We saw the cop waiting when we went outside," she said as he drove. "I figured he wanted to talk to you alone, and he didn't realize it was Walter standing next to me."

"And I'm sure Walter didn't want to talk to him," laughed Billy.

"So what did he want?"

"Seems our Miss Remington isn't sharing with the locals," said Billy. "He wanted to know what was going on. Turns out he's the son of the first officer who came to the house that day."

"Did you tell him anything?"

"Same thing I told that detective."

Katie stared at him for a moment, keeping her thoughts to herself.

When they arrived home, she looked at him and said, "Would you make love to me again?"

Billy smiled, took her hand, and led her inside.

They climbed the stairs to her bedroom and proceeded to undress each other. They made love slowly, stretching it out as long as possible. When they finally finished, drained and thoroughly sated, Billy went downstairs, grabbed a couple of beers, and then rejoined Katie in her bed.

They cuddled and made small talk, and then Katie brought up her brother again.

"It's funny," she said, "but sometimes I have a hard time remembering my brother. I guess it's just age. Every once in a while I'll take out his old scrapbook and look through it, just to remind me of him."

"Scrapbook?"

"Yeah, my big brother kept a scrapbook. Way before it became popular, I know."

Billy couldn't imagine what Vinnie had kept in a scrapbook, so he asked.

"Oh gosh, he would put anything and everything in it. He had pictures from our vacations to Disneyland and York Beach, some newspaper articles about little league games where his name was mentioned; stuff like that."

"I never would have guessed," said Billy. "Do you have it here, at the house?"

"Yes, it's in a closet in the room where you're sleeping. Well, where you usually sleep," she amended, a sheepish smile on her face. "Let's put some clothes on, and then I'll dig it out. Would you like to see it?"

"Sure," he said. Billy went to the guest room and got dressed while Katie did the same, and then she joined him.

The scrapbook was well hidden under a half dozen boxes of odds and ends, but Katie knew right where it was and found it immediately. "I believe he received this as a Christmas present from one of our grandmothers," she said. "I don't think anyone ever expected Vinnie to use it, but he seemed to take to it for some reason."

"He never mentioned it that I recall," said Billy.

"I'm not surprised. It's more of a girl thing, don't you think?"

They took it downstairs. Katie grabbed a couple more beers, and then they settled onto the couch.

The scrapbook was in good shape considering its age. It was brown with gold trim, and the cover was plain, although something had obviously been taped to it once.

"It used to say, 'Vinnie's Life' on it," said Katie, "but it was just a piece of paper, and it ripped off one day during one of my moves." She opened the book to the first page, and memories of his childhood friend began flooding back to Billy.

Page one was all about Disneyland, which the Maki's had gone to in 1963. There was a picture of Vinnie and Katie with Donald Duck, an admittance ticket, and a postcard of Snow White and the Seven Dwarfs.

Page Two contained a newspaper article. The name *Vinnie Maki* was underlined in red, now well faded, and the article said *Vinnie Maki had a single and made a nice running catch in the outfield for the Pirates.* Vinnie had written *My first hit* to the side of the article.

More stories from the papers and souvenirs from various vacations were found on the following pages. Only about ten of the forty pages the scrapbook contained had been used, and a few minutes later Katie said, "That's it," and closed the book. As she did, a flash of white caught Billy's eye.

"What's that?" he said.

"What?"

"I thought I saw something in the back as you closed the book."

"Oh," said Katie, "that's just something he stuck back there. I don't know why."

Billy picked the book back up, reopened it, and found what had caught his eye. "It's a betting slip," he said.

"That's what I thought it might be," said Katie, "but all I've ever seen are those football cards."

The slip had been placed four pages from the back of the book. There was no tape on it. Billy examined the paper closely. It had previously been folded over once, and the writing on it was faded, but he could still make out what it said:

K Derby   Advocator   Win 2K DA21

"I don't know where he found it or why he put it here," said Katie. "He certainly never bet on a game. What does it mean? Do you know?"

Billy turned to look at her and said, "Yes, most of it anyway. K Derby would be the Kentucky Derby, and someone bet two thousand dollars on Advocator to win. That was a hell of a lot of money back when we were kids. I don't know what the DA 21 means, but it's probably some code for the bookie who took the bet."

"So where would Vinnie get something like this?" asked Katie.

Billy examined the slip again, and in the upper left hand corner, barely visible, he noticed a faded brown spot. "Has this always been there?" he asked.

"I think so. I've never taken this out of the book, so it must have been. Why?"

"Did you ever show this scrapbook to the police?"

He saw the startled look on her face. "The police? Why in heaven's name would I show this to them?"

"Because," said Billy, "I'll bet this brown spot is dried blood, and I'm guessing that this is Vinnie's famous clue."

Katie looked at him, completely dumbfounded. "You think this is what got my brother killed?"

Billy saw the shocked look on Katie's face. "I do," he said. He examined the small slip of paper again, and then asked, "Is it possible that Vinnie knew anything about bookies or betting back then?"

"I don't think so," said Katie. "Remember, I was only eight at the time. I know what a football card looks like now, and I knew in high school, but when I was eight? No way. And I doubt that Vinnie knew either."

"Did your dad ever bet or play the football cards that you know of?"

She thought for a moment, trying to recall a past that had long ago turned hazy. "Well," she finally said, "I think I saw him with one once or twice, and I know he bet on the Super Bowl once. Mom nearly killed him when she found out, and dad was so nervous he couldn't sit still during the game."

"That would have been after this," said Billy. "The first Super Bowl wasn't until 1967."

"Oh, it was later than that," she said. "I think I was on college break. Maybe '72 or '73."

"Well, if this clue meant something to Vinnie, then he must have known about betting and gambling back then, and he must have had an inkling about who was involved."

Katie was at a loss. "I have no idea," she said. "Should we take it to the police?"

Billy sat back on the couch and took a deep breath. He liked the fact that she had said *we*. After all, there was no reason for her to become involved. Although if certain people found out she had been in possession of the clue all along, perhaps she would be involved. The police seemed to be actively invested in the case, and whoever had left those notes for him and Walter certainly seemed interested. Billy wondered if their lives were on the line here.

"I don't know," he finally said. "What do you think?"

"I'd love to know who killed my brother, or should I say who ordered him killed. But after all these years," she paused, and gazed at the ceiling for a moment, "maybe we should let sleeping dogs lie. Those notes you and Walter received scare me. I don't want anything to happen to either of you."

"They scare me too," said Billy. He had no desire to be the next person found floating in Brooks Lake. "If we never say anything about this, I imagine everything will all die down pretty quickly. Unless the cops come up with a DNA match, which I doubt they will, they've got nothing."

"Whoever had Vinnie killed must be dead," said Katie. "We'd just be going after some relative or successor. So the question is, is that worth it?"

"Maybe we should call Walter and get his thoughts. After all, he's involved in this too."

"But will knowing about this put him in even more danger?"

"I don't know," said Billy. "I need to see what year Advocator was in the Derby. Maybe this is from a different year and we're just obsessing for no reason."

Katie watched as Billy googled the 1966 Kentucky Derby on her computer. He found the results right away. "Look here," he said. "Advocator came in second to a horse called Kauai King."

"So he lost the bet because the horse didn't win?"

"Right," said Billy.

"This guy who was killed in the woods bet two thousand dollars on a horse race?" said Katie, obviously shocked. "But wasn't he just a factory worker, as I recall? How could he afford to do such a thing?"

"My guess is he was in deep to the bookie, owed him a lot of money, and tried to get out of it with an all or nothing bet. When he lost, he owed the bookie so much there was no way he could pay. He'd probably lost all of his savings by that point and had nothing to fall back on."

"And it got him killed."

"I'm afraid so," said Billy.

"I wonder if his wife knew."

They were silent for a while, each lost in their own thoughts. Finally, Katie spoke up. "We should call Walter, let him know what we've found, and see what he thinks?"

Billy thought it over and decided it wasn't a bad idea. "Okay," he said. "I'll give him a call now." He went into the kitchen, picked up his cell phone that was lying on the counter, and called his childhood friend.

Katie sat on the couch holding her brother's old scrapbook. She had looked through it a dozen times or more over the years and had seen that paper in the back more than once. It had meant nothing to her, and she never considered that it might have something to do with Vinnie's death. Of course, she had no reason to think that. She had always thought Vinnie's death was an accident.

On more than one occasion she had thought of taping it in the front of the book for Vinnie, but it didn't seem that important. Other times she had nearly thrown it away. In the end, she always left it where it was, thinking that was where it was meant to be.

Katie heard Billy still talking to Walter, so she decided to step outside for a moment. The air was beginning to turn chilly, but it felt good to her. She couldn't believe she had made love to her childhood crush these past few days. *After all these years,* she thought. It had been amazing, a sexual explosion within her that she hadn't felt in years. But still … he was scheduled to go home soon. She wondered if there was any chance she could keep him here.

Billy came outside a few minutes later. "There you are," he said. "I wondered where you had gone off to."

"Thought I'd get some fresh air," she said. "What did Walter have to say?"

"Well, first off, he doesn't want us to tell anyone that we've spoken to him. He'd rather not be involved in any way."

"I can understand that," said Katie

"I can too," said Billy. "Next, he suggests we keep it to ourselves. If we do decide to tell the police, he suggests we do it anonymously."

"How do we do that?" asked Katie.

"Walter said we could turn it over to Curtis and let him contact the cops. He could say a client of his wanted them to have it, but wanted to remain anonymous; attorney client privilege and all."

"Would that work?" she asked.

"I don't know," said Billy, shaking his head. "They'd have to know it came from one of us, and they'd probably think we've been hiding it all these years."

Katie turned to look straight at him. "So the answer is no."

"I guess so. We could go to Curtis for advice. See what he thinks."

There was a swing on the porch, and she led Billy to it. They sat and rocked quietly for awhile, arm in arm, her head lying softly against his shoulder. When he started to get chilly, she went inside and brought him one of her sweatshirts. The arms were a little short, but it fit well enough.

Billy started talking about his mother, and the things he wished he'd done differently.

Katie listened, and offered comfort where she could. When it appeared he was finally all talked out, she said, "What are we going to do, Billy?"

"About the clue?"

"No, about us?"

"What do you ...," he started to say, and then it hit him. *Us.* As in, *a couple.* Katie was asking if the past few days were just a quick vacation fling or something more. "Oh," he said, letting it trail off.

"I know you haven't thought about it," she said, "what with all that's been going on, but you're supposed to go home in a few days. I'm just wondering if there's any chance I could change your mind about that. 'Cause Billy, I think I love you."

He looked at the amazingly beautiful woman beside him and felt his heart skip. "No one has said that to me in a long time." He caressed her face and brought her to him, kissing her ever so gently. "So much has happened so fast," he said.

"I know," she said, "and I'm not trying to pin you down or anything. You've had a lot on your mind, what with your mom's funeral and all, and now this stuff with Vinnie. It's just …." She paused, and let the moment linger for a bit before continuing. "I've always been in love with you, Billy. And I know we've hardly seen each other in the last forty years, but the fantasy in my head never died. Sometimes I'd even think of you while I was making love to my husband. Call me crazy, but when you said you were coming home for the funeral, I just knew you had to stay with me. And I fell in love with you again the minute I saw you. I just knew."

He took her in his arms and hugged her, holding her tight, and not wanting to let go. "I don't know what we're going to do," he whispered, "but we'll figure something out."

They sat on the swing in a light embrace for another hour, barely speaking. Eventually they went indoors.

That night they slept naked in Katie's bed, spooning, his hand cupping one of her breasts

.

TWENTY

Simon Taylor awoke on Thursday morning thinking about Maria. It had been a week since he'd seen her, and he realized how much he missed her. They had spoken on the phone nearly every day since he'd been gone, but that wasn't the same as being with her, holding her hand, or sleeping next to her in bed.

He smiled as he thought of how things had changed in the past week. His mindset had transformed ever since he had received his messages from Thomas last Thursday evening. Nora had told him he must move on, much as she had said in the dream he'd had of her. He had moved on before the dream physically; had been dating Maria for a few months at that point. But mentally he was still fixated on Nora, and that had continued after the dream.

Now the message appeared to have finally taken hold. He needed to move on with his life. Nora had reiterated that again, and he knew that Maria had been hinting the same thing to him for weeks now.

He felt alive again, refreshed, and ready to take on the world. It was a good feeling. Nora would always hold a dear place in his heart. Their marriage had been a good one, and they had taken plenty of time to spend with each other on their numerous vacations. Their trips to Maui, Pompeii, Switzerland, and other locales would always be special to him, but they were in the past.

He was ready to build a life with Maria and her son Enrique. *Life is short,* he thought, *and time passes quickly.* He grabbed his cell phone and called her number.

She obviously noticed who was calling before she answered. "Is this my doctor friend?" she said.

"Good morning, Maria dear," he replied. "How are you?"

"I'm doing great," she said, "although I seem to be very lonely at night."

"I'll fix that for you if you can just wait a while longer. Hopefully Enrique can keep you occupied until then."

She gave a quick laugh, and he could picture her perfectly over the phone.

They talked for just a few minutes more. Maria had to leave for work, and Thomas was yelling that breakfast was ready.

Simon was all smiles as he disconnected the call. A quickening of the pulse seemed to overtake him whenever he talked to Maria. It was not the same as the feeling that had stayed with him after his dream of Nora, but it was similar. He had found another woman who could make his body tingle, and he decided at that moment what he needed to do when he returned to Florida.

He would ask Maria to marry him.

"You seem happy this morning," said Thomas, as they were eating the french toast and bacon that Elizabeth had made for them. "Are you looking forward to tonight?"

Simon wasn't about to tell him what was really making him smile, and simply said, "I am."

He had been doing regressions for years now, and had worked with smaller groups many times at the conferences they attended, but tonight would be the first time he worked at a local gathering.

"You'll like it," said Thomas. "I've done this many times over the years. You get an eclectic sort of crowd, maybe even a few non-believers who come to see what all the fuss is about. The Unitarian church is pretty open-minded and always lets me do my thing there. Mostly, though, you'll get the same sort of seeker that we see at the conferences. Believers who want to know more about past lives and want to hear from their loved ones who have crossed over."

"Sounds like fun," said Simon. "How long do you expect us to be there?"

"Well, working alone I'm usually there for a little over an hour. I would suggest we each do no more than forty-five minutes."

"No problem," said Simon, as he finished the last bite of bacon on his plate. "Fifteen or twenty minutes for the regression, then the rest of the time to hear their stories."

He thought it would be fun.

Billy and Katie awoke to a flash of lightning and a roll of thunder. The downpour began a minute later; its pounding on the roof indicating it was no light shower. Billy had rolled away from her during the night. Now he crept close and began kissing her softly on her neck and back.

"That feels good," Katie said. She rolled over to face him and kissed him on the cheek. Then Billy caressed her nipples, rolling them gently between his finger and thumb, and a moment later began licking and sucking on them.

Katie began stroking him, and in no time he was hard. "Let me get on top this time," she said, and she knew by his smile that was fine with him.

She sat atop him and leaned forward, letting him suck on her breasts a bit longer. Then she gently lowered herself onto him. He started to move with her, but she stopped him. "Just lie there," she said, "and let me do the work." Again she teased him, bringing him to the brink and then letting up, but eventually there was no stopping him.

"You're wonderful," he said, when it was over.

They stayed in bed for another twenty minutes, cuddling and listening to the downpour outside, and then they realized they were hungry, and they headed downstairs.

Billy made blueberry pancakes and bacon while Katie started the coffee. She was happy to see he didn't seem lost in the kitchen, and Billy reminded her he had been single for a long time now. "I can vacuum and do laundry too," he said.

She gave him a smile and replied, "I love you more every minute."

They took their breakfast out onto the porch and watched the rain come down. When they finished, she took the plates inside, and then brought out the coffee pot and refilled their cups. She snuggled up next to him on the swing and said, "So, have you thought about what we should do?"

He'd been thinking about the fact that he lived a thousand miles away and was wondering how they were going to solve that problem, but he knew that this time she was talking about the betting slip.

"Well, we have three choices," he said. "One, keep it to ourselves; two, take it to the police; and three, go see Curtis and get a lawyer's opinion. We know Walter would vote for number one if he could, and I think we have to take that into account, because he's a part of this too."

"True," said Katie.

"That being said, I don't think we can just ignore it, and taking it to the cops scares the crap out of me. So I'm leaning towards talking with Curtis and seeing what he has to say. What do you think?"

"I don't want to ignore it either," she said. "I think I owe it to my brother to see this through. I'd want to take it to the police if it weren't for those notes you two received. That still scares me. So I agree with you, we should take it to Curtis and see what he has to say."

"Okay then, I'll give him a call in a bit."

They sat on the porch until the rain stopped. "Should we call Walter and let him know what we're doing?" Katie finally asked.

"No, he didn't want to be involved, and it might be best if he didn't know. And we won't tell Curtis we talked to him about it. Agreed?"

"Agreed," she said.

Billy took out the card Curtis had given him and dialed the number. The phone was answered on the second ring.

"Law offices of Curtis Armstrong, how may I help you?"

"I'd like to speak with Mister Armstrong, if I could," said Billy. He learned that Curtis wasn't due in the office until eleven, but fortunately he had an opening at 11:30, so Billy made an appointment for then.

They arrived at Curtis's office ten minutes early. It wasn't a fancy place by any means, simply a storefront on Main Street in Greenfield. However, the inside was nicely decorated with thick carpet and comfortable furniture.

The secretary, Heidi Greenblatt, according the nameplate on her desk, greeted them warmly and offered coffee. Both declined, although Katie asked for and received a bottle of water.

"Let me see if Mister Armstrong is ready for you," said Heidi. She went to the door leading to the back office, knocked twice, and then opened it and stepped inside. A moment later, she came back out and said, "Go right on in."

The office was warm and a shade dark for Billy's liking, the heavy velvet curtains on the back window blocking much of the daylight. The walls were lined with law books, like every other lawyer's office he had ever been in.

Curtis was sitting behind a massive oak desk that appeared to be newer than any of the other furniture. Paperwork was scattered about the desk, and a pile of folders was stacked on one edge. His diplomas hung on the wall behind him, and one of the bookcases had family pictures sitting atop it.

Curtis arose as they entered. "Welcome," he said. "I didn't expect to see you again so soon."

"Neither did we," said Billy.

They shook hands with the lawyer, and then he and Katie each took a seat in front of the desk. Billy pointed to one of the pictures and said, "I didn't know your dad played basketball too."

"No better than me, I'm afraid. That's a picture of him in his high school uniform," said Curtis. "So what can I do for you?"

"We have a situation that we'd like your opinion on," said Katie, "concerning my brother."

They saw Curtis's eyes open wider.

"Really?" he said. "Well, I'll be happy to help in any way I can. It certainly seems to be the case that won't die." He realized his bad choice of words as soon as they left his mouth, but Katie seemed to pay no attention.

"You're well aware of the details of the story, I assume," she said.

"If you mean the confession of that Membrino guy, yes I am."

"He claimed Vinnie had a clue which led him to assume, correctly as it turned out, who was responsible for the killing of the bodies we found," said Billy.

"Sure, I read that," said Curtis. "I'll never understand why Vinnie didn't tell the police if he had a clue. If I recall correctly," he continued, looking at Billy, "you said he told you back then he had a clue, but you didn't believe him."

"He asked me to go with him that night," said Billy, "but I wanted to watch television. And you're right; I never believed he really had any clue about the murders. None of us did."

212

Curtis loosened his tie and sat back in his chair. "But apparently he did. So what does all this have to do with today?"

"We think we've found the clue," said Katie.

They watched as Curtis's mouth dropped open. For a moment he just stared at them, but seemed unable to speak. Finally, he softly said, "You're joking?"

"Billy had a scrapbook. It's been in my possession ever since my dad divorced my mom," she said. "Every once in a while, when I think about Vinnie, I take it out and look through it. It's just some mementos from trips we took and newspaper articles with his name in it; you know, little league games and such.

"In the back of the book was a piece of paper, which I'd seen before but never paid much attention to. I figured it was just something he was keeping for whatever reason and simply hadn't gotten around to taping in the book yet. I never in a million years thought it could be a clue to the murders, and I didn't even know he had a clue until Membrino's confession."

"He never mentioned it to you back then?" asked Curtis.

"No," said Katie.

"And what makes you think what you've found is the missing clue?"

She turned to Billy. "You explain it," she said.

"It's a betting slip," said Billy. "It concerns the Kentucky Derby in 1966, which was held a week or so before the murders. Someone bet $2000 on a horse named Advocator to win. Turns out he came in second."

At first Curtis just mumbled "Hmm" as he digested what Billy had told him, and then he said, "You could buy a nice car for $2,000 back then. That was a hell of a lot of money to be betting on a horse race. Was there anything else on the paper?" asked Curtis.

"A code of some kind," said Billy. "Probably the bookies." He thought Curtis would ask what it said, but instead the lawyer moved on.

"Did you bring it with you?"

"No," said Billy, and Katie gave him a questioning look. She knew Billy had the paper in his pocket. "We thought it best to put it in a safe place for now."

Katie hoped that Curtis hadn't noticed her surprised look, but he seemed to be zeroed in on Billy.

"So why come to me?" asked Curtis. "Why not go to the police?"

Billy and Katie looked at each other for a moment, and then Katie spoke. "It was a long time ago, Curtis. I'm not sure what the benefits would be of reopening all these old wounds."

Curtis pursed his lips. "I see."

Katie explained the three options they had come up with, and the pros and cons of each. Curtis listened with rapt attention, occasionally jotting down a note on the pad in front of him. Finally, Katie said, "There's one other thing."

"What's that?"

She looked at Billy and said, "You tell him about the notes."

"Notes?" Curtis gave Billy a questioning look.

"I received a note on my car windshield the other day, warning me not to tell the cops anything," he said. "Turns out Walter received one too. I thought it was odd, since all the participants in the murders must be dead or dying by now. Since we obviously didn't know anything new, I wondered what the point was."

"Did you tell the police about these notes?" asked Curtis.

"No, neither one of us did. To be honest, I don't really enjoy having to deal with cops much, and like I said, I didn't see the point."

"But now things have changed, and you want my advice."

"Exactly," said Billy.

Curtis leaned back in his chair, gently swiveling left and right. He gazed at the ceiling, the ends of his fingers touching in a pyramid shape. "You're certain the paper you found came from the body?" he finally asked.

"Well, we can't be certain," said Billy, but the date is right, and there was one other thing."

"What's that?" asked Curtis.

"There was a spot in the upper left corner, rusty looking. I think it was dried blood."

"And is Walter aware you've found this clue?"

"No, we didn't tell him," said Billy. "No need to involve him, I don't think. Not now, anyway. If we do end up going to the cops, I imagine they'll ask him if he ever saw it."

"Anything else you need to tell me?" asked Curtis.

"No, I think that's it," said Katie. "Any ideas?"

"Okay, listen," said Curtis. "I have a few friends in the police department. Let me make a few inquiries into the investigation. See how they're coming along, whether they have any new leads or not. I'm sure their searching for all the information they can find on Richie Membrino. If they haven't come up with anything, then maybe you two should just lay low. Whoever those notes came from might not want to hear that a new clue has come to light. They'd have to figure it came from you or Walter. Let me see what I can find out and get back to you."

Call him a coward if you must, but anything that kept Billy from talking to the police was fine with him. "Okay," he said, and Katie concurred.

"When are you heading home?" asked Curtis.

"I'm supposed to fly back to Sarasota on Sunday," said Billy, "but ...." He turned to look at Katie, gave her a little smile, and finally said "... that could change."

"Okay, I'll get back to you sometime tomorrow, by three at the latest. That way, if you decide to go to the police, you'll have time before you leave."

"This is all confidential, right Curtis?" asked Katie.

"Attorney-client privilege," he said. "Don't worry; I'm just going to talk with the police as an interested bystander. They'll never know I talked with either of you."

"Thank you," she said, letting out a sigh of relief.

They arose to shake hands with Curtis, and then left the office. As they walked to the car, Katie said, "I think that went well."

"I hope so," Billy said.

"But why didn't you show him the betting slip?"

Billy wasn't sure what to tell her. The aura around Curtis had changed instantaneously when they mentioned they had found the clue, and he had immediately become suspicious of the lawyer. It was a spur of the moment decision to keep it in his pocket.

"Just a hunch," he finally said.

"You saw something in his aura, didn't you?"

He turned to look at her and nodded. "Maybe it's nothing," said Billy.

"And ...?"

"And maybe we just made a big mistake."

TWENTY ONE

Paul Stephens arrived home just after noon that Thursday. He had worked a twelve hour shift and was exhausted. His father, back home after his stay in the nursing home, was sitting on the couch watching candlepin bowling.

"Hey pop, how you feeling?" asked Paul.

John Paul craned his neck around to see who was talking to him. "Oh, it's you. I didn't hear you come in."

"Forget to put your hearing aid in again?"

"What?" asked his father, but as soon as he did he realized what Paul had said. "Oh, guess so." John Paul arose and went into his bedroom. When he came out a moment later, he said, "That's better. So what's up?"

"Nothing much. Long day at work is all. How are you feeling?"

The old man smiled and feigned a punch on his son's arm. "Fit as a fiddle," he said.

Paul was constantly amazed at just how fit his father was for a man his age. John Paul walked at least a mile every morning, and he did exercises that were recommended in the latest book by Doctor Oz. Of course, the doctor suggested they be done three times a week, but John Paul did them every day.

"How's the shoulder?" asked Paul.

"Just dandy, son. Don't worry about me."

Phyllis came into the living room at that point and said, "I thought I heard your voice out here. Come have lunch. I made grilled cheese sandwiches and tomato soup."

They all trooped into the kitchen and sat down to eat. Paul liked to dunk his grilled cheese into his soup, which always drove his father nuts.

"Why must you do that?" his dad asked him. "Put crackers in your soup like a normal human being."

"Why must you put ketchup on scrambled eggs?" asked Paul, which was something that drove him crazy.

"I like 'em that way."

"Well, I like to dunk my sandwich. Okay?"

John Paul just shook his head. They ate in silence for a minute, and then he asked, "Have you heard anything more about the case?"

"No, nothing," said Paul, as he reached for another sandwich. "Detective Remington isn't exactly sharing info with us, although I doubt there's much to share anyway. I talked to Billy Wilson for a few minutes after his mother's funeral yesterday. He said he didn't know anything new, although I guess he told them that if the Maki kid actually did have a clue, he must have taken it off the body in the woods."

"Really," said John Paul. He thought about that for a second, and then said, "Well, that makes sense. Pretty hard to figure how it could have come from the old lady."

"I don't see how it helps them much."

They finished eating, and the two men went back into the living room while Phyllis stayed in the kitchen to clean up.

"Tell me something, dad," said Paul, as they settled themselves onto the couch. "When I talked with Wilson, he said he had never talked to you. I know he stayed behind when you took the two other boys back to the scene, but how come you never talked to him after Vinnie died?"

"Well," said his dad, pausing and rubbing his chin as he tried to recall the past, "the Greenfield detectives were in charge of the case by then, of course, just like they are now. They never really asked for much help from us. I did go back out to the scene with the Chief after he returned from vacation. That was the day he found the bullet in the tree."

"Did the Chief ever talk to any of the boys?"

"Well now, let me think." Again his dad stared off into space. Finally, he said, "No, I don't think so. We did stop at the Maki's that day so he could express his condolences."

"It seems strange that nobody ever followed up with the kids. You know, see if they remembered something new they had forgotten to mention the first time, particularly after Vinnie died."

"Maybe the Greenfield detectives did. I don't know. And you have to remember, we all thought the Maki boy's death was an accident."

"You didn't think it was too much of a coincidence, his dying so soon afterwards?" asked Paul.

"Oh, I'm sure it crossed my mind, but there was no evidence of foul play. Kid was found floating in the water. No signs of a struggle that I could see."

"You were there? I don't remember that."

"Sure," said his father, "I was first on the scene again. You probably didn't know that because it's not in the report of the other murders. Separate case, or at least we thought it was back then."

"Hmm, that must be it," said Paul. "Still, I'm surprised you never mentioned it."

"Maybe I did," laughed John Paul, "and we both forgot. After all, you're no spring chicken anymore either. Say, where's that Wilson kid staying?"

"He's no kid anymore, dad," Paul said with a smile. "He's in his sixties. He's staying with Katie Maki out at her place."

"Ah. Well, you look tired. You should get some sleep."

"I'm gonna do just that," said Paul, and after he finished eating he headed off to bed.

John Paul waited twenty minutes to make sure his son was asleep, and then he headed for his car. He had decided to make his own visit to Billy Wilson.

Katie and Billy returned home after talking with Curtis. The rain had ended and the sun was trying to break through the clouds. They ate a light lunch, and when they finished Katie said, "Come with me. I want to show you my meditation garden."

"You have a meditation garden? How come I haven't seen it?"

Katie just said, "Follow me," and took his hand in hers.

They went out the front door, turned left, and walked about forty yards. Billy thought they were heading into another part of the forest, but just as he was about to ask, Katie swerved to her right and said, "Over here."

Billy turned, took three steps, and drew in a breath. "Oh my," he said. "It's gorgeous."

"Did it all myself," she said.

She had cleared out a small portion of the woods and built her own Japanese garden. It was blocked from the driveway by a line of trees and some dense foliage.

"You're kidding," he said. "What kind of tree is that?" he asked, pointing off to his left.

"That's a Japanese maple. I have a number of them here, plus some cherry, willow and evergreen trees. Let me show you around."

They walked a path that meandered through the garden. "You don't want to know how many bags of pea gravel I had to buy to make this path," she said.

They came upon a small pond, surrounded by native plants, and Billy was surprised to see fish swimming in it. Another area had a running fountain, and lanterns dotted the landscape as they walked.

"Solar powered," said Katie. "I'm a bit surprised you didn't notice them at night, but it is well hidden."

"I had no idea this was here," said Billy.

They came upon a wooden bench and sat down.

"Do you meditate?" she asked.

"Off and on. It used to be more on, now it's mostly off," he said.

"I've been doing it for about four years now," she said. "When the weather is nice I come out here; otherwise, I sit on the couch or on my bed. Of course, I've missed it these past few nights because we've been doing other things."

"We were, weren't we?" he said, and felt his face flush for just a moment.

They sat down and listened to the sounds of nature. Billy could understand why she liked living out here. It was calm and quiet, and he imagined that being away from the hustle and bustle of the city could make for a very relaxing life. Still, he enjoyed living in Sarasota.

As if reading his mind, Katie asked, "So, you missing home right now?"

"It's so different out here," he said. "I was wondering if I could stand it on a permanent basis."

"You used to live here, Billy. Was it so long ago that you've forgotten what it was like?"

He thought about her question, but didn't answer. He had enjoyed growing up here, but he was used to living in Sarasota now. He enjoyed the sunshine. Could he really come back to a place like Dearborn now, after all this time?

She didn't press him for an answer. She knew two things for certain; she had no intention of ever leaving this area, and she wanted him to stay. Whether he would or not was a decision he was going to have to make.

They were quiet for a while, simply enjoying nature, and then she said, "Tell me more about auras, Billy. What is it that you see?"

He was grateful for the change of subject.

"All bodies are energy," he began. "Energy flows both within and around your body. You've heard about the colors of the chakras?" he asked.

"Yes, I know about the chakras of the body. And I've read a little bit about auras too. But what do you *see*."

"I see colors flowing around your body. Sometimes it's a smooth, even flow, and sometimes it's a jagged, fractured flow. The colors all have meanings to me. Some shades indicate a happy, positive person, while other shades may show a more negative side. For instance, right now you have a lovely flowing green around you. That shows me you are in a loving mood and you enjoy being in this garden.

"On the other hand, another shade of green, jagged instead of smooth flowing, would indicate a person who was jealous or envious of another. That's where the phrase 'green with envy' comes from. Other phrases, such as 'seeing red' or 'feeling blue,' all indicate apt descriptions of a person's aura at that moment."

"And does black mean death?" Katie asked.

"Not always, although as a kid I thought it did for a long time."

"Because of your grandfather?"

"Yeah. As I recall, he was gray and black when I first saw him that night, but the black was growing by the time he left. When I heard the next day that he had died, I did associate black with death. But the truth is, black can also indicate hatred, malice, fear or depression, and gray associates with those also. Not everyone with a black aura dies, but I don't like seeing it in any event."

"So what did you see around Curtis that caused you not to show him the betting slip?"

"Well, to begin with, even though he was acting friendly to us, his aura showed a shade of spiking blue that I associate with arrogance, so that had me a bit on edge to begin with."

"I don't see him often," said Katie, "but I have had that impression of him before."

"Then when I mentioned the clue, his aura went haywire for a moment. A deep red shot out of him in all directions, not only an angry red but an anxious one. It's a color I associate with selfishness, and I've discovered over the years that it also corresponds with hatred and revenge. The clue really shook him up, and I didn't know why. That's why I kept quiet about where it was."

"Is Vinnie's clue still in your pocket?" she asked.

"It is. Why?"

"Because I think we should hide it for safe keeping, and I believe I have the perfect spot."

"Which is?"

"Give it to me," she said, and Billy complied. Katie took it and headed for the center of the garden. A statue of Buddha sat over the area, and by his side was a small pyramid shaped item that appeared to be made of copper, barely three inches tall. Katie picked it up, unhooked a clasp, and opened one side of the pyramid.

"You're supposed to write a wish on a piece of paper and put it in here," she said, "but for now I think it's a good hiding spot."

Billy watched as she deposited the paper inside, and then closed the hinge and put it back in place. He was about to say something to her when they heard a car coming up the driveway.

John Paul Stephens had just knocked on the front door when he noticed Katie and Billy coming out of the woods. "Hello there," he called out to them.

Katie had no idea who the man on her porch was. "Can I help you?" she asked.

He waited until they reached him, and then said, "I'm John Paul Stephens. I've come to talk to Billy Wilson." He looked at Billy and said, "I take it that's you."

"It is," said Billy. He recognized the name immediately, and then introduced Katie and told her who the man was.

"Ah, yes," said John Paul. "The past week must have been very shocking for both of you."

"You could say that," she said, and then she suggested they all go inside.

Billy and the retired cop sat in the living room, while Katie went to the kitchen and made a pitcher of iced tea for them.

"My condolences for your loss," John Paul said to Billy, as they waited for Katie's return, and Billy thanked him.

Katie came back with the drinks, passed them out, and then sat on the couch next to Billy.

"So what can we do for you?" asked Billy, who was surprised to see how spry the old man looked.

"Well, my son has been keeping me apprised of the case concerning your brother," said John Paul, looking at Katie. "As you may or may not know, I was the first cop on the scene the morning he was found."

"I didn't know that," she said, "but then again, I was only eight at the time, and of course I never spoke to the police, so there's no reason I would."

"You were first on the scene for the murders too," said Billy.

"I was. Not that it helped me much."

"Have you heard anything new about my brother's case?" asked Katie.

"No, nothing new. My son is a bit frustrated because the Greenfield detective working the case isn't keeping him very well informed."

"You say you came to see me," said Billy. "What is it that I can do for you?"

He looked Billy in the eyes, and he paused a moment before answering.

"That case has haunted me for years," he finally said. "We never came close to solving it. Almost no clues to speak of. Now," he turned to look at Katie, "we find your brother was murdered by the same people. We should have figured that out, I guess, but we never did."

Katie could see the pain in his face. "There was no reason for you to put the two together," she said, although in her mind she thought otherwise.

"No, we should have. I've never believed much in coincidence. I guess because the Greenfield cops had taken over the case, we just let it slide. I'm sorry for that now."

He paused again, his mind drifting to thoughts of long ago, and then he turned back to Billy. "My son tells me you believe this mysterious clue Membrino talked about was on the body in the woods."

"I do," said Billy. "I know Vinnie looked at Mrs. Potter's body, but I'm pretty sure he never touched it. As you may remember, he's the one who rolled over the body in the woods. My guess is he saw something that none of the rest of us did, and he put it in his pocket. Why he would do such a thing I have no idea."

They spoke for a few minutes more, but it was obvious Billy wasn't going to tell John Paul anything he didn't already know.

They could see the disappointment on his face. Katie looked at Billy and gave him a questioning look. He knew she was wondering if they should mention the betting slip to the retired cop, and he gave a slight shake of his head no.

John Paul may have been old and retired, but he'd seen that look more times than he could count, and he knew something had just passed between the two of them. *They're hiding something,* he thought. He asked a couple follow up questions but got nowhere, and a few minutes later he arose to leave.

"Did my son give you his card?" asked John Paul.

"He did," said Billy.

"May I see it?"

Billy fished it out of his wallet and handed it to the old man.

"I'm just going to write my number down on the back. If for some reason you can't get ahold of him, just call me. I can get him a message."

"Okay," said Billy, and a moment later they stood on the porch and watched as John Paul Stephens trudged back to his car and drove away.

After returning inside, Katie said, "Don't forget, we have that show at the church tonight with Simon Taylor and Thomas Mann."

"I'm looking forward to it," replied Billy. "I can't wait to see the look on Simon's face when he sees me again; if he remembers me, that is."

"How could anyone forget you?" Katie stroked his cheek with her hand as she smiled at him. "Do you think we should go see Walter beforehand and give him an update?"

"We could do that, although he did ask not to be involved. What time is the thing at the church?"

"Seven. We could stop by the Marriott around five or so. The church is close by, so it won't take us long to get there from the hotel."

"Sounds like a plan," said Billy.

They went back out onto the porch and relaxed on the swing. They were quiet at first, both enjoying the sight of hummingbirds at the feeders.

Katie broke the silence. "Billy, I'd like to ask you something."

He turned to face her, and was sure he knew where the conversation was going. *Would he still be going home in a few days? Would he stay with her a while longer, or maybe forever?*

"What's that?" he asked.

"What happened to you after ...," she paused, not really sure if she should continue.

"After what?" he asked.

"After Jenny died."

She saw his face crumble, a look of something like fear overcoming it, and was immediately sorry she had asked. She started to apologize, but before she could get a word out he held up his hand.

"It's a fair question," said Billy, an obvious shaking to his voice. "If there's a chance that you and I are going to move on together in life, than you should have all the facts about me."

"I don't mean to hurt you."

"I know," he said, "and I would never want to hurt you either. I've never really discussed it with anyone." He stared out over the tree line for a moment before saying, "Perhaps it will be cathartic."

He spoke for the next forty-five minutes.

Katie never interrupted him.

TWENTY TWO

BILLY'S STORY
PART FOUR

He was lost; oh, of that there was no doubt.

He lost his belief in God, yet cursed Him at the same time for haunting him with this gift of seeing auras. For a long time he lost the will to live, and suicide was a daily thought running through his brain.

His parents and Marylou helped get him through the first few days, but they had their own lives to live and had to move on.

He stayed in his house for a short time but knew he wouldn't last there for long. What had once been a home so full of life and the sounds of happy children was now empty. He put it on the market just six weeks after the tragedy and moved into a studio apartment on the outskirts of town.

He attempted to do his job at the bank, but in reality he was just going through the motions. He had trouble trying to concentrate for long periods of time, his mind wandering to dark corners where it shouldn't be going. His work slipped and his bosses were noticing.

Days went by where he couldn't tell you where he had been or what he had done. He knew the bank couldn't put up with him much longer. He had been a terrific employee, and they felt bad for him, but his work was slipping and mistakes were being made. They were relieved, yet saddened, on the day he gave his notice. He had four weeks of sick time built up, and his boss broke the rules and paid him for all of it.

Billy began to roam the country with no plan in mind and no end in sight. He could afford to do this because of the life insurance. He and Jenny had discussed insurance many times. They had whole life policies on all of them, which would provide enough money to cover funeral costs and pay off major debts. Billy thought that was enough, but on occasion Jenny would suggest they needed more. He kept fending her off, claiming they had enough bills and shouldn't be making any more.

He was unaware she had done anything on her own without telling him, but she had. They belonged to an auto club which had travel insurance coverage. Jenny had signed up for it. She always took care of the bills and never told him about the new insurance.

The policy had only been in effect for nine months, but unlike many insurance companies, they paid quickly and without question; three-hundred thousand dollars for Jenny, one-hundred thousand for each child. Along with their whole life policy, it came to just over five-hundred and forty thousand dollars. He would have gladly given it back to have his family together again, but he couldn't, and so he became a wanderer.

He moved from Pennsylvania to Maine, where he rented a cottage near the ocean. He'd lie in bed at night listening to the sound of the waves, and once tourist season was over he would meander along the beach during the day. He stayed just over a year, but when winter moved in again, he decided he'd had enough of cold weather and headed south. Two months in North Carolina, then three months in Georgia, and then a stop on the Gulf Coast in Sarasota, Florida.

He stayed in cheap hotels that charged by the week or month, and spent most of his time on the beach. Once Easter came and went, and the northern crowd had gone back home, he found a permanent spot near the water.

He occasionally had sex with strangers he met, but the AIDS crisis was in full bloom by then, and he turned down more opportunities than he accepted.

He stayed in Sarasota almost two years, but eventually the urge to move on hit him again, so he packed his few belongings and headed out. He went to Louisiana in 1991, where he found his first post-banking job as a blackjack dealer on a riverboat cruise line. It lasted three months, and turned out to be the longest he would stay at one job for the next four years.

He moved to Oklahoma, then Indiana, then Kansas, rarely staying in any one place for more than a few months. His parents and sister couldn't keep up with his movements, and for long periods of time they had no idea where he was.

He was drifting through life with no desire to do anything and no worries about what would become of him. He didn't care. Whether he lived or died mattered not the least bit to him. His main goal was to avoid looking at people. He didn't want to know if they were happy or sad, and he certainly didn't want to know if they were about to die.

In time, he finally grew tired of his constant moving and the avoidance of his fellow man. He knew his ability would never leave him. He had to decide to start living life again or just end it, and much to his surprise he suddenly realized that death didn't hold that much interest to him anymore.

He thought he would choose a small town with a small population, but shocked himself when he found just the opposite. He arrived in Denver one day in 1994, took a look around, and suddenly decided he was home.

He rented a small apartment over a garage in a cul-de-sac in the suburbs. He stayed away from downtown Denver whenever possible, however. There were too many people there, and the aura overload would damn near drive him crazy.

He found various jobs as a waiter and did tax returns for people he met, but mostly he kept to himself. He tried to pay attention to the people around him, and once in a while he would offer some friendly advice to an acquaintance whose aura showed a problem.

For exercise he would hike alone in the Rockies. The workout refreshed him, and the quiet and solitude calmed his inner demons.

In the summer of '95 he found his first full-time job in eight years. The local YMCA needed a bookkeeper, and Billy was finally tired of doing nothing. He had invested some of his insurance money in stocks, which he didn't want to touch, but his cash on hand was running low. They gave him a cubicle in a small office, and he only had to deal with half-a-dozen fellow employees. He would wander the building on his breaks, and enjoyed watching the kids playing basketball in the gym. On rare occasions he would even shoot some hoops with a few of them.

He stayed in Colorado just over six years, but in time the urge to move on returned again. The death of his beloved wife and beautiful children began to move to the back of his memory banks. Oh, Billy still thought about them every day, and the pain was still there, but life was about looking forward, not back, and he was accomplishing that a little more each day. However, the auras he saw continued to be a source of constant disruption in his life.

His car was packed with what little he owned, and he was just about to call the phone company to shut off his service, when his mother called to inform him of his father's death. He flew home for the funeral, his car and all his belongings waiting for him at the airport in Denver.

Marylou barely recognized him when she first saw him, and his mother spent most of the time haranguing him about how he needed to end his pity party and grow up. They would rarely speak again in the years that followed.

He flew back to Colorado, found his car in the long term parking lot, and headed out. He once again wanted to find someplace where the population was low, and since he missed living by the water as he had in Sarasota, he chose California.

He tried a variety of small towns on the ocean—Trinidad, Rockport, Bodega Bay—figuring fewer people meant fewer black auras. He still mainly walked with his head down, avoiding as many people as he could. Occasionally he would bump into poles or mailboxes, drawing strange looks from those around him.

He didn't care.

Oh, he was better by then, for sure. His family's shock at his appearance made him decide to take better care of himself. He paid more attention to his grooming and began to work out at local gyms. He even started to smile again, and when he gave a five or ten-dollar bill to a homeless man or woman on the street, he would feel a spark of satisfaction.

And then one day the flame was finally lit.

He was wandering the streets in Bodega Bay when he saw a sign in a storefront window. There was a psychic fair not far away that had just started a half hour before. He decided to go, having nothing better to do, and headed that way.

The fair was being held in the back room of a Knights of Columbus building. It was a small room, barely big enough to fit in a half dozen vendor tables, and with room for six readers sitting at card tables along the back wall.

He decided to have a reading just for the hell of it, and checked out the five women and one gentleman sitting behind the tables. He eliminated three of them immediately, judging by their auras that they had little or no psychic intuition and were just making shit up. The man, and a woman next to him, seemed genuine enough, but both were busy.

Then he saw the elderly lady in the corner, and he was struck by the golden glow around her. This was someone he knew he could trust, and as luck would have it her table was free.

Her name was Orlana, and she appeared to be in her eighties. Her hair was white, her face was more wrinkled than any face he had ever seen, and the veins on her hands stood out sharply.

She didn't smile at him as he approached; instead, she stared as though she were reading his aura. As he sat, she said, "You troubled man. Lots of unhappiness around you."

"Can you see my aura?" he asked.

"No need see aura," Orlana said, "written all over face."

She handed him a deck of cards, which seemed to be older than she was, and told him to shuffle them. After he did, she took them, placed them on the table, and told him to cut them into three piles. Then she picked them up and said, "Gonna tell you what you need to know."

Her hands shook every time she turned a card over, yet to Billy it seemed as though she wasn't even paying attention to the cards. She simply stared at him as she talked.

"You holding on to lots of pain; old pain, I think."

He nodded, and was shocked to find that tears were already building behind his eyes. *This lady can see my soul,* he thought, and suddenly he wasn't sure he would be able to withstand what Orlana was about to tell him.

"Your spirit is lost, and your search has not brought you any closer to it."

He just stared at her, unable to speak.

"We all have sadness, we all have crosses to bear, but you come to this life for a reason, and it's time you got around to doing it."

"What is my purpose for being here?" he asked, and he heard her make a grunt that almost sounded like laughter.

"You know purpose," said Orlana, and when he started to protest she held up a shaking finger to him. "You know purpose," she said again, "but you no want to know. It's time to let the pain of your past go. No can do nothing about that. Long gone. You still have many years to go, and it's time to get busy and start living again."

The reading was supposed to last for twenty minutes. Orlana went well over that time limit. She talked about his gift as though she knew what it was, and told him it was time to start using it for good. She said his father was there, and even brought forth his name. "Carl wants you to move on, live again. We all have sorrows. Get past them."

He started to protest, but she cut him off.

"You're angry with God, and hate your gift," she said.

He looked her in the eye and nodded as a tear finally ran down his cheek, and that was when he realized her eyes were dead. Orlana was blind.

"Now it's time to let go," she said. "They call it a gift for a reason. You could do so much good for people, but first you must forgive. Forgive God, forgive yourself, and forgive those who don't listen to your advice. We all have free will to make our own choices. When you leave here today, you will have free will to listen to what I say or call it rubbish. It's up to you."

"How can you see all this?" he asked.

Orlana finally let out a smile. "I have a gift too. No need for eyes anymore. I see well without them."

Billy stood, and felt compelled to give the woman a hug as she sat in her chair. He wanted to thank her, but no words would come.

"Time grows short," she whispered. "Don't waste it."

The reading blew his mind but also gave him hope, and it finally shook him out of his years-long doldrums.

In the years that followed he would go to a number of psychic mediums for messages. Some were very good, some were obvious fakes, but none of them would ever measure up to Orlana.

He began reading spiritual literature—Walsch, Dyer, the Dalai Lama—and started to believe his family was not dead, but simply on another plain of existence. He thought Jenny was his soul mate, and he would be with her again in another lifetime. Over time, he finally began to believe that Orlana was right. He could, and should, use his ability to help people.

He decided to move again, but this time he was looking for the one spot that called to him, and he knew where it was. He returned to Sarasota. Shortly after arriving, he secured a job as a counselor at a Boys and Girls Club, helping kids stay out of gangs and off drugs.

The black auras were still around; he saw them often. However, he understood the circle of life better now. If he passed someone on the street whose aura showed they had a short time left, he silently blessed them and wished them well on their journey to the other side. He developed a small circle of close friends, and while none of them knew of his gift, they all knew there was something different about him.

"If I tell you to change your plans," he would tell them, "listen, and do as I say, or have your will in order."

They would generally smile when he said this, and yet their own intuition would tell them to listen to him.

Occasionally, of course, it didn't matter. Someone who was going to die of a heart attack could die anywhere. On other occasions it saved lives, like the time he told a friend not to go on a fishing trip. None of those who went ever came back.

The one area he hadn't overcome, however, was in relationships. Quite frankly, he was afraid to get close to anyone for fear of losing them. He dated casually and had sex occasionally, but for the most part he remained closed off from any true connection with women. Yet he was getting older, and he didn't want to be alone for the rest of his life. He wanted that someone special in his life again. He was just having trouble taking that first step.

One thing he had studied and understood perfectly well was synchronicity; things happening at a particular time, in a particular order, to produce a particular result. It was not coincidence, which he didn't believe in at all. Billy was certain there was a plan for every person's life, which was determined before they were even born. Sometimes you veered off the path, and that's when your guides and angels quietly set things up to push you back on track.

Then one day, while roaming the aisles of a local bookstore, a paperback fell off the shelf right in front of him. He took it as a sign and picked it up. It was *Memories of You,* by Doctor Simon Taylor. He bought the book and read it in two nights. The author page in the back of the book said that the doctor lived in Sarasota. Billy decided to give him a visit.

Synchronicity at work.

TWENTY THREE

When he finished with his tale, Katie simply turned to him and hugged him. "Oh, Billy," was all she said.

"Now you know all my secrets," he said.

They spent the next ten minutes in complete silence, staring at the scenery and holding each other, and then they went inside and prepared for the night's events.

They arrived at the Marriott just after five to find the dining room half full.

"Convention just arrived this afternoon," said the hostess, as she showed them to a table away from the crowd.

"We'd like to speak with Walter when he has a moment," Katie told her. "Just tell him his best friends are here."

They ordered glasses of white wine from the waitress, and Walter appeared before the wine arrived.

"I've already placed your order," he told them. "You're both having the Chicken Picatta, and don't even think of objecting, because it's delicious."

Katie and Billy both laughed, and when the waitress returned, Billy said, "Apparently we've already placed our order." She looked confused, but Walter just shooed her away with a wave of his right hand, and she knew better than to argue.

"So what's up?" he asked, after the waitress was out of earshot.

"We went to see Curtis to tell him about Vinnie's clue. He's going to check with some friends on the police force to see how the investigation is going. We wanted to get his

237

thoughts about whether or not we should turn it over to the police."

"Couldn't keep it to yourself, eh?"

"It's my fault," said Katie, "I really think I owe it to Vinnie to find out what really happened to him."

"It's not your fault," said Billy. "We decided together."

"But ...," said Katie, then let it trail off.

"But what?" asked Walter.

"Something about Curtis wasn't right," said Billy. "The news seemed to shock him; made him angry and upset. He tried to hide it, but it was obvious to me. I was going to show him the slip, but decided not to when I saw his reaction."

"We've hidden it for now," said Katie. "Billy and I thought you should know."

"Quite frankly, I'm not sure what to do at this point," said Billy.

"Oh God, this whole thing just keeps getting more bazaar," said Walter. "I really think we should let sleeping dogs lie, don't you?"

"We're going to keep it to ourselves for now," said Katie, "and wait to hear back from Curtis."

"I think that's best," Walter replied.

They chatted for a few minutes more, and then Walter arose, saying, "I'd better get you that dinner you came for."

The meal was delicious, as they knew it would be. More conventioneers arrived, and Walter was too busy to return to their table, so at 6:45 they departed the hotel and headed for the Unitarian Church.

Neither one paid any attention to the lone man sitting at the table next to theirs. When they left, he picked up his cell phone and made a call. After a short conversation, he said, "I understand," and hung up.

Simon and Thomas arrived at the Unitarian Universalist Church at six-thirty and discovered that half of the seating capacity had already been taken.

Thomas looked at his friend and smiled. "Apparently having you here is a good thing. I normally only get about fifteen or twenty people at these events, and it looks like there's more than that here now."

They had already discussed how they would proceed. Simon would go first, and after a short talk about reincarnation, spiced up with some of the stories he had heard over the years, he would do a group regression. It would be much shorter than individual regressions he did in his office, of course. When it was over, he would ask if anyone would like to share what they received.

Thomas would go after that. He felt that people may have questions after going through their regression with Simon, and perhaps he could bring through messages from loved ones that could answer those questions.

The crowd continued to filter in, and one of the church members had to bring in more chairs from an adjoining room. Simon and Thomas waited in a side room until just before seven, and then entered the stage area where they would be performing.

Simon took his seat and gazed out over the audience. The crowd seemed to be about ninety percent women, which paralleled what he usually saw at the conventions. In a roomful of fifty people you could often count the men on one hand.

Stragglers were still coming in as the clock neared seven, and Simon suddenly noticed a couple enter and take seats in the back. The man appeared to look at him and nod as if in recognition. Simon smiled back and tried to think of who it might be, for the man did look familiar. Perhaps it was someone who had been at the Boston conference.

The pastor of the church, Rev. Martha Gallagher, entered the stage just after seven. She told Simon and Thomas that they had a full house and were closing the doors to anyone else, and then she introduced them to the audience. "I believe Dr. Taylor is up first this evening," she finally said. She turned to Simon and quietly whispered, "All yours."

Simon arose and addressed the audience. "Good evening. It's a pleasure to be here with you tonight. While I have performed thousands of regression sessions in my office and at various conferences around the country, this is my first time doing them in a setting such as this."

He talked for a few minutes about interesting cases he had come across over the years. When he mentioned Jill Palmer, he saw heads bob throughout the hall, and knew that many of them had read his book. He then told them his next book would be about past-life lovers he had brought together in this life, and he heard a variety of *Oohs and Aahs* go through the crowd.

He began the regression much the way he would in his office, with the toes to head relaxation technique followed by the walk down the circular stairs, and then he took them through the doorway to their past lives.

"Look at the way you are dressed," he said. "Try to determine the time period and the country you are in. Are you male or female? Are their family members present? Try to discover your name. Look closely at the people around you, and try to determine if they are people you know in your present life."

He gave them time to wander around in their past lives, though of course the time spent there was much shorter than it would have been in his office. He then brought them back to the present and asked if anyone would like to share what they discovered.

The tales they heard in the next few minutes were as different as night and day. People had returned to lives in China, Peru, Uganda and many more countries. Some people seemed to have gleaned a great deal in the short time they were regressed, while others were rather fuzzy about what they had seen.

The most compelling story came from a man in the second row. He had tears in his eyes as he recounted how he had lived in Kansas during the Civil War and fought against his brother, he for the North and his brother for the South.

"I knew the unit he was in, and he knew mine, and one day, wouldn't you know it, we were in the same battle, fighting on different sides. I guess I was killing his friends and he was killing mine. We finally fought them off and they retreated, and then we went out into the fields to see if we could help any of our wounded. That's when I saw him, lying in the mud face up. He had been shot in the gut and bled out. His eyes were open, and I leaned down and closed them. It was the saddest day of my life, for we had always been close until the war started."

The man received condolences from people seated next to him, as though his brother had just died yesterday, not 160 years or so ago.

"Did you recognize him as someone you know in this life?" asked Simon.

"I did," the man replied. "He was a dear uncle in this lifetime. We were again very close. I often said that I loved him like a brother. Sadly, he passed just a few months ago."

Billy and Katie were seated in the back row, having cut their entrance a bit close and making it inside just two minutes before the doors were closed.

"What did you receive?" Katie asked Billy.

"Not too much, I'm afraid," he replied. "I think I was in Africa, but I have no idea what country it was. It was very dry, and I was part of a small tribe of nomads who all looked like they were starving. How about you?"

"Well, I was a young girl in Mexico, somewhere around the turn of the century, I think, and if I'm not mistaken, you were my sister."

He gave her a strange look, as if to say she must be kidding. "No way," he said.

"It was funny. We were playing in a field outside of our home. I don't think we could have been more than four or five years old, and when I looked at my sister, I could swear it was you looking back at me."

"Well, it looks like your guy is about to take the stage," said Billy, "so we'll have to continue this later."

Thomas Mann arose from his chair as Simon sat down. He greeted the crowd, commented on how many had come, and said it must be because of Dr. Taylor, for he had never seen a crowd this large at the church before. He gave a quick explanation of how he worked for those who were there for the first time, and then he dived right it.

"I have a message from someone named Mia," he said, and a lady in the middle row began wildly waving her hand.

Thomas gave messages from the beyond for the next forty minutes, and Billy was beginning to think that neither he nor Katie would be receiving one.

Just then a troubled look came over Thomas Mann's face. "I have a very distraught young lady here on the other side," he said. He appeared to look toward the ceiling as he mumbled, "Tell me your name, sweetheart; tell me your name."

He took a quick glance at the audience and said, "I'm sorry. I'm having a hard time getting this one to calm down. It seems she is a bit young."

Again his head turned up, and he said, "Slow down so I can understand you." He paused a moment, and then continued. "That's better, much better. Okay, you're name is Ruth, and your daddy's in trouble."

Billy nearly shot out of his chair. "That's my daughter!" he cried.

Thomas looked at the man in the back row who seemed so certain he knew who was coming through. "You had a daughter named Ruth who has passed?" he asked.

"Yes," said Billy, a little too loudly.

"What is your name, sir?"

"Billy Wilson."

Simon stared at the man who had jumped out of his seat so fast. It was the same man he thought he had recognized earlier, and now the name seemed familiar also. Suddenly it came to him. This was the Billy Wilson whom he had seen at his office in Sarasota a few weeks ago. He was sure of it. *What the heck is he doing here?* wondered Simon.

Thomas seemed to be speaking with the spirit of Ruth while Simon was making the connection, and then Thomas turned his gaze back to Billy.

"Sir, I need to speak with you in private after we have finished here," he said.

Billy sat back down, shaking like a leaf, and turned to look at Katie.

She could tell he was stunned, and she thought she might look the same. "What did she mean, you're in danger?" she asked, even though she knew Billy didn't have the answer.

"I'm guessing all this stuff with your brother is about to hit the fan," he said.

The evening's events ended minutes later, although it was twenty minutes before the crowd filtered out, as many people came up to Simon and Thomas, thanking them or asking questions.

Billy and Katie waited, not so patiently, for everyone to leave, and then they approached the duo.

243

"I know that man," Simon said to Thomas. "He was at my office in Sarasota just a short while ago for a regression."

"In Sarasota?" said Thomas. "So what is he doing here?"

"My question exactly," replied Simon.

When the couple arrived at the stage, Simon repeated what Thomas had just asked him. "Billy Wilson, what are you doing in Massachusetts?"

"Hi, Doctor Taylor. Long time, no see, eh?" Billy introduced Katie to the two men, and then Thomas suggested they move to a side room that was just down a short hallway.

They entered the room, which had a small table and four folding chairs. The room was filled with books and served as the church's library.

When they were all seated, Billy explained. "I'm here because my mother just passed away. Her funeral was yesterday. I grew up next door to Katie. When we were kids, her brother and I and two other friends found a body in the woods, and then a second one in a house. Three days later Katie's brother died from what we thought was a drowning, but recently a man on his death bed confessed to killing him."

"Oh my," said Simon, "I believe I read about that on the plane coming up here."

"Yeah," Thomas nodded, "it's been a pretty big story up here the last week or so. Elizabeth called me just after I arrived in Boston to tell me about it."

"Anyway, some strange things have been going on ever since I arrived here, and when you said we may be in danger, well," said Billy, pausing just a moment, "I think you might be right."

"Ruth was your daughter?" asked Thomas, to confirm what he'd earlier been told.

"Yes," said Billy. "My wife, son, and daughter Ruth were killed in a car accident many, many years ago."

"I'm sorry to hear that," said Thomas, "but I can tell you she was definitely here tonight, and she was very worried for your safety."

"Is she still here?" Katie asked before Billy could.

"No, she left quickly," said Thomas, "but I do have a message for you from her."

Billy and Katie glanced at each other, and she reached out for his hand.

"Go ahead," said Billy.

"She said you were both in grave danger, and that it was very, and I mean very, close at hand. She was nearly frantic as she said this. As you saw, I had a hard time getting her to calm down. She was talking so fast I couldn't understand her at first."

"We noticed," said Katie.

"She said that events were now moving quickly and that you needed to be on your guard at all times. Then she mentioned a book you once read. I'm not quite sure what it means, but I believe she said your death day is near, but it's not your last one."

They were all surprised to see Billy actually smile.

"Ah," he said, "I guess my little Ruthie has been watching me for some time."

"Would you like to explain that to us?" asked Simon.

"I read the book many years ago. I can't even tell you the title, it's been that long. In it, the author spoke of an Indian tribe that believed we choose a set of death days before we are born. One would be shortly after birth, in case you realize you've made a mistake in returning. The others would be spread out over time. Basically a death day is a chance to exit when you've had enough. If you've ever been in an accident, or near accident, and realized that one small change may have resulted in your death, then that may have been a death day that you decided not to use."

"I've never heard of that," said Simon.

"Neither have I," said Thomas, "but apparently your daughter believes you have a death day at hand, although it's not your last one. I suggest you proceed very carefully."

"We will," said Katie, "believe me, we will."

The group chatted for just a short while longer, and it was nearly nine-thirty when Billy and Katie prepared to leave.

Suddenly Thomas spoke up. "I have an idea," he said. "Why don't the two of you stay with us tonight? Simon is visiting me, and I have another bedroom that you could use."

"There's no need for that, I don't think," said Billy.

"Well, I'm sure you would be safe there, and I'd love to hear this story of yours."

"Me too," Simon chimed in.

"We couldn't impose," said Billy.

"I think it would make Ruthie happy," said Thomas, and a moment later Billy and Katie agreed to spend the night at the Mann residence.

It probably saved their lives.

TWENTY FOUR

Walter left the Marriott just after nine that night and pulled into his driveway ten minutes later. He was tired, and felt like he had just worked a sixteen hour shift, instead of just eight.

He had been debating lately how much longer he wanted to work before retiring. He had plenty of money and certainly didn't need the job, but he had always enjoyed cooking and running a large kitchen. On the other hand, he wanted to travel while he still could. He had visited Italy once many years ago and had always looked forward to returning. Perhaps it was time.

He ambled up onto his porch and noticed the light wasn't on. *Must have burnt out,* he thought, and made a mental note to replace it in the morning.

He entered his home, hung his jacket on the coat rack in the hall, and headed straight for the kitchen. He grabbed a bottle of Beck's from the frig, thinking a beer would taste good about now, and then he headed back to his living room.

The voice that came out of the darkness startled him and stopped him short.

"Hello, Walter."

He nearly jumped out of his skin. He turned, and saw a shadow of someone sitting on his couch. "Who are you?" he managed to say, "and what are you doing in my home?"

The intruder switched on the light that sat on the end table, revealing the gun in his hand. "Come sit over there, if you would," he said, pointing to the chair opposite him.

Walter froze where he was, staring at the silencer on the end of the pistol.

"Please," said the man, "or I'll shoot you where you stand."

Walter walked to the chair and sat down. "If this is about Vinnie," he finally managed to say, "I haven't told the cops anything."

The man smiled at him, but it wasn't a smile that gave Walter confidence.

"I believe you," said the intruder. "However, I am interested in what your friends have told you. You know, the ones who came to see you tonight."

"How …," he started to say, and then realized he knew. "Have you been following us?"

"My associates and I have been keeping close tabs on you and your friends."

"But why?' asked Walter. "Why are you so interested in something that happened so long ago? Who cares anymore?"

"Oh, my associates still care a great deal," said the man. He laid the gun on his lap, thinking there was no way such an overweight slob could suddenly attack him. "Please tell me everything you and your friends discussed tonight."

"It was nothing important," said Walter, his voice shaking, his attention focused on the gun. "We're pretty certain everything is going to blow over in no time."

"I was sitting nearby," said the man, and he noticed Walter's surprise. "I heard things. Now tell me exactly what was said, and don't waste my time."

Fear coursing through him, Walter tried to recall exactly what he had discussed with Billy and Katie. He quickly realized that any mention of the betting slip would put them in grave danger, if they weren't already. He tried to sum up their conversation without mentioning it, but when he finished he knew instantly his attempt was futile.

"You seem to have forgotten something," said the man. "You discussed a certain clue, did you not? " The man noticed

Walter's face drop and his shoulders slump, like someone who realizes he has been defeated. "Now, where is that clue?"

"I don't know," said Walter, sweat now pouring off his brow. He wanted to protect his friends, but he saw the man pick the gun up again and point it right between his eyes.

Walter's courage broke. "It's hidden somewhere in her house. I swear I don't know where. Please don't shoot."

A big grin broke out over the man's face. "Ah, now that wasn't so hard, was it?" he said.

He picked up his cell phone and made a call, telling his associates what Walter had just told him, and then he arose and started walking towards Walter. "Come into the kitchen with me. I have a drink all ready for you?"

"A drink?" said Walter, thoroughly confused. He struggled to get out of the chair, and then led the way into the kitchen, the gun poking into his back. The intruder made him sit down at the kitchen table, where a tall glass filled with brown liquid sat before him.

"I knew you would want a beer when you came home," said the man, "and I see I was right." He pointed to the bottle of Beck's still in Walter's hand. "You can put that one down, however, because I have a better one for you."

He paused, smiling again at Walter as he held the gun on him. Walter had not noticed the glass on the table earlier. "Of course, you might not like this one so much. I added a little something. People will probably think you had a heart attack."

"What?" was all Walter managed to say, the color draining from his face.

"Your choice," said the man, suddenly all serious again. "A beer, or a bullet in the head. Decide now, or your face won't look so pretty in a minute. "

With that he raised the gun to Walter's forehead.

Walter chose the beer.

TWENTY FIVE

Billy and Katie spent a quiet Friday morning at the Mann's before heading home. They enjoyed coffee and warm cinnamon buns for breakfast, and they delighted in the company of Thomas and Elizabeth Mann, and Simon Taylor.

They had all stayed up till just after one in the morning. First Billy told them the story of the fifty year old murders and the death of Katie's brother, and then he spoke of the recent goings-on.

Thomas told them once again how worried Ruth had been, and that they needed to be extremely alert in the days ahead.

It was just after ten when they left the Mann's residence. "You two be careful," Thomas said to them as they were about to leave. "I mean it."

"Do you have any more messages for us?" asked Katie.

"No," he replied, "just a feeling in my gut."

Katie suggested they stop in at Shelburne Falls on the way home. Billy thought she might be putting off going home, and he couldn't say he blamed her.

The town was fairly quiet, it being a little too early in the year for the tourists. They leisurely strolled the streets and window shopped, and Katie purchased a lovely orange and green vase from the glass blower's store.

It was two o'clock by the time they arrived home, and they both saw a police car in the driveway. Billy pulled up behind it and said, "This can't be good."

The driver's door opened and they both saw Officer Paul Stephens get out.

Paul waited for them to exit their vehicle before approaching.

"Officer Stephens," said Billy, "what brings you here?"

"Bad news brought me here, and I'm afraid more bad news awaits you inside."

"What?" said Katie. "What do you mean?"

"Follow me," said Paul. "When I arrived I went to knock on your door. I noticed it was ajar, so I took a look inside. I'm afraid you've been ransacked."

"Oh my God!" cried Katie.

"I searched the house. Whoever did this was probably long gone. I was just about to call it in when I heard you coming," said the officer.

They entered the home to find chaos. Tables were overturned, papers were scattered all over, and drawers had been removed, emptied, and tossed on the floor. Katie went to check out the kitchen as Billy gazed at the mess in the living room.

"The upstairs is even worse," said Paul. "Drawers and paperwork everywhere, and I'm afraid they've destroyed a great deal of her camera equipment."

Katie came back from the kitchen and went straight into Billy's arms.

"You want to tell me what they were looking for?" asked Paul.

They stared at each other, and Billy could feel Katie shaking. She gave him a small nod, and said, "I think it's time."

"Okay," said Billy, and he turned towards Paul. "Let's sit down."

They cleared away some debris, and then Katie and Billy sat on the couch while Paul took the opposite chair. When they were all settled, Paul said, "First off, I'm afraid I have even worse news."

"Worse than this?" said Katie.

"I'm afraid so."

They both looked at the officer anxiously, wondering what else could be wrong.

"Walter Logan has had an apparent heart attack. He's hanging on by a thread."

Katie turned and clutched Billy, a look of stunned disbelief on her face, while Billy stared at the officer as if he hadn't heard him right. "But we just saw him last night," he managed to say.

That got the officer's attention, but he set it aside for a moment. "He didn't show up for work today, and wasn't answering his phone when they called, so the hotel sent an employee over to check on him. His doors were locked, but she looked through his kitchen window and saw him lying face down on the floor."

Katie was sobbing, her face buried in Billy's shirt.

"I can't believe it," said Billy.

"To be honest, I don't either," said Paul. "The timing is just too remarkable."

Katie sat up at that, staring at the officer, and Billy said, "What do you mean? You don't think it was a heart attack?"

"It's a little too convenient for me." He looked at Katie and continued. "The news about your brother comes out, and a few days later all this happens. Sort of sounds like what happened fifty years ago, doesn't it?"

"You think we're in danger too, don't you?" asked Katie.

"I do," said the officer, "and after seeing your home I think it's rather obvious, although I have no idea why. Hopefully you can tell me that now."

Billy thought for a moment, and then nodded his agreement. He turned to Paul and said, "There's been a new development."

They told Paul Stephens everything.

252

"It started last week," said Katie, "when Walter found a note on his car windshield. It told him not to tell the police anything."

"I have a copy upstairs," said Billy, and he started to get up, but Paul held up his hand.

"Later," said the officer. "It's a disaster up there, and if they found it, they probably took it."

"Walter called me and told me about it," continued Katie, "and then Billy arrived for his mother's funeral. The same note was put on his windshield while he was visiting his old home."

"Tell me about that," said Paul to Billy.

"I went to visit the old neighborhood to see what it was like now. I stopped in front of the house I grew up in, and the man who lives there now saw me and invited me in. I was there for about an hour, and I recounted the tale of the murders to him and his wife. When I came out, I found the note on my windshield. It was exactly like the one Walter received. They were both photocopies of the original."

"So you were being followed," stated Paul.

"I guess so."

"And we can assume you're still being followed."

Billy turned to Katie and saw the worried look on her face. He imagined his face looked the same. "We didn't understand it," he said. "We couldn't figure out why anyone would care after all these years. We thought it would all blow over, so we decided not to go to the police about it."

"And then what happened?" asked Paul.

"And then we found Vinnie's mysterious clue," said Katie.

"What!" said Paul, nearly jumping out of his chair. "You're telling me that after fifty years this clue suddenly turns up. Please tell me you haven't been hiding it all this time."

"No," said Katie, "at least not knowingly. It turns out I did have it all along, but I never knew it."

She explained it all to him; the scrapbook, the betting slip, what was on it, and how Billy confirmed the slip was from 1966.

"And you didn't tell anyone about that either, I suppose?" asked Paul.

"We decided to take it to a lawyer and get his opinion on what to do," said Billy. "We went to Curtis Armstrong. He was a friend of mine as a kid. In fact, after Vinnie died, Curtis replaced him in our little group."

"I know Armstrong," said Paul. "Bit of a weasel if you ask me. So what did he say?"

"He said he'd check out how the investigation was going, see if they were making any headway, and get back to us. He said he'd call back this afternoon, but I haven't heard from him yet."

"And did you give him this clue?" asked Paul.

"No," said Billy. He looked at Katie, and then back at the officer. "We hid it."

"Hid it? I hope to hell you didn't hide it here."

"No," said Billy. "If you'll follow me, we can go retrieve it now."

Paul looked a bit confused as Billy and Katie stood up and headed outdoors. They led the way to the Japanese garden, and Paul realized how well hidden it was.

"I never would have known this was here," he said.

"I didn't know it was here until Katie showed me," said Billy.

Katie walked to the center of the garden, and then she leaned over and picked up the small copper piece in the shape of a pyramid. "During certain ceremonies," she said, looking at the officer, "you put your wishes in here and lift them up to the gods."

She opened one side of the metal pyramid and reached in. The betting slip was still there. She took it out and handed it to Paul.

He gazed at it for a moment, then motioned to the nearest bench and said, "Sit down there, if you would. I have a few more questions."

Billy and Katie did as instructed.

"Okay," said Paul, "you say you saw Walter last night; tell me about that."

"He was working at the Marriott," said Billy, "so we went there for supper, and he came out to talk to us. I had already told him over the phone about the betting slip, so I just updated him on our visit to Curtis, and then he went back to work."

"And had a heart attack a few hours later," Paul said. "Way too coincidental for me, and if you were being followed, I'm sure he was too."

He thought for a moment, and then continued. "So fifty years ago, you kids find a body in the woods that's been shot in the head, then you find Mrs. Potter dead in her home, also shot. Somewhere in that time Vinnie comes upon this paper, which no one else saw, pockets it, and decides to do his own investigation."

Billy and Katie followed along, neither speaking.

"He goes out a few nights later and ends up in Brooks Lake, because according to Richie Membrino something on this paper lead him right to the person who was involved in the murders; which probably means if he'd just given the paper to the police, they could have solved the case in no time."

He looked at Katie and said, "Man, my dad's gonna be pissed about that."

"As he should be," she said, wondering what the hell her brother was thinking about so long ago.

"So now it's fifty years later and this Membrino character confesses to drowning your brother. At the same time, your mother passes away," he said, turning his attention to Billy, "which has nothing to do with the case, but unfortunately brings you back to the area. You and Walter receive these notes about not going to the police, and it apparently scared you enough to not tell the police about them."

"I guess it scared us a little," said Billy, "but for the most part we just didn't understand why anyone would care after so many years, and we had nothing new to tell the police anyway."

"But you knew you were being followed, and you should have assumed they were going to continue to keep tabs on you as long as you were home."

"I never noticed anyone," said Billy.

"So last night you went to see Walter, and he came out and talked with you at the table."

"Yes," mumbled Katie, still stunned by the news about her friend.

"They must have followed you there," said Paul, "and seen the three of you talking. For all we know they heard you, and when you talked about finding the clue they got nervous."

"It was a busy night." said Billy. "There was a convention that had just arrived, but we were seated away from them, almost by ourselves."

"Almost?" said Paul.

"There were a couple tables close to us that had people sitting in them, but I didn't pay any attention to them. Do you remember anything, Katie?"

He watched her face turn to a look of shock. "There was a man who came in right after us. He was sitting right behind you, Billy. All by himself."

"Probably heard everything," said Paul, "then waited for Walter to get off work and followed him home. Or already knew where he lived and was waiting to greet him."

"Poor Walter," said Katie, and the tears began running down her cheeks again.

Paul gazed at the sky, thinking for a moment. "We have to assume," he finally said, "that Walter told him about this clue, and that's what they were looking for when they ransacked your place. You're lucky you weren't home. Where were you, by the way?"

They explained that they had stayed at a friend's house without going into detail, and then the trio headed back to the house.

Paul called the Greenfield police station on his cell phone and asked to speak with Sylvia Remington. It took them a minute to track her down, but she finally came on the line.

"Detective Remington," she said.

"Detective, it's Paul Stephens from Edgeworth. I'm at the home of Katie Maki. The place was broken into and ransacked. We need a forensic team over here right now. And ...," he said, pausing for a moment as he took a deep breath, "you'd better get over here too. We have a break in your cold case."

"What sort of break?" she asked.

Paul could hear a hint of excitement in her voice, and paused again for a moment before saying, "Vinnie Maki's famous clue just turned up."

TWENTY SIX

Sylvia Remington made it to the Maki residence in record time, siren blaring and lights flashing. She had just finished a call with the Northampton police, getting an update on Walter Logan, when Officer Stephen's call came in.

The attack on Walter Logan had caught her off guard. Her investigation into the cold case of Jack Luongo and Greta Potter had been proceeding slowly. She thought she had made some headway into discovering who the associates of Richie Membrino were, but there had been no reason for her to believe that anything more connected to that case would appear now, fifty years later.

However, when she first heard that Walter Logan had suffered a heart attack, she immediately thought that was suspicious. Much like Paul Stephens, Sylvia didn't put much stock in coincidence.

The local Northampton police had no reason to suspect that it was anything but a heart attack, so they were surprised first when Detective Remington called, and secondly when she insisted they do a thorough search looking for signs of foul play.

Sylvia arrived at the Maki residence ten minutes before the forensic team and found a local cop sitting with Katie and Billy.

Paul introduced himself. While he had talked with the detective over the phone, it was the first time he had met her in person.

"Stephens," she said. "You're the one who talked to Membrino."

"That would be me," Paul replied.

"So tell me what happened here," said Sylvia.

"The home was broken into sometime between last night and early this afternoon," said Paul.

"We didn't come home last night," added Katie. "We stayed at a friend's house."

"What did they take?" asked the detective.

"No way to tell just yet," said Katie. "The house is a complete mess."

"So what were they looking for then?" said Sylvia.

"This," said Paul, and he held up a kitchen baggie holding the betting slip.

Sylvia Remington looked at the bag as a slight frown appeared on her forehead. "What's that?" she finally asked.

"Apparently it is the famous missing clue of Vincent Maki," said Paul, and he watched as Sylvia's chin dropped down an inch and her mouth formed a small O.

"My brother had this in a scrapbook," said Katie. "I never knew what it was, and I had no idea it had anything to do with those murders. Billy here figured it out once he saw it."

"Trouble is," said Paul, "they discovered it a few days ago, but didn't tell us. They were in Northampton yesterday to see Walter and talk it over with him. I figure someone was listening in, and that's why Walter Logan was attacked."

Sylvia just stared at Billy and Katie, her eyes looking as if they were about to explode. You didn't need to be an aura reader to know how angry she was.

"My guess is that these two may well have suffered the same fate had they come home last night," continued Paul.

"I think we should sit down somewhere," said Sylvia, "so I can hear the whole story."

The forensic team arrived at that point and was about to enter the house, so Katie suggested they go sit in the Japanese garden.

"What a lovely place!" exclaimed Sylvia after they entered. "You must do meditation here."

"I do," said Katie.

"A wonderful exercise," said Sylvia. "I do it every day. Helps keep me focused and even keeled. I need that on this job."

Billy was surprised. He didn't think a woman like Sylvia Remington would have anything to do with meditation. However, the smooth flowing aura of green and blue that surrounded her showed that she did indeed love the garden.

Unfortunately, her mood changed once Billy and Katie relayed their account of the past few days, starting with the notes on the windshields, and then the discovery of the clue, none of which had been told to the police.

"Unbelievable," she said, shaking her head. "And it may cost Walter Logan his life."

"We just didn't think it would matter after all these years," said Billy, for what seemed like the thousandth time.

"Hmm," said Sylvia, and she gazed at the sky for a moment, lost in thought. She finally came back to the present and looked at the two of them. "You two are obviously in danger. I'm going to assign a police officer to stay with you around the clock. If you don't want to stay here, we can put you up someplace."

Billy looked at Katie. "What do you think?" he asked.

"Will we be okay if we stay here?" she wondered.

"Like I said," the detective replied, "I'll post an officer with you. You should be fine."

"Okay," said Katie, "then I guess I'd like to stay. I have a house to put back together."

Two hours later, the forensic team and Detective Remington left. Officer Philip Rivers of the Greenfield Police Department was assigned the first shift of guarding Billy and Katie.

"I'll be right outside," he told them after everyone had left, and Katie thanked him.

She and Billy then began the long task of picking up the house. They started upstairs. One of the first items Katie found was Vinnie's scrapbook. It had been tossed aside rather harshly by the look of it. The cover had a dent in it, and one of the pages was bent in half.

"They probably were excited when they found it, since it had his name on the inside cover," said Billy. "Then once they found nothing of interest, they just threw it aside."

They cleaned her bedroom first, and other than a broken picture frame and glass nothing was too amiss.

The room Billy was staying in was just the opposite. All of the boxes Katie had stored in there had been opened, their contents strewn around the room ankle deep in spots, and the empty boxes had been thrown upon the bed. Billy and Katie simply filled the boxes back up, no rhyme or reason to how they did it for the moment, and then they moved on.

The last room was the worst for Katie. Her photography studio had been completely destroyed. Cameras were smashed on the floor, light stands tipped over and the bulbs broken, photo albums torn apart.

"Oh my God!" she cried out upon entering, and then she burst into tears.

"There was no need for them to do this," said Billy. He hugged her and tried to comfort her as best he could, but he knew the damaged camera equipment was worth thousands of dollars and would be hard for her to replace.

"They've ruined me," she finally said.

He saw her shoulders sag in defeat, and for the moment Billy couldn't think of anything to say.

They picked up the room slowly. Katie stopped often to leaf through an album looking for damage, often pointing out pictures to Billy and describing the occasion to him. As they finished cleaning the room, she asked, "Why would they destroy everything like this? What was the point?"

Billy thought for a moment, and then said, "This was most likely the last room they looked in. They hadn't found anything up to this point, and they were angry. They took it out on your photography stuff, unfortunately."

She sighed deeply, then looked at him and said, "Let's go downstairs."

They checked on Officer Rivers, and Katie brought him some iced tea.

"Thank you, ma'am," he said.

"Would you like to come inside?" she asked.

"No," he said, "I think I'll stay out here. I'll circle the house every once in a while, but I imagine if anyone approaches it will be from the road. Best if I'm outside."

She thanked him, and told him to come inside if he needed anything.

Officer Rivers just smiled and said, "Will do," and then he turned and headed for the side of the house to make his rounds.

The downstairs area was much easier to put back together, there being little paperwork of any kind, and the kitchen left pretty much unscathed. When they finally finished, they sat down and ate some chicken salad that was in the fridge, but neither of them had much of an appetite. Billy ate just a few bites, and Katie mostly drew designs in her food with her fork.

They decided to simply have a glass of wine, and Billy had just finished pouring two glasses when the phone rang.

Katie answered, and a moment later mouthed to Billy, "It's Curtis."

He tried to get the gist of the conversation, and understood that Curtis had heard about Walter and was offering his condolences. It appeared Curtis thought Walter had died, and Katie was telling him that wasn't the case, at least not yet. Katie told him about the break-in, and then Billy heard her say, "new information?" and "sure, come on over."

After she hung up, Billy asked, "Is he coming over now?"

"Yes. He says he'll be here in half an hour."

Billy took a glance at the wall clock and noticed it was almost eight.

"He said he found something out about Richie Membrino and who his associates were, and he wants to tell us about it in person."

"Maybe he should just go to the police."

Katie frowned and said, "I didn't think of that. Perhaps I should call him back."

She was surprised when she redialed his number only to receive no answer.

Billy took out his wallet, removed the business card of Officer Stephens in case he needed it, and laid it on the kitchen counter next to his car keys. Then he and Katie took their wine outside and told Officer Rivers that Curtis was on his way.

"Sure, I know Armstrong," said the cop. "No problem."

They sat in the swing for a while, and Katie wondered how she would ever replace the damaged photo equipment.

"I'll help you," said Billy.

She looked at him and smiled, the first smile he had seen from her in awhile.

"That's sweet of you, Billy," she said, "but I'm talking a great deal of money here. Besides, it's not your problem, it's mine."

"But I want to help," he said.

"We'll talk about it when all this has died down ... if you're still here."

If I'm still here, Billy thought. The big question. What was he going to do when all this was over? Go home to Sarasota, or stay here with this beautiful lady he was falling in love with?

She saw the sudden serious look on his face, and said, "Don't worry, I'm not pressuring you." Then she gave him a quick kiss and said, "All in good time."

He drew back from the kiss and was about to reply when he was suddenly startled to see her aura changing rapidly.

She noticed the look on his face and immediately said, "What's wrong?"

"Your aura. It's getting darker, greyer. Something's not right."

Just then Officer Rivers came around the corner after making another round of the house, and Billy saw his aura had turned much darker than it had been. He was about to speak to the cop when they suddenly heard the sound of a vehicle approaching, and all three heads turned at once.

"Something's wrong," said Billy to Officer Rivers.

The cop looked at him in surprise. "It's probably just Curtis Armstrong," he said. "You told me he was on his way."

"I know," said Billy, "but something is very wrong."

He turned to Katie and said, "Let's get in the house," and then he turned back to the cop and said, "Be very careful out here. Something is definitely not right."

Billy and Katie quickly moved back indoors.

Philip Rivers watched as they went, puzzled as to what had gotten into Billy all of a sudden, and then he turned his attention back to the approaching car. He had been a cop for twelve years and had learned to trust his instincts, and for whatever reason he thought that Billy Wilson might be on to something.

However, when the car pulled into the driveway and Curtis Armstrong exited the vehicle, Philip Rivers relaxed a bit. He didn't know Armstrong well, but he had seen him in court on numerous occasions and recognized him immediately.

Billy watched the lawyer approach from the living room window and saw his aura spiking wildly. *What the hell is going on,* he wondered, and then something clicked in the back of his mind. He remembered being in the lawyer's office and seeing the picture of Curtis's dad in the basketball uniform. It was red, with yellow stripes and a white number twenty-one. And his dad's name was Donald Armstrong;

DA21

The code on the betting slip.

He returned his gaze to the window just in time to see Curtis pull a revolver from behind his back, and then he turned around and yelled "RUN!" to Katie as the explosion of the weapon resounded through the air.

TWENTY SEVEN

Katie dropped the wine bottle she had just picked up and looked at Billy in shock.

He was running towards her and pointing to the back door. "GET OUT," he yelled, "AND RUN."

She reacted immediately this time, throwing the door open and racing down the steps towards the woods.

Billy followed hot on her heels, grabbing the business card from the kitchen table as he passed, not even breaking stride. He took a quick glance back, and was surprised and happy to see that Curtis was just entering the house. He took his cell phone out of his pocket as he ran and called the number on the card. When the voice on the other end answered, Billy simply yelled, "Help! Katie Maki's place! Curtis Armstrong is trying to kill us!"

He didn't wait for a reply, because when he finished yelling he heard the screen door on the back porch slam shut and knew that Curtis was coming.

They had already received their first piece of good fortune, although they didn't know it. Curtis had not heard Billy yell run the first time, because it coincided with the gunshot fired at Officer Rivers. Curtis had then bent down to check on the man, realized the shot had been fatal, and mumbled, "Sorry, Philip, but I never liked you that much anyways."

When he heard Billy yell run the second time, he simply smiled and arose slowly. It confirmed to him his prey was inside, and Curtis was sure there would be no escape for them.

He entered slowly, not wanting to take the chance that they might also be armed, and so he missed seeing them scoot out the back. However, as he was about to search the house, he saw them through one of the kitchen windows. They were heading for the woods.

Curtis made his way to the back door and stepped outside. They were at least fifty yards ahead of him and about to enter the denser part of the forest. He stood on the porch and took aim, then fired off two quick shots at the fleeing Billy Wilson.

Billy heard the bullets zip by him, one slamming into the trunk of a tree and the other one snapping off a branch. Katie was ten yards ahead of him, and Billy wished he was in as good a shape as she was.

That's when he noticed she was barefoot. Katie had taken off her sneakers when they sat on the swing. Now she was running through the woods in bare feet, and she wasn't even breaking stride. Billy was amazed.

Curtis began following them, but he wasn't gaining on them. The lawyer had put on weight over the years, and his shoes were not meant for running in the woods. They kept slipping on fallen pine needles, and once he nearly went down. He knew he couldn't keep up with them, but he thought he had them trapped, and it would just be a matter of time.

Katie reached the fork in the path first and headed right. By now, Billy was right behind her, and he quickly noticed her aura turning darker still.

"Stop," he cried out suddenly.

"We can't stop!" yelled Katie.

"The other way," said Billy. "Your aura."

He didn't have to explain, thank God. She immediately turned around and headed back to the fork, now taking the other path. They could hear Curtis in the distance, although at the moment they couldn't see him.

Billy glanced at Katie's aura again. It was still a dark grey turning towards black, but at least it was lighter than it had been a minute ago. Perhaps they had a chance to survive in this direction.

The inevitable finally happened when Katie stepped on a sharp rock and screamed out in pain. Billy quickly put his arm around her, and together they continued on as best they could, but Katie was noticeably limping, and they both knew Curtis would now be gaining on them.

"There's a dense thicket of bushes up ahead," she said to him. "We should try to hide there. Otherwise he's just going to catch us once the trail ends."

He saw the area she was talking about and remembered it from the other day. It was about twenty yards short of the bench she had made. They pushed through the overgrown brush and fell to the earth. Curtis came around the bend less than two minutes later.

Katie tried to be quiet, but she was breathing hard and her foot was killing her. She also heard Billy's labored breathing and thought it was even louder than hers. They both held their breath as Curtis neared their hiding place.

Somehow the lawyer ran by them at first, but he didn't go far before stopping. The noise they had been making as they ran through the woods had stopped. He listened closely, but couldn't hear anything that resembled running, and he determined they had gone into hiding somewhere nearby. He turned and started to backtrack.

"Don't move," Billy whispered to Katie, knowing how silly it had been to say as soon as it was out of his mouth. They heard Curtis's approaching footsteps, and both of them wished they could have burrowed underground. Billy shut off his cell phone as quietly as he could so no sudden ringing would give them away, and then he laid it on the ground.

"I know you're here somewhere," Curtis finally said. "How about you just come out so we can have a nice talk."

He slowly surveyed the surrounding area, seeing and hearing nothing at first. Finally, he spotted a glimpse of color that didn't fit in with the rest of the forest.

"Ah, there you are," he said, and a moment later he bent down and pointed the gun through the bushes at Katie.

Neither Billy nor Katie could see the gun, for the bushes were too dense at that point, but they heard the rustling and knew Curtis had found them.

"Come out now," demanded Curtis.

Billy arose first, and then helped Katie to her feet. Together they reentered the clearing and faced Curtis.

"Surprised?" asked Curtis.

"DA21," said Billy, "your father's uniform number."

"Very good," said the lawyer. "When did you figure that out?"

"Too late, obviously," said Billy. "It hit me as you were walking up the drive, just before you shot Officer Rivers."

Katie was clutching him, and he felt her heart pounding against his chest. His heart was doing the same. When he glanced back at her, he was surprised that her aura had not yet turned black, as he expected it to be, but was still a dark grey.

"You two love birds need to separate," said Curtis. He motioned with the gun for Katie to move to her left, until the duo stood about ten feet apart from each other.

"Vinnie was obviously a quicker study than you," said Curtis. "Of course, he had been over my house a few times— you had too, Katie—because your father liked to do a little gambling from time to time, and my dad was the man to see for that."

"I don't remember being at your house," said Katie

"Too bad," replied Curtis. "Anyway, your brother had seen the picture of my old man in his basketball jersey, and he must have seen some betting slips laying around too, 'cause when he saw that code on the betting slip you two found, he knew right away where it had come from."

Billy listened quietly and kept looking at Katie. He was startled to see her aura actually becoming greyer and less black, and he couldn't understand why. He looked for an opening where he might try to wrestle the gun from Curtis, but Curtis was smart. He wasn't standing close enough to them for something like that to work. Yet when he looked back at Curtis, he suddenly saw his aura getting darker, and Billy knew something was up.

"After that my old man made me make friends with you." Curtis saw the surprised look on Billy's face and said, "What, you think I wanted to hang out with you guys? My dad wanted to know where this clue was that Vinnie had, and we thought sooner or later one of you would blab about it. But you really didn't know, did you?"

"Not until we found it the other day," said Billy. "Guess we took it to the wrong lawyer."

Curtis gave a little laugh at that and said, "Guess so." Then he took a deep breath and said, "Now I'm afraid there's going to be two more bodies found in the woods."

"When did you become a killer?" asked Katie, the sound of fear mixed with anger in her voice. "How many people have you killed?"

"Actually, that cop was the first. Usually I'm just the lawyer who keeps all my crime buddies out of jail. My younger brother actually runs the gambling in this town now, along with some drugs, prostitution, and a little money laundering."

Something was going on that Billy couldn't figure out. Katie's aura was still not turning black, as he expected it should be if they were about to die, yet he had no idea what he could do to stop that from happening. His cell phone was still behind the bushes, yet he felt an incredible urge to do something to try and save the woman he loved.

Meanwhile, Curtis's aura was turning darker by the minute. Billy had no idea why, but he felt certain that if he just came up with a plan it would work in their favor. Whatever he was going to do would have to be done quickly, however, because Curtis wouldn't be wasting much more time before shooting them.

Billy turned to look at the woman he was falling in love with. He didn't know what his own aura looked like, but if he had to sacrifice himself to save her, he would. He couldn't bear the thought of her life ending because he had stood back and done nothing. It was time to act.

Curtis saw Billy suddenly reach both hands into his pockets. "Whoa there, cowboy," he said, but then he started to giggle as he saw Billy remove a wallet with his left hand. "What, are you going to try to buy your way out of this?"

"I have money," he said. As he raised the wallet up high with his left hand, hoping to draw Curtis's attention, his right hand pulled out the only other item he had on him.

"Money won't save you now," said Curtis, "and the time for chitchat is over."

"You're right," said Billy, and he side-armed the item in his right hand towards Curtis, as though he were trying to skip a rock on the water.

"RUN!" he once again yelled to Katie as he charged Curtis Armstrong, hoping that at least she could get away in the three seconds his foolish action might buy them.

Curtis turned his head to the right and felt something hit him on the left cheek, and then he spun back around and fired at the onrushing Billy.

Billy felt a searing pain go through him, and then his legs gave out and he tumbled to the earth. He turned to look at Katie in time to watch her scream.

The second shot took him completely by surprise, and then all went dark.

TWENTY EIGHT

Simon awoke Saturday morning to the sound of Thomas Mann banging on the door of the guest bedroom and calling his name."

"Simon. Simon, are you awake?"

"I am now," Simon replied. He stood up and ambled to the door. "What in blazes is so important? Am I late for breakfast?" The look on Thomas' face immediately told him it was more than that.

Thomas barged into the room, a newspaper in his hand. "Look at this," he said, and handed the paper to Simon.

The paper had been folded to show the headline on the right hand side of the front page. It was obviously a late addition to the paper, as the story itself was quite short. Simon glanced at the headline and took a quick intake of breath. The article was listed under a large *BULLETIN streamer.*

SHOOTING IN DEARBORN LEAVES TWO DEAD, ONE WOUNDED

"Take a minute to read it," said Thomas.

Simon scanned through the story quickly.

A shooting in the early morning hours has left two men dead and another in serious condition. Police say the incident occurred in the woods behind 58 Travesty Lane in Dearborn. Names of those involved have not yet been released pending notification of next of kin. However, it is known that one of the dead is a Greenfield Police Officer. Police would only say that it

*was part of an ongoing investigation and no more information
would be released at this time.*

"I looked the address up online," said Thomas. "The house belongs to Katie Maki."

"Good God," said Simon, "do you think it's them?"

"Too much of a coincidence not to be, don't you think?"

"The way this reads, it seems the person in serious condition is also a man. Perhaps Katie is alright."

"I didn't think of that when I read it," said Thomas. "Let's hope you're right."

"Is there anything we can do? Someone we could call to find out?" asked Simon.

"That's not a bad idea. I know a lady who works as a dispatcher in Greenfield. I'll give her a call."

They went downstairs. Simon headed into the kitchen for coffee and found Elizabeth making toast, while Thomas went to find his phone.

"I hope those two are okay," said Elizabeth, as she handed Simon the pitcher of cream. "They seemed like such nice people."

"I hope so too," said Simon, "but it doesn't sound good."

It took nearly fifteen minutes for Thomas to return to the kitchen.

"Well?" asked Simon questioningly.

"I got a hold of the dispatcher," said Thomas. "She's pretty broken up. It seems the officer who was killed was a Phillip Rivers, who she knew quite well. He was apparently at the house to protect Billy and Katie, because her house had been broken into and ransacked, most likely while they were staying here with us."

"Oh dear, that's awful," said Elizabeth.

"However, she didn't know the names of the others who were shot, although it was her understanding that they were both men."

"So Katie is okay, at least."

"It appears so," said Thomas.

They put on the television to see if they could get any updates. They had to sit through two hours of Saturday morning cartoons and an infomercial for the most amazing knife set ever, but at eleven-ten that morning the station broke into their regular programming for a *Breaking News story*. The Greenfield Chief of Police was about to hold a live news conference.

By noon the story was the lead item on every channel in the state.

Billy awoke in his hospital bed nearly twelve hours after being shot in the woods.

Katie had been dozing off and on by his side, holding his hand all the while. Now she felt his arm twitch, looked up, and noticed he was slowly looking around the room.

Billy had an IV drip in his arm, a breathing tube in his nose, and his stomach hurt like hell. He glanced at Katie, managed the tiniest of smiles, and in a raspy voice asked, "What happened?"

"You were shot in the stomach," she said. "You were in surgery for nearly six hours. They had to remove your spleen, and you damn near bleed to death."

He found his thinking was slow, like trying to swim upstream against the tide, and Katie noticed his brow drop and his forehead wrinkle as though he were thinking hard. Finally he managed to mumble, "Why are we still alive?"

Before she could answer, he fell back to sleep.

He awoke again four hours later as a nurse was checking his vitals. This time Katie was joined by both Paul and John Paul Stephens, plus Billy's sister. Marylou and her husband had flown home to South Carolina Friday night. Upon receiving a call from Katie just after midnight, she had boarded another plane at six this morning and flown back.

"Well, our patient is awake," said the nurse, one Stephanie Gilmore.

"How am I?" asked Billy.

"Oh, I think you'll make it," said Stephanie. "Let me get out of here so you can visit with your friends."

Katie held a glass of water for him, and Billy managed to take a few sips through the straw. "Someone want to tell me what happened?" he finally asked.

"Well, you solved a fifty-year old murder case," said Paul Stephens, "and my dad had way more excitement than a man his age should reasonably expect."

They all saw the confused look on his face, and smiled as one.

"Katie," said John Paul, "why don't you tell him the story."

Katie was still sitting to Billy's right. She again took his hand, squeezed it gently, and said, "You're my hero."

"How?" was all he could think to ask.

"You threw something at Curtis, and then you charged him."

"I remember that," said Billy, "and then I was shot. Then I heard a second shot and figured I was dead."

"The second shot was mine," said John Paul.

Billy was thoroughly confused as he looked from one to the other.

"When you used your cell phone to call the police," said Katie, "in your haste, you dialed the number John Paul had written on the back, and it's a good thing you did, because he was visiting a friend less than a mile away.

"He relayed the call to the police and then headed over to my house. He found the body of Officer Rivers out front, entered the house, saw the back door wide open, and assumed whoever was there had gone out that way.

"If Curtis had shot us right away after catching us in the woods, he and John Paul would probably have met on the path as Curtis returned to the house. But Curtis took a while to catch up to us, and another minute to locate us, and then he wanted to talk, and that gave John Paul enough time to find us."

"Timing is everything," John Paul broke in. "I arrived just as you were throwing whatever it was at Curtis. He shot you, and then I shot him. For an old guy, I can still shoot pretty well, as it turns out."

"I try to tell him he's not on the force anymore," said his son, "but old habits are hard to break. He should have waited for the *current* police to arrive, but if he had you two wouldn't have come out of the woods alive.

"Katie told us everything Curtis had admitted to, and the Greenfield police have been rounding up Curtis's brother and some of his associates all morning."

"Is Curtis dead?" asked Billy.

"He is," said John Paul. "I couldn't take a chance that he would get off a second shot at you. I aimed for the chest and hit my target. He probably never knew what hit him before he died."

Billy suddenly thought of Walter. He looked at Katie and asked, "How's Pokey?"

"Walter is going to make it," she said. "He was poisoned, but I guess they forgot who they were dealing with."

"He drank enough poison to kill a 250 pound man," Paul said. "Unfortunately for them, they were about 100 pounds short if they wanted to kill Walter. His size actually saved him."

Billy suddenly stared at John Paul. "Who were you visiting at that time of night?"

John Paul broke out in a big grin, but it was his son that answered.

"Turns out my dad has a girlfriend," said Paul. "Surprise, surprise."

"I want to thank you," said John Paul Stephens. "That case has bothered me for fifty years, and I thought I'd go to my grave not knowing what had happened. I'm pretty sure that once everyone is rounded up, we'll know the identity of the person who killed those two people that day, and because you called the wrong number, I was able to close the case myself. Damn, I feel good."

And everybody laughed.

Except Billy, because laughing hurt too much.

Sunday morning, Simon stopped in to see Billy before heading for the airport. Katie had finally gone home to get some sleep and wasn't due back for another hour.

Billy smiled as he saw Simon enter. "Hey doc," he said, "good to see you again."

"Same here," said Simon. "When we first heard the news, we were afraid our attempts to help you had fallen short. How are you feeling?"

"Sore, very sore, but I'll be okay, thanks to you and the Mann's. You probably saved our lives."

"Well, that was mostly Thomas, I'd say. I think someone from the other side was pretty insistent about not letting you go home that night."

"Are you heading back to Sarasota today?"

"I am," said Simon. "In fact, I have to get a move on if I want to catch my plane, but I had to stop in and check up on you."

"Thank you, Simon."

"So will I see you again in Sarasota, or have you found a reason to stay here?"

Simon was smiling broadly at him, and Billy smiled back.

"Time will tell," he finally said.

"Be good, Billy," said Simon, and then he turned and headed for the door. Before leaving, he took a final look back at the man in the bed and said, "Seems to me the answer is obvious."

Billy left the hospital five days later. A nurse pushed his wheelchair out to the car as Katie walked by his side. Billy could see the love emanating from her aura, and he was certain his looked the same. He would recuperate at her house in the woods, and that would take some time. He was under strict orders from his doctor as to what he could and could not do.

"We'll work things out as we go," Katie had told him.

He knew what she was really getting at, but his decision had already been made. He had found a love that he never thought he would ever find again, and he was not about to let her go.

They arrived at the house, and Katie helped him into the living room.

"This is your hangout for the next few days," she said. "You're going to take it easy, follow all my rules, and let me take care of you. No climbing stairs for now."

"Yes, ma'am," he said, smiling brightly, "but I hope it's for a lot longer than just a few days."

She looked at him, a nervous countenance to her face, and said, "Is that what you really want?"

"Yes, ma'am," he said again.

"You want to stay here, with me, as a couple?"

"More than anything in the world," he replied.

Her face lit up, and she bent over and kissed him. "I'd hug you," she said, "but I don't want to hurt you. And you'd better never call me *ma'am* again."

Billy felt a feeling of joy coursing through his body. He knew it wouldn't be easy. He'd lost Jenny and Ruthie and Tommy, and the pain had been unbearable for so long he had doubted this moment would ever arrive; doubted he would ever let it.

But perhaps it was time.

Orlana had told him he needed to start living again. Billy thought he had done that, but now realized he had only gone part way. To be fully living, you needed to be fully loving. He had withheld that love for so long.

No more.

EPILOGUE

Billy spent his first few days at his new home slowly recovering. He walked gingerly around the house, increasing his time a little more each day, trying to get his strength back. The pain from the surgery was difficult at first, but it was slowly subsiding.

Katie proved to be a tough taskmaster. Billy felt he should be allowed to climb the stairs and sleep in his bed after a few days at home, but she wouldn't allow it. Finally, on Monday morning, ten days after he'd been shot, he suggested they take a walk in the woods.

"Are you sure you're up to it?" she asked.

"I was ready three days ago," he replied, "but that ornery lady who was watching over me wouldn't let me out of the house."

"That ornery lady just wants what's best for you," replied Katie, "because she loves you."

Katie had given away all of her upcoming photo sessions to the few local photographers in the area. There was no way she was going to leave Billy alone in the house, save for a few excursions into town for supplies. Besides, her equipment had been ruined to a large extent, and she didn't know how long it would take to replace it, or how she would pay for it.

"I will replace it all," Billy had finally told her, "and buy you even better stuff than you had."

"We're talking a lot of money here, Billy," she replied, and that was when he informed her that she was dating a man who was quite well off.

She hadn't believed him at first, and he was forced to explain.

"Jenny had taken out a policy I didn't know about, and I received a huge sum of money after they perished. It didn't interest me at the time. I stayed in a lot of cheap apartments and never spent extravagantly. Most of it is gone now, that's true, but I did invest a portion of it way back when, and I never touched it. Mostly blue chip stocks that have grown nicely, and then there's the two hundred shares of a stock called Amazon I bought when it first came out."

"What!" cried Katie, too surprised to say anything more.

"It split three times after coming out, so I think I have about twenty-four hundred shares now. Last I checked it was worth nearly two million dollars; probably more by now," said Billy. "I never really cared, but I'm pretty sure I can buy you whatever photography equipment you might ever need."

"Oh Billy," she said, and hugged him ever so gently.

They made their way out the back door and into the forest. They walked slowly, and Katie wrapped her arm around him just in case he lost his balance.

When they came to the fork in the road she looked at him, thinking he would go right and avoid the spot where they had almost died.

But he fooled her.

"We have to go this way," he said, pointing to the left.

She thought it was some sort of cathartic cleansing he felt the need to do, and she was totally surprised when he told her the real reason.

"I have to find that thing I threw at Curtis," he said.

"Why?" asked Katie. "It just looked like some cheap plastic box."

"It was a cheap plastic box," he said. "Just help me find it."

They arrived at the spot of their near demise to find crime scene tape still wrapped around the trees. Katie pulled it down, and she was happy to see that recent rains seemed to have washed away any sign of blood from the ground.

They recreated the scene that was still so fresh in their minds. Billy stood where he had been, and Katie played the part of Curtis Armstrong.

"I raised my left hand with the wallet in it, and then threw the box at him with my right," said Billy. "I think it hit him, but I'm not sure. What happened after that?"

"It did hit him on the cheek, and then you yelled run, but I was so surprised by what you did that I just stood there and watched as you charged towards him. He ducked like this when you threw the box," she said, as she recreated Curtis's movements, "and then he turned back and shot you, and he was about to fire again, but John Paul shot him from over there." She pointed to where the retired officer had been.

"It's funny we never heard him approaching," said Billy.

"I think we were too involved with Curtis at the time," replied Katie, and Billy had to agree.

"Okay, so where do you think my box landed?"

"Good Lord, it could be anywhere."

"It couldn't have gone far," said Billy. "It was just a small plastic box."

"I don't understand why it's so important to you," said Katie.

"Just look for it," he replied.

She began to prowl the grounds, lifting leaves and moving twigs, knowing Billy shouldn't be bending over too much. The police and paramedics had trampled all over the area, and Katie thought it would be hiding under a leaf somewhere.

She suddenly had the thought, *maybe he wants to put it in a scrapbook,* and laughed out loud.

When he looked at her, she just said, "Tell you later."

Barely two minutes went by before Katie suddenly exclaimed, "Here it is!" The plastic was cracked, having obviously been stepped on more than once. She handed it to Billy, and his expression quickly lost its excitement.

The box had opened when it struck Curtis, and its contents were missing.

"Keep looking," he said.

"For what?" asked Katie.

"You'll know it when you see it," was all he said.

Ten more minutes went by, and Billy suddenly had the sinking feeling that some raccoon had found what he was looking for and walked off with it. He was also becoming quite tired, and knew they would have to head back soon.

"Is that it?" Katie suddenly said, pointing to something between them about three feet in from of Billy.

He reached down, wincing a bit as he did, brushed aside some pine needles, and picked up what Katie had seen.

"It is," he said. "Thank goodness."

He took two steps and handed it to her.

One look told her she was holding no ordinary coin. "Oh my," she said. "What is this?"

"It's my good luck coin," replied Billy. "To be precise, it's a 1909 Barber quarter, minted in New Orleans. Given to me by my grandfather on the night he died. I was five."

"This must be worth a lot of money," she said. "What the heck was it doing in your pocket?"

"Well, when I'm home I usually have it stored in a safe place. But it's always been a habit of mine to take it with me when I travel. You know, for good luck."

He smiled at her, and she just shook her head.

"I guess it works," she finally said.

They walked slowly back to the house, hand in hand, speaking little.

The next night, as the movie they were watching was just finishing, Katie turned to him and said, "I think you're ready to sleep upstairs."

"I've been telling you that for the last week," said Billy.

Katie gave him a loving grin. "Look at my aura and tell me what I'm thinking."

He gazed at her for a moment, and then smiled broadly. "You're thinking you should take me upstairs and make love to me."

"Wow, you're good," said Katie, and a moment later Billy was allowed to go upstairs for the first time in two weeks.

AUTHOR'S NOTES

This is the 3rd book in the Simon Taylor series, although Simon is really just a sidelight here to Billy Wilson. In actuality, this is the joining of two different books, neither of which I deemed long enough to publish.

The idea for the murder mystery part of the story came to me as I was driving home from work one day. At that point WHISPERS THROUGH TIME wasn't even out yet, and TRACES OF YOU hadn't even been thought about, so the story was obviously sitting on the back burner for a long time. I started writing it after TRACES was finished, but became bogged down around 40,000 words.

In the meantime, I began the third Simon book, but found I was getting nowhere with it, and that's when the idea hit me to join the two. I'm guessing my guides and angels turned me in that direction.

I am a spiritual person. I believe in past lives and reincarnation, and I have been helped many times by my guides. For instance, in both WHISPERS and TRACES, I thought I had finished the books and was ready to publish. In WHISPERS case, I was finishing the epilogue when I suddenly heard a voice say, "You know ..." and they then informed me about something I had written twenty chapters and five years earlier (yes, that book took a long time to write—I met a lady, we were married, and the book sat silent for a few years). My guides suggestion made the ending that much more special.

In TRACES, I had finished the book and was quite happy with it. Five days later, I was at my job, riding in a golf cart down by the waters of Sarasota Bay, when suddenly my guides spoke up again. It was another "You know …" moment, and they reminded me of something I had written in the very first chapter of the book. I couldn't believe I had forgotten about it, and again it made the epilogue so much better.

One more story. I had a dream one night as I was writing TRACES. In the dream, a man came to me and said he was going to help me with my writing. The next morning I looked the name up online, and discovered he was a German author who had won the Nobel Prize in 1929. His name was Thomas Mann. Since he was helping me anyway, I decided to use his name in the book, and obviously he made it into THE AURA READER also.

My writing is geared to the spiritual community. I've included not only past-life regressions in the books, but have also featured mediums, tarot card readers, a lady who channeled Saint Martin de Porres, and a shaman. I've known many fine people who have these abilities, and yes, I have also run across a good number of fakes too. I hope that even those of you who don't believe in such things are still able to enjoy my books.

As for me, I will keep on writing. One more Simon book is a must, for we all must know where his life with Maria Vasquez will take him, and the fact he has never had a regression of his own has to be rectified, I think. I hope you will take the journey with me.

Sincerely,
Barry Homan
June, 2017

ABOUT THE AUTHOR

Barry Homan lives in Massachusetts with his wife Karen and their cat Gizmo. He can be reached at bfh6771@msn.com. Your comments, both positive and negative, are always welcome.